THE FIRE WITHIN

BEING AN ACCOUNT OF
THE BATTLE FOR KING'S ROAD PASS

JOHN B. CHEEK

ALSO BY JOHN B. CHEEK

Bragg For Hire

For my wife, Robin,
who always asks whether the story has a girl.

AUTHOR'S NOTE

This is the story of a battle. It was fought in the long dark of deep time, in a past beyond memory or record. You, Reader, may fairly ask how I came to know of it. I will tell you it was given to me in a dream. Its stage was set before my slumbering mind by some unseen hand, and the players came forth to show me who they were: their struggles, their cares, their loves, their triumphs, their sorrows. And all of it was laid before me so complete and so clear it seemed I watched it, waking, in the light of a summer noon. And when they were done, and the long dark fell again over that stage, I knew those players had desired me to tell you their stories, so you would know them as I do.

This I have done.

As you will see in these pages, we Humans were on the field that day, neither more nor less than we are now; but our hour on this Earth had not yet waxed to its present fullness. For we shared the field and this Earth with others then: other beings. Beings our scientific time dismisses as relics of a more credulous age: an age that saw creatures as real as ourselves in the shadows of a twilit wood, or the spoiling of a pail of milk fresh the day before.

Those other beings would meet our cold disbelief with their own incredulity. The Orkh would strike his sword and shield together in a thunder of arms. The Aelf would yip her ancient battle cry and rap the hard leather of her cuirass.

Each would say to us in our unbelief: *Is not my spirit, too, a fire within me? Am I not also made from flesh that yearns? Do I not also strive to be greater than I am, because I will it to be so?*

We, too, walked this Earth once. We, too, lived. You have forgotten.

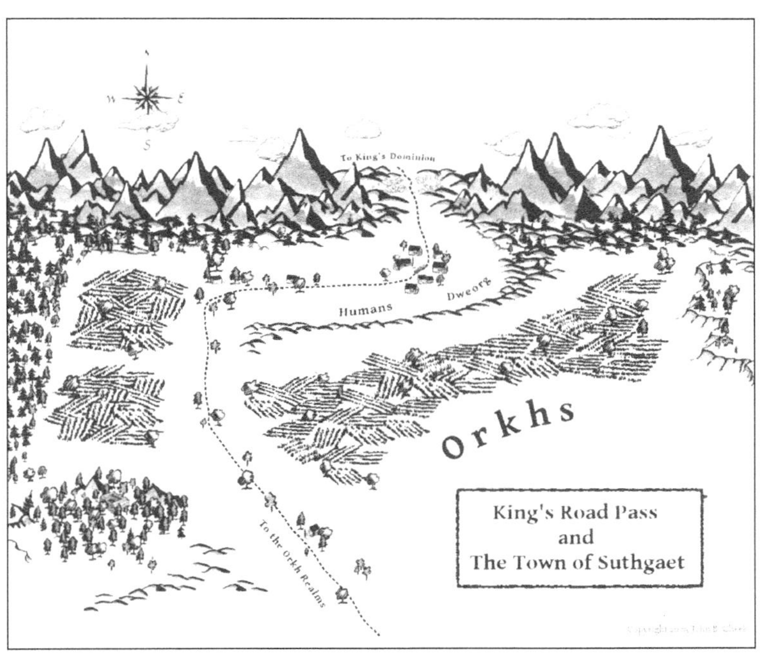

To King's Dominion
Humans
Dweorg
Orkhs
To the Orkh Realms
King's Road Pass
and
The Town of Suthgaet

1

OF ZARA

Zara raised her eyeglass and studied the Orkhs through it. She was seeing the main body now, coming toward the pass from the south over the roads and across the fields. Even the van was distant still and the Orkhs marched in route column: thin black lines that moved slow and silent over green and wrinkled land. The sun, new-risen, shone its light on their spears so it seemed the Orkhs carried with them many torches of silver fire.

But those dark columns held no interest for Zara now, for they were many leagues from where she sat her cat-sí on the crest of a long, steep-sided ridge. She brought down the glass and shut it. What interested her far more could be seen without the glass: skirmishing parties of Orkhs sent forward to clear and hold the southern approaches to the pass. She could see them now, not a mile out: beating every thicket and wading forward through fallow fields deep with late summer grass.

They would come to the ridge soon.

Zara looked about herself. It was good ground here. The crest of the ridge was broad and treeless, and the earth beneath Te'a's paws was firm and dry. The south slope, facing the Orkhs, was not so tall as she'd like, but it was steep and well-rutted with long, stony rain gullies.

Better still, the line of the ridge ran straight east and west, along the southern edge of the Human dwelling here, forming a natural line of defense for both the dwelling and the pass behind it. Cenred's Human warriors, when they came, could make their shield wall here, looking down on the Orkhs as they came.

This was good ground; and it was, without question, where this coming battle should be fought.

Zara reined Te'a around to face her Second, Salf Kve-ma. He sat his own cat-sí, a brown, at a respectful distance. He was tall for an Aelf and sat high in the saddle. His close-cut hair was silver and his face, once handsome to her, was cloven in two by an old wound: a long, ugly stripe of puckered skin that passed over his nose from one cheek to the other. An Orkh had given him that wound, long ago, at a time when things were different between them.

"Bring up the *kansa*," Zara said to him. "We will hold this high ground until the Human warriors come down the pass road to relieve us. Put First Claw on the right, over there, dismounted." She pointed west with a gloved hand. "Tell Tra'am not to extend his line past that barn, the tall one. Third Claw will dismount and defend the ground here. Tell them to make a show of it, and build fires on the back slope. They are to make enough smoke for five times their number."

Salf nodded. "It will be done, my lady."

Zara drew herself up the saddle to look south again. Her duty here was clear: the ridge must be held. She couldn't fail in that, for failure would mean disgrace and another disgrace would ruin her.

"What of Second Claw?" Salf asked.

Zara didn't answer at once, but opened the glass again and brought it to her eye. She regarded the far off columns once more, judging their speed and distance, then glassed the skirmishers she could see. Yes, there was time in plenty to harry the beasts. She snapped the glass shut and lifted a finger to command Salf's attention.

"Second Claw will form on me, here," she said. "We will ride out against these Orkhs and drive them off. They cannot be permitted to do their work unmolested. Then we will return and hold our place here until the Humans come. You will ride with us, Salf."

As she said this, the urge to action rose hot in Zara: she had something to prove and now was the time to do it. But Salf didn't reply at once. Instead he urged his cat-sí closer to her, as if to speak in confidence.

Here it comes, she thought. *He will seek to drop the leash on me, as my father the king told him. But I won't have it, not today.*

But her look of warning failed to deter him. "My lady," Salf said, leaning close from his saddle so only she could hear. "That tree line yonder hides water and mud, who knows what else. Our lines will be broken, and we robbed of the advantage of our mounts. This foray is needless, lady. If we—"

Zara cut him off with a hand. "Ware, Salf! I will not hear your cautious murmurings today. I command here, not you, and not my father's words of caution."

The Second studied her. "In truth the words are mine," he said. "And your father did not choose me."

"Lies do not become you, Salf. I know well you are my father's hobble on me."

The Aelf's mouth made an unhappy smile and the scar seemed to echo it. "I begged your father for the boon of this posting."

Zara sat back in the saddle, surprised. "A boon?" she said. "For this? Whatever for?"

Salf looked at her then as if the answer lay plain on the ground between them, but he spoke no answer aloud. Instead he asked quietly: "Do you truly believe this attack wise, Zara-ena?"

She stiffened: he did seek to thwart her, and now with soft words. "Form up the Claw for advance, *Ritzar*," she said harshly. "A double line with sabers. I will lead. You will ride the tail. You have heard my wishes, *Ritzar* Kve'ma. Execute them."

Salf pulled back, wounded by the formal address. But when she didn't draw the barb, he moved away with only a murmur of acquiescence.

Zara glared after him. He was a tall, ugly bird perched on her shoulder to squawk caution into her ear. That was the price of her father's consent to this command. But she knew caution and glory were not bedmates; and there was glory in plenty to be won here, and her lost honor to reclaim.

She had only to reach out a hand and seize it.

Zara's blood quickened at the thought of redemption here, and under her Te'a responded. Not with words, but with a warm eager pressure against the walls of Zara's mind. Zara permitted the cat-sí's intrusion for a time, but found Te'a urging her to care also, in her own wordless way: offering Zara memories of repose in deep grass and long sleeping under a cool sun.

Zara closed her mind to it. *Not you also! Bend your thoughts toward war today. This is a day for boldness and steel!*

The cat-sí fell away, chastened, and Zara looked down to the green fields below the ridge. "We shall give steel to yon black-hearted beasts," she said aloud in her own tongue, "and all shall harken to it."

As she waited for Salf to do his duty, Zara studied the plain below the ridge. It was a mix of crop fields, hay meadows, and woodlots, each bound neatly by walls of gray field stone. In the middle distance was Salf's tree line: a winding belt of green marking the course of a stream. It ran east and west, parallel to the ridge, and the trees concealed only a narrow strip of ground immediately beyond. Farther out the land was clear and open, rolling gently for two leagues or more until finally it swept under the feet of the approaching columns.

When Salf signaled readiness, Zara turned to see he'd formed the riders of Second Claw into two lines, one behind the other, centered on Zara and her guard. Nearby the horn-aelf waited to relay her commands, and the banner-aelf held aloft from her saddle the *kansa*'s scarlet and green swallowtail on its tall pole.

Satisfied, Zara drew the curved saber from her back. Behind her the Aelfs of her guard did the same. Then the warriors of the claw brought out their own steel to shine whitely in the sun. They were one hundred forty-eight strong now, and well-blooded by long months of war. They'd been two hundred once, and her *kansa* more than six hundred; but the grind of war had pared them down, leaving a hardened core that knew well its work of war.

She lifted the saber and yipped to them. The riders called back the ancient *ritzan*, high and yodeling. She heard no reluctance in that cry.

Be damned to you, Salf!

She lowered the saber to point down the slope and the horn-aelf lifted his long horn to sound the forward ride: a long, trilling note that would carry far over any field. Te'a responded to it with a powerful, thrusting leap that flung both cat-sí and rider far down the slope, ending with a wild gallop south over short grass. Zara clucked for restraint, but privately she was glad the cat-sí had set aside her doubts to share in her rider's eagerness for battle.

The claw's advance was swift. The fields were level and even, and the great cats ran smoothly over them, leaping the gray stone walls. But from the first the Orkhs had seen them, and already they fled south: scattering from their hides and from brushy copses of hickory and oak, like great black beetles flushed from beneath a stone. These were scouts and messengers, and watchers of the roads: not meant to stand, nor could they, against any cavalry.

The Orkhs were swift but the cat-sí were swifter, and the claw blooded its sabers. Zara rode down a short, loping Orkh clad in boiled leather and rusted mail. She struck the back of its neck, nearly severing its head, then slid the blade free as she passed and rode on without looking back.

Salf appeared then. He pushed his cat-sí close to Te'a, riding knee-to-knee with Zara. His saber was bloody and he held it out from himself.

"My lady!" he shouted. "They flee! The work you set for us is done!"

Zara flung out a hand to ward him away. "No!" she cried. "We will drive these beasts to the Hells! Follow me!"

Her blood was up now and she twitched the reins to urge Te'a away from her Second. The line of trees was just ahead now, rising tall and green across her path. Orkhs were disappearing into its depths even now, escaping her.

"To me!" she called, holding the saber high to be seen. Hearing her, the horn-aelf sounded the rally to banner.

The claw had scattered in their chase but now it responded to the call: coming together to remake its lines to either side of Zara. The *ritzan* rose again from them, louder now, and together the claw entered the trees in pursuit of Orkhs.

"Re-form on me on the far side!" Zara cried to Salf, and the Second nodded before disappearing into the dense green.

Zara urged T'ea in behind him. But what she found here was no trickling stream, easily leaped, as she'd hoped. Instead the belt was wide and dense, and it concealed tangles of briar and piles of rotten deadfall that themselves hid pots of dark mud and wet sand.

Te'a wound her way through it, slowly, leaping what obstacles she could and moving around others. Around them, others picked their own ways through: some moving lightly around undergrowth, while others sought to bull their way through by main strength.

Doubt rose in Zara but she thrust it away. This was no matter: the claw would form its lines again on the far side and carry on. Perhaps she would gallop it within bow shot of the Orkhish infantry still plodding forward under their heavy armor and weapons. Word of that daring feat would spread quickly, and all on the field would marvel at her. This pleased Zara and she smiled at the thought of it.

She heard shouting ahead, beyond the trees. This was good: her riders were slaying Orkhs again. Zara urged Te'a to more speed, eager to take the lead again. But when the cat-sí pushed her broad shoulders from the trees into sunlight, Zara reined her hard.

What's this?

What Zara was certain she would see was open, empty ground leading south and Orkhs fleeing over it. But what she found was a company of Orkhish spear, seventy-five yards from where her riders emerged from the trees, unwitting.

She swore.

The Orkhs had been resting or waiting for something, and they were surely as surprised as the Aelfs; but they recovered swiftly. Shouts rose in their hideous, croaking tongue, and they rushed to form a hollow square: leveling their spears outward to form a steel porcupine no cavalry riding the Earth could penetrate or frighten.

But this was not the only threat. Orkhish archers in the center of the square lifted heavy bows and began to work them: loosing arrows at Zara's riders as they came out from the trees. Already a half dozen cat-sí lay on a lawn of short grass verging the green belt. Some kicked their hind legs still, as if to flee, even as death took them. Their riders lay nearby, pitched from the saddle by heavy arrows.

As Zara struggled to draw her thoughts together, two riders emerged from the brush. The first was shot from her saddle before drawing another breath of open air; the other escaped, wheeling her cat-sí to crash back into the trees. Arrows followed her.

Sudden fear made Zara weak. *Gods! What have I done?*

She looked along the tree line for Salf but he wasn't there. The banner-aelf followed her still, but the horn-aelf was nowhere to be seen: surely struggling still in the heavy brush. Zara ordered her guard back into the trees with instructions to halt everyone they could find. There was nothing good to be done here: even if the claw was properly assembled for a charge, it would never crack that awful phalanx of spears. A square was meant to break cavalry, and it would do murder if given the chance.

Zara bent low over Te'a neck and she urged the cat-sí to run along the tree line. Ahead a dozen riders emerged from the trees at once, unwarned and unwary. The Orkhs turned their bows on these and their cat-sí reared, screaming in pain.

"Go back!" Zara shouted to them, pointing her saber northward. "Go back!"

A white cat-sí burst from the green ahead of Te'a. But before its rider could swing his head around to Zara, a dark-fletched arrow sprouted from his left eye and he was flung backward over the cat-sí's haunches as if snatched by a rope.

Zara left him and moved on. More bodies lay in her path:

cat-sí and Aelf. Each arrow-killed. Then a rider approached her at full gallop. It was Salf. The horn-aelf trailed close behind him.

"Sound retreat!" Zara shouted. "Sound retreat, damn you!"

The horn-aelf swung the horn to his lips and sounded it. The notes were clear and bright, but it was a call no Aelf wished to hear. Zara twisted in the saddle to peer in both directions along the tree line, but she saw no living cat-sí or rider still in the open. There were only those who lay on the grass before the Orkhs.

"Go!" she shouted to Salf. "Get everyone back to the ridge!" Then, speaking to Te'a in both word and thought, she said: "Flee!"

The cat-sí turned to leap into the wood, crashing over thick brush. Briar tore at Zara's leggings and arrows spattered through the leaves about her head. Then from behind her rose a thunderous roar of many cruel voices: the Orkhs celebrating their victory.

They were laughing at her.

They fled north, scattered and disheartened. They did not re-form beyond the trees, but ran for the ridge, each making their own way. Zara slumped low and unseeing over Te'a neck as she rode, letting the cat-sí find her own path. The great blackness was open before her again, the one she couldn't let herself fall into. It tugged at her, promising comfort in surrender. She resisted its beckoning call, as ever she had, but still a black fog lay over her, shadowing the world to gloom and despair.

Salf rode near. She didn't wish to speak to him. "Are you well?" he called.

She made no reply and he rode on. He would know what to do without her: take the claw to the ridge and assemble it there with the others to make what defense they could. Salf didn't need her for that. Perhaps he didn't think he needed her for anything. Perhaps he was right.

A presence touched Zara's mind then: it was Te'a. The cat-sí also sought to know if her rider was well, but her asking was a hazy feeling of questioning, not the closely pruned thoughts that were Salf's words. But Zara didn't answer the cat-sí either. She closed her mind and kept that great blackness to herself. No one could know the secrets of her heart. Not even Salf. He no longer understood her.

In time Zara straightened and took the reins again. The gloom held her still, but the imperative of duty moved her now. She guided Te'a across the fields and up the slope of the ridge to its crest. She saw Salf there, in the distance, calling in Aelfs and restoring order to confusion.

She watched him work, wondering at the boon he'd spoken of. Had he truly sought to come with her? She'd been certain her father had forced him on her, to put a thumb on her head; but now Salf claimed to be his own Aelf. Zara wasn't certain she believed that, but for all their trouble he'd always been honest with her.

Just then a rider on a white cat-sí broke away from the circle of Aelfs clustered about Salf and made a course toward Zara. This was certainly a messenger, doubtless carrying more ill-news to lay on her distress.

The Aelf came up to Zara and sketched a bow from the saddle. "*Ritzar* Kve'ma's respects, lady," she said, "and he bade me say word has reached him the Dweorg have cleared the pass. They are said to wait east of this Human place." The messenger gestured with plain distaste toward the buildings. "The Dweorg are the first to come down, lady. No word on the Humans."

"Very well," Zara said with far more decision than she felt. "Inform Salf I will deal with the Dweorg. He is to carry on."

The messenger wheeled her cat-sí to gallop away and Zara clicked for Te'a to descend the back slope of the ridge. Then she turned the cat-sí east, toward the Dweorg. Her guard followed: twenty mounted sabers commanded by yet another chosen by her father. She was surrounded by the marks of his untrust, and all knew it. With a victory here, she would have a free hand to replace both Salf and Gar'an, the guard commander. Her father might not like it but he would respect it. He would not argue with success.

Zara turned her gaze to the Human dwelling as she rode past. The wooden buildings of it squatted together, leaning and filthy, at the foot of the south slope of the pass. The road off the pass, the King's Road as the Humans called it, fell down that slope to run a straight course between the buildings before leaving their south end to turn due west some distance short of the north slope of the ridge. The road was rutted and treacherous with holes; and its side streets were fouled by rubbish and castoffs: the accumulated offscourings of lives carried on indoors in a single place.

A few had chosen to remain there: barring themselves into wooden tombs that coming black tide would burn with glee. But Zara cared little for this, for she cared little for Humans; and she was unpleased with this alliance forced upon her kind. But forced it was, for this wide pass through the southern range—lying below tall granite peaks and high white snow fields—was a open doorway into Human and Aelfin lands alike. Whether her people would wish it or not, common cause must be made and the beasts turned aside here or not at all.

Soon she and Te'a passed beyond the eastern edge of the buildings. She saw the line of the ridge bent northward here to drive toward wooded foothills lying east of the pass, below the mountains. Within that bend lay a broad field left fallow: it was overgrown with tall grasses and many purple wildflowers, and on it rested four long columns of Dweorgish foot.

Zara shifted Te'a's line to move toward the nearest. The Dweorg were yet another ally of need. They were an over proud race and vain, demanding courtesy from all but giving it to few, certainly not to Zara herself. The creatures were crudely made: their faces sullen and heavy, their hands thick-fingered and overlarge, producing unlovely work of which the Dweorg were far too proud. They rode no animal for work or war and strayed nearly never from their high-walled hilltop forts. When they did go to war, they brought nothing but footmen such as these: armored in heavy plate. The Dweorg here carried that armor on their backs now, bound up in tall leather sacks so their columns looked more like lines of washerwomen carrying their labor to the river than an army come to war.

She met the near column toward its middle and passed forward toward the van. She commanded the field here, for now at least, so both courtesy and prudence demanded she deal with these Dweorg in person, as distasteful as it might be. Nearing the head of the column, she found an older Dweorg wearing the heavy gold necklace of a war leader. Suspended from its lower links was a bluntly fashioned silver pendent in the shape of a leaping stag. This Dweorg had a personal guard also, and they edged closer to their charge as Zara approached.

She ignored the affront, halting Te'a somewhat less than a polite distance from the leader to put on the face of diplomacy and raise her right hand in greeting. Then she spoke her name and made to the Dweorg the sign of instruction, intending to speak in Hands, for she spoke no Dweorgish and few Dweorg had any Common or Aelfan.

The leader gestured behind himself with a thick finger and another came forward to stand at his side: a younger Dweorg of lesser rank. He surprised Zara by addressing her in the Common, though his words were marred by the unpleasant clicks and deep growls of Dweorgish.

"My Lord Ocksyn welcomes you, my lady Aelf," the younger Dweorg said to her, "and acknowledges the Dweorg must hear your words. He will relay them to . . . out greater leader."

Zara almost laughed at this despite her gloom. *Welcomes me, does he? Surely like the arrival of a pox.*

"Thank His Lordship for his generous welcome," she said. "His presence here is needful and timely, and he is correct he must hear my words. They are now for his legions to take position on this high ground." Zara pointed toward the ridge. "With his right against that gully and his left set against those heights." She pointed now to the foothills that came down to meet the line of the ridge. "The Dweorg will have the honor of holding the left."

The younger Dweorg translated this and as he did the war leader's hard gaze followed Zara's finger. Then he looked her fully in face for the first time and spoke at length in his own tongue. Whatever he said caused yet more pairs of Dweorgish eyes to fix upon Zara in doubt.

"My Lord says he knows of you, lady Aelf," the translator said. "He asks why your king permits the dishonored to command his warriors. My lord would have slain you then, on that field, had it been in his choosing to do. He wonders why the Dweorg should take words from the dishonored."

Zara squeezed Te'a's reins and drew in a breath to contain her anger. *Not this, you stinking pizgaz!*

She thought to simply cluck to Te'a and ride away with dignity, but the Dweorg's words couldn't go unanswered: the challenge was too direct, and too many ears had heard it. Zara lifted herself to sit straighter in the saddle and leaned over the war leader to emphasize her height above him on the cat-sí.

"It is no business of yours, Dweorg," she said, the words cold and flinty, "what the King in the Wood shall do or shall not do. Nor shall you presume to pass judgment upon his wisdom." She lifted a hand from the reins then and made the sign for a master closing discussion with an apprentice.

The Dweorg's guard stirred at this but he ignored it, holding his gaze steady on Zara. When he spoke the tone was cold and deliberate, and he waited for the translator to relay each sentence as he said it.

"I was there that day, Aelf, when you and your kind rode your beasts away." The Dweorg pointed a finger at Te'a. "No

Human now alive beheld that day, only their grand-sires. But my eyes beheld it. From my place in the war-wall, I saw it. And the woe that followed. Many of my people went to sit with the gods that day because of you, Aelf." He spat the word.

Old arguments thronged in Zara, ready to hand. But she pushed them down. They hadn't sufficed then and they wouldn't suffice now, and certainly not for this dung-smelling Dweorg. She'd had her reasons then, on that field, and they'd seemed good to her then. They seemed good to her now, many score of years later. She could have won the Succession that day, with that one magnificent blow. And she'd thrown her fist boldly to strike it.

But it was not to be.

Her moon was waxing then. She was the sixth and least of her father's brood, yet she'd won command of the left wing of his Woodland Army: eight companies of cat-sí riders, four of foot, two of archery. It was a post of high honor, freshly wrested from another by rite of the knife. But the winning of that high place had not banked the fire of her ambition. It grew higher still, and she raised her eyes to places higher still: to command of the Woodland Army, to the council table of her father the king.

Even to the throne itself.

So that day she ached to strike a blow that would turn her rise into an unstoppable force, and she wrung her scouts dry until something emerged: a swampy mire that anchored the Orkh right and which all thought impassable.

It might yield, the nervous scout had said. *Just here,*

perhaps. But I'll not vouch for what lies beyond it, lady. I did not go there.

But the warning fell on deaf ears, for it seemed now to Zara a door had opened before her. She gave the archers and foot to her Second with orders to hold the left while she gone, then took every Aelf who could mount a cat-sí and rode them far left, seeking a passage into the rear of the Orkhs.

She found that mire, riding long and far to get there, and she drove her riders through it in the wan light of a quarter-moon. But the dry way was narrow, and many Aelfs strayed from it, seeking advantage. Their cat-sí were deeply mired, and many became lost or bewildered in that strange and trackless place.

When Zara emerged on the far side, she didn't know how many riders remained to her, but she pressed on, heedless and without counting. But her luck seemed to turn when she came upon the Orkhs' baggage train just where she thought to find it, and now her raid seemed a perfect stroke. The Aelfs struck that train like a thunderbolt as the sun rose, and Zara rode among them saber bared with a jubilant grin on her lips. For the eye of her mind fixed already on the bold future she would make for herself.

But fate turned against her again. The Aelfs were too few and the Orkhs too many. The toll of the mire had been too great. The riders were driven away with great loss, many scattered beyond recall.

But this, while terrible, was not the greatest of Zara's troubles that day. The Orkhish commanders were no fools and they divined correctly that Zara had stripped the allied left to the bone to make her force, and the line there was thin and frail. So as the sun rose the Orkhs made a hurried assault against it, swinging wide to strike its end with no fear of repulse or envelopment by cat-sí cavalry.

The Orkhs broke the Aelf foot first, then the archers. Then they smashed into the Human center from two sides, front and left; and finally they routed the Dweorg holding the right, whose support was swept away. It was a black day for the Free Peoples, and the stain on Zara was blacker still. No argument would efface it. No mere words could wish away the shame of it. Only deeds could bring her back.

Great deeds. But they couldn't be done here, trading words with a surly Dweorg.

"I hear you," Zara said to him. "But squawking as crows over an ancient corpse will not bring up more shields. Do as I instruct, Dweorg. Soon the Human Aetheling will come and you will not have to take your words from me."

The war leader didn't reply to this, but turned his back on Zara and walked away slowly with exaggerated dignity. His guard followed after, casting dark glances back to her. Zara remained where she was until the Dweorg columns began to move again, bending themselves separately toward those places she'd commanded. Satisfied, she wheeled Te'a around and urged the cat-sí into a gallop back toward the ridge.

"Eleven dead," Salf said. He wore a bandage on his left arm now, where a ricocheting arrow had bruised him deeply.

Zara sat Te'a still, her head turned from him.

"Eighteen wounded," he continued, "but only three not expected to return to their duty. Ten mounts dead, including three who were put down." The Aelf's tone was neutral, but

Zara could hear the tight disapproval behind it. She knew him well.

"How many Orkhs?" she said.

"Difficult to say, my lady. It was a running fight when the killing started. Disorderly."

"How many, Salf?"

He lifted his hands. "Perhaps forty? More? Again, it's—"

"Yes, it's difficult—you said. Put seventy-five in the dispatch. No, ninety." Fewer than seven to one would get even Zara recalled by her father and she couldn't have that. It would be the end of her.

"Yes, my lady," Salf replied, then he moved into Zara's view. The desire to speak was plain in the set of his head.

"Yes, what is it?" she snapped. "Out with it!" She wanted the Second to say his piece to her and begone, so she could brood in the dignity of solitude.

But his eyes held less reproach than she'd expected. "My lady, respectfully—"

"Oh, respectfully, is it? So it's hard words from you, is it, Salf?"

The Aelf moved to center himself on his feet, as if to do a hard duty, but his voice remained quiet. "No, Zara-ena, not harsh words. Only truth. This ridge was all we needed. Honor and prudence required nothing more of us. Nor would Aetheling Cenred have required more."

"To hell with Cenred!" she spat. "Do you follow orders like a slave, Salf, when opportunity presents?"

The Second drew breath and flushed. "That was no opportunity! It was—" He stopped himself.

"It was what, *Ritzar*?"

Salf shifted his stance again, as if to make a new approach. When he spoke again his voice carried a complex emotion Zara chose to ignore.

"My lady," he said, "this desire for redemption, it ill-becomes you. It is not needful and others are made to pay the price of it. None here doubt you." He caught her eye. "I do not. I never have."

Zara snapped the sign of anger at him. She felt her will returning. "I do not desire your good regard, Salf! It is the work of warriors to die, whether it is today or tomorrow." She could hear her arrogance but didn't care. "The chance for glory is fleeting, Salf, always. It lingers only a moment before winging away to another. When it comes, it must be seized with both hands. We have spoken of this many times."

He opened his mouth to reply but she carried on. "And what is need in war?" she said. "None know. Not I. Certainly not you. Our charge today may have set in motion a chain of happenings, one leading to the next, unknown to us now, that will turn the tide of battle tomorrow. The fortunes of war are dimly seen, *Ritzar*, or not at all, until the end is known."

He looked unswayed by this speech. "I see eleven misfortunes of war," he murmured, "and not dimly."

"That will do, *Ritzar*. Return to your duties. Report to me in two hours on the wounded, not before. You may go."

Salf looked to say more but checked himself and sketched a bow, then he departed. Zara frowned after him. *Damn that Aelf!* He didn't understand. He never had. This coming battle might be the one to decide this new war. If not that, then certainly it would decide the balance of many powers and interests before the next campaigning season. She must put herself on the right side of that balance.

Zara draw herself up in the saddle. Today had gone awry, yes, but this was only the first day. The players here were yet making their opening moves. She would redeem herself here on this field; and if more Aelfs must die for that to happen, then this also was the fortune of war.

<h1 style="text-align:center">2</h1>

OF EARIC

"I'm with child," Aere said.

Earic pulled his face from hers. "What?"

He'd heard the words, but they were so unexpected and they'd drawn up so many emotions so quickly, it was all he could think to say.

What?

"I'm with child, Earic," she said again with patience for which he was grateful. "It's yours, Earic. There's no other."

He stared at her, that single, effectless word lingering between them still. She was the warrior he was not: an archer of Hengar's Company in the King's Own, and she wore the scars of her long campaigning. Across her cheek lay the curled, pitted flesh of an old burn: the touch of an Orkh's flaming brand. And the upper half of her left ear was long lost to a sword, giving her a charming air of being lopsided. Earic thought from the first these scars became her, telling the story of a fierce warrior devoted to her duty.

But she was also far below his station. For she came from common crofters living beneath a sod-roof and working the lands of another for a third part of its meager yield. Fierce or not, Aere was no match for the son of an earl, even the youngest son such as Earic was. So even before today he was determined to end their dalliance when the ground froze and the Fyrd went home and to winter quarters. He would return then to his father's halls, alone, and wait there for campaigning to resume in the spring.

Now all his workings were overset.

"I had thought . . . I thought we were careful," he said.

Aere smiled and took his chin in her fingers to square his face with hers. "The gods will make it rain when they wish, Earic. Are you not happy?"

He moved his eyes from hers to study his warring emotions. His gaze fell on her longbow leaned against the wall of the loft. She'd left it there, straight and unstrung, when he came to him.

A child. Perhaps a son.

Earic wondered whether he should acknowledge it. Could he acknowledge it? What would his father say? His mother would certainly be ill-pleased.

"Earic," Aere said, drawing his eyes back to hers. "Speak to me."

She was right: he should say something. Earic drew breath, searching for a place within where he could stand firmly to face her. But he couldn't find that place. Winds like he'd never known buffeted him. She was his first love. Or was it truly love? Perhaps it wasn't, but only a passing desire he would soon forget. He didn't know. How could he know? And did it matter? They could never wed: he was high born, she low.

Earic yearned now to return to those first days when they were new to each other. It had been so right then, so easy to slip into this world of their own making. But now: now it was complicated, and so suddenly. Or maybe it wasn't. He could leave her now and never return. None whose opinion mattered would think less of him.

It was hot in the loft now, even in his nakedness, and Aere's gaze lay on him still, waiting. There were many questions, but only one answer he could give her now.

"Yes," he said. "I'm very happy."

She smiled at him, but seemed troubled as she leaned in to kiss his lips. "Then wear a happy face, my lord," she said.

He accepted the kiss then said, "His name shall be Gar, the little arrow from your bow."

She laughed at this, but shook her head. "No. Her name shall be Eoforhild, a fierce warrior like her mother."

"You don't look so fierce now," he said, "lying bare in a farmer's hay."

Aere covered herself with her hands. "You are deceived, good sir! Were you an Orkh, you would see my true steel!"

They laughed and then each looked away across the loft. Earic didn't know what he felt for this woman: except he felt something—maybe something strong. He wished again she was high born. If the gods did indeed order the world as they wished, as Aere had said, it was certain they were cruel.

"We must put some thought to this," he said at last, giving voice to the thing that lay between them.

Her eyes darkened. "Will you cast me away?"

"No!" he said, but it was too quick, too loud: false even to his own ears. In truth, he had thought to cast her away, even before now. In his night thoughts he'd even told himself that when the time came for their parting, the fire of their togetherness would have gone to embers to kicked apart and left to die.

"No," he said again, quieter. "I will not cast you away."

Her gaze sharpened. "Then will you take me for wife?"

Earic jerked. "I cannot!"

Her mouth grew hard. "Cannot? You are the son of a high ealdorman! You may do as you wish, Earic! There are few in this world who can say so much. Your father will give us a house. Land and horses. What would an acre or three be to him? We will be happy!"

Earic scrubbed his face with his hands. Hay clung to him and his skin itched. "My father would not give us a house," he said, "nor leave to marry. He would disown me, that's what he would do. He would see even the asking of it as a shame on our house."

Aere sat up, casting about for her clothing. "So we're a shame, are we? Our child is a shame too, is it? It's your shame, Earic Eadwulfing, not mine!"

Now she was standing, holding her tunic in her hands. She pulled it over her head and shook the skirts out over her legs, then she drew the belt closed with shaking fingers.

"What of me, Earic?" she cried. "I carry your child in my belly. Who will have me? What will become of me? Will you throw a purse from your horse as you ride past?"

He opened his mouth to deny it, but she cut him off. "I will go," she said. "There is no need to follow, and no need to call for me again. And no need for a purse." She took her bow from the wall and her leather quiver of white-fletched arrows that sat beside it, and moved toward the hayloft ladder.

Earic stood now, shedding motes of hay to shine in the orange light from the open hay door. Moments before the nakedness of his body had felt right, but now it seemed duplicitous, as if he'd never intended to do more than ravish her.

"Aere!" he cried, but then no more came to him to say. He didn't know what to say that would be truth, or wouldn't hurt her more.

She regarded him from the top of the ladder. Her face was set in an expression he couldn't read, but the warrior burned in her eyes.

"This," she said, gesturing with the bow to the loft around them, "was enough when it was we two rolling in the hay. I didn't need anything from you then. I do now."

She fixed the quiver to her belt and swung herself onto the ladder, then climbed down out of his sight.

Earic lowered himself back to the sun-warmed hay where they'd lain. What he'd said to her was the truth: he could not wed her. It was an iron law of the world in which he lived. He could flee that world, but this would mean turning his back on everything he knew: his family, his work here, his birth. The price was high.

He decided then he would not decide; or not here, not now. He was aware this was a kind of cowardice, but he couldn't think clearly and he had a meeting with his Witanmen in an hour, followed by a council of war in Cenred's tent, to hear the final plan for the Fyrd's move down the pass road. The fight with the Orkhs was coming soon and he needed all he had for that.

He looked around the loft for his breeches. He would

certainly protect Aere—protect them—whatever else happened. He'd done it before, months ago, early in their togetherness: calling in a favor, perhaps overreaching, to move Aere from the band of her liege to Hengar's Company in the King's Own. He'd concealed from her his hand in this, allowing her to believe it was a mark of confidence by some other.

The King's Own was newly formed for this war: conceived—in part by Earic himself—as a reserve to meet whatever contingency might arise on the field. It possessed a company of heavy infantry to plug gaps in the shield wall, a cohort of lighter infantry to repel flanking attacks, archers to counter the enemy's own, and cavalry to exploit advantages and run down broken and fleeing foes. It was a versatile tool kept ready to hand; and best of all, it waited in the rear for a problem that might never happen.

Aere would be safe there. Or as safe as may be in war.

Earic found his breeches and put his legs into them, then stood to shrug on a green officer's tunic. Then the baldric went over his head and the sword on it fell to settle by his hip. It was only a symbol of his office, for he hadn't drawn a blade in anger for many years. It was his aptitude for tactics and for the movement of armies, not any skill with the sword, that first pulled him up to a seat at Cenred's table. He'd been twenty-four then. Four years after that, the High Aetheling made Earic the Master of Scouts, a job he loved. But he'd grown soft in those years, and untrained. The sword would feel heavy and awkward in his hand.

He drew on his boots, leaning against a post, then moved to the ladder and clumped down its dirty treads. He went to the barn door, but did not leave until he'd spent a full minute peering out from within. He searched for eyes that might be surprised to see a high officer, and the son of a well-known ealdorman, leaving a lonely barn close in the wake of a common woman. But he saw no one and left the barn in the direction of his tent, resolved to attend to his duty.

The map that lay on Earic's work table was a poor one. It had been drawn by one of his scouts, likely in the saddle, and it betrayed a remarkably lazy eye for detail. There was no key and no estimate of distances, and long wavering lines that might have been water or fences or contours meandered randomly across the wrinkled parchment. But this would have to do, because it was all he had. Little of the King's Dominion was mapped, none of it south of this pass; so two days ago Earic had sent a scout to draw the land. This dereliction of duty was the result. There was no time to send another to do the same work.

Frowning at the map, Earic pushed away thoughts of Aere to focus on framing the battlefield in his mind. Four others, the Witanmen who advised him, stood near, waiting for him to speak.

"This place is not ideal for a fight," he said, addressing them. "The pass itself is a problem. It's too wide and too flat at the top to be held as a choke point, so we have to find another defensive position. And it must be south of the pass, since the King has ordered no Orkh may place a boot into the Northlands."

He placed a fingertip on the map, at a place where the scout had drawn two pointed buildings as a child might. "This town at the south foot of the pass is Suthgaet, an unclever name. Below the town is an open plain running south a hundred leagues or better toward Orkh country. It's flat for the most part, certainly here.

"To the west and southwest of town is flat farmland, extending west toward forested land, and north to the foothills of the range. That whole area out west will be an easy place for the Orkhs to cross in force, getting into our rear quickly and cutting off our line of retreat back up the pass road. It's what I would do, at any rate. So, gentlemen. I need ideas for holding this gods-forsaken piece of flat ground to the west, this farmland. Aetheling Cenred will ask me about it later, at council."

Earic straightened then and looked around the table, catching eyes. The competence of the men here varied widely. Two had been pushed on him for lack of a better place to put them, and now they marked time on his Witan as placeholders, eating stores and offering little in return. The other two Earic had handpicked, using every bit of his good will with Cenred to draw them away. They were thoughtful and hardworking, and Earic listened to them.

One of these was Behrt, who paused to see if another wished to go first before clearing his throat. The man was no warrior, but he had a keen eye for the motions of war. He swept a fingertip over the scout's map.

"As you say, sir," he said, "this area to the west is most troublesome. Nearly all the harvest will be taken in by now and there's been little rain for a week or better, so the ground there will be firm and dry." The man rubbed his neck. "The first thing, the obvious thing, is to put cavalry against this forested land to the far west, to threaten the Orkhs' flank when they do come. The second thing—well, the more important thing actually—is this building here, if the map is to be believed." Behrt placed a fingertip on a sketch of a tall building with a outwall around it. It lay some distance southwest of Suthgaet. Exactly how far was not the least clear.

I'll have that scout's skin for a tent door.

"I saw that," Earic said aloud. "A farmstead, I suppose. A large one by the look of the wall. But it's isolated, or seems so. There might be a lot of open ground between that stead and the town."

"If the Orkhs take that place, sir, it'll be impossible to dislodge them," Behrt said. "And it's a perfect step-off for a quick attack, since it shortens their approach." The man paused, thinking. "On the other hand, a well-supplied company, maybe two, would be hard for the Orkhs to push out. And they would have to leave that place in their rear, garrisoned, when they came toward us. It would make their work more difficult in a place where we want it as difficult as possible. Sir, I consider it imperative we take and hold that farmstead. The wall makes that place a fortress, right on our front."

Earic studied the map, but thoughts of Aere intruded. Did she really think he could wed her? It would be the ruin of him. "I agree, Behrt," he said. "I'll urge that notion on Cenred." He looked around the table then. "Anyone else? Other thoughts on this area to the west, or do we agree?"

They did agree, and Earic turned his attention to the order of battle. This was Cuthred's particular duty and Earic raised an eyebrow at him. "Who'll be late?"

"Eadred's Legion, most likely, sir," Cuthred said. "He's moving on the roads through the vale to the north. More or less here, if the map ran to that. His people caught it hard at Fenric's Ford, so he'll not be pushing them. He'll be the last up, I think, barring the unforeseen."

Earic almost laughed at that. Yes, there was always the unforeseen, wasn't there? Had she done it of a purpose? Surely not. He wasn't a wealthy man. His father was, but the youngest son of any ealdorman was left to struggle for himself.

"What of Ceadda?" Earic asked.

"He's drawn up to us this last day. He'll follow us down and into position tomorrow. He and Eadred, and the others coming late, ought to move west of town to block that farmland. Raedmund's people, also. He has archers and this is his Hundred, so he knows the ground."

"I agree," Earic said. He pursed his lips. "Cenred intends to put the Dweorg on the left. Thoughts?"

"I would also," Cuthred said, "but they may feel lonely there. It'll be the safest place on the battlefield—far from that farmland."

"Ill-used is what they'll feel," Earic said, "and their tender honor slighted. So they'll be unpredictable. More so than usual. But we need a rock on the left. Maybe we can find something for them to do. What about the Orkhs? Anything new?"

Cuthred turned up his hands. "No, sir. I'm sorry. Their cavalry has put up a tight screen, so our information is nearly a day old. Same as you heard then. The main body coming up from the south, and more coming from the southwest. A rumor of Trolles, but only that, a rumor."

"Commanders?" Earic asked.

Cuthred looked more confident at this. "Ugash has taken command of the army coming from the south. He killed Graz some days ago. We're certain of that. I don't reckon Ugash will shed any of the aggressiveness he showed as an independent commander. I'm sure you'll remember The Hollows, sir. He'll push us hard, very hard indeed. He might even have something in his sleeve."

"Such as?"

Cuthred shrugged. "No idea, but that's his way. He'll work to get us off balance then knock us over with something we didn't expect. That's another reason Behrt thinks—we think—this farmstead, or whatever it is, is important. Taking it will force him to react to us, if nothing else comes of it."

Earic grunted in agreement. He was convinced about the farmstead. "Who else is out there?"

"The new round of up and comers," Cuthred said. "Ool-gorash, The Beast, Nah-car. Tsov-ar-kan, of course.

"Tsov-ar-kan," Earic said, musing over the name. "He's the truly ambitious one. I expect he'll make a move on Ugash soon, before he can consolidate power. Interesting. I presume Prince Mar-gul still has the army coming up from the southwest?"

"Yes, sir," Cuthred said. "He'll be in a natural position to take up the Orkhs' left and occupy this farmstead, unless we get to it first."

"He's under Ugash's orders?"

"We don't know, sir, but probably yes. The Prince is a hothead though, even for an Orkh. He could do something unexpected, too. His troops are veterans and spirited, and he's a clever bastard himself. That west side of the field will be hot."

"Agreed," Earic said. "Anything else?" He looked around the table, but there was nothing. "All right, get out there and find me more information I can use. And gods damn it, get me a better map!"

When the others had left, Earic fell into a camp chair and put his head in his hands. Thinking about the battle to come was easy: the problems were clear for the most part, and the range of possible solutions easily seen and weighed. He was good at that. But he had a poor head for dilemmas he couldn't parse with logic. And that was exactly what this child was: a messy, intractable problem he couldn't think his way out of it. He couldn't push counters across a map table to find the dispositions to make the problem dissolve.

He set his chin in his hand and thought again of sending Aere away and never seeing her again. Men of his rank denied bastard children every day, and he would be believed out of hand by those whose opinion mattered. Aere's word would count for nothing, and she would soon be side aside and forgotten.

His heart squeezed at this and he shied from the thought.

If he took them in, acknowledging the child and marrying Aere as she wished, he would be forever the nobleman who fell: living out the remainder of his life in a rude cot on paltry land, or moving from place to place and calling nowhere civilized home.

Earic thrust himself from the chair and strode from the tent into open air, hoping his problems might seem less constricting there. He chose a random direction and stalked across camp, passing many gray tents, his eyes fixed on the ground. His heart pounded in his chest. How could she do this to him?

Damn her! Damn her to Hell!

He walked for hours, unseeing and unhearing, and heeding no one. Until finally another voice spoke, intruding on his thoughts.

No, Earic Eadwulfing, it said, *damn you to hell. For it was you who did this.*

The sun had passed behind the high peaks in the west and the hour came for Cenred's council of war. Earic set aside the question of Aere, as he could, and turned his steps toward the Aetheling's tent. It stood in the protected center of the encampment, tall and wide, and its great canvas bulk shuddered under a strong evening breeze. Flags stood at its poles, snapping in the same air, and all about the tent the vanguard of the king's Fyrd, his army, rested and waited.

It was a war camp like any other Earic had known: men and women, warriors all, gathered about cook fires that grew brighter as the gloom deepened, and they filled their bellies with supper as only soldiers uncertain of their next meal can do. What talk Earic heard from them was pensive and quiet; but he heard laughter also, and boasting, and rowdies who called out in jest to comrades passing by. There was confidence here. He could feel it. This was not their first taste of war: the Fyrd had campaigned through the summer, in the hilly east, repulsing the Orkhs' first searching fingers of invasion. But now the hand and arm came behind, reaching to seize and hold open this wide doorway into Human lands.

He looked north, higher up the pass road, as he walked. Aere was up there, somewhere, with the King's Own. He imagined the others huddled about her like a guard, protecting her—protecting *them*—from Orkhish steel. Earic drew a long breath to steady himself against his fears. All would be well.

"Welcome," Cenred said to them, shifting his papers around a large wooden map table. "This will be our last council before moving down into position."

The man was an Aetheling, a cousin of the King, though distant. He had come up in the last war, finding fame and favor in a gallant four-day rearguard action Earic had studied once. Then a Thegn of Foot, Cenred had used rough terrain, a difficult river crossing, and a most remarkable cunning to confuse and delay a far larger force of Orkhs. This had allowed the king's Fyrd to flee a trap its commander had blundered into.

Now it was Cenred who commanded the Fyrd, and he'd recognized early Earic's own talents, lifting him to his current station over others more senior. For this mark of trust Earic felt a large measure of gratitude and even affection for the old man, far more than he felt for his own rigid and unforgiving father. But he didn't envy Cenred this command. The risks were great: defeat here, or even withdrawal, would open the door wide for these approaching horde to rampage unchecked across Dominion lands.

So they were met now: the Thegns and Ceorls who commanded the Fyrd's warriors, together with others like Earic who thought and planned in support. The air in the tent was overwarm with torches and tense with expectation.

Cenred continued: "Before we get to details, I want to impress on you the need for haste. Our time advantage now is very slight. So each of you will urge haste in all things. Aylett will give you the final dispositions in a moment. They've changed since we last met. But each of you knows what I expect of you on the field. Opportunity must be exploited, even without orders. Unexpected threats must be countered promptly, and with firmness. Do not ask me for permission to do what you know must be done."

His eyes on them turned sympathetic now. "I know it's been a long campaign. I know your troops are tired and foot-sore. But we must stop these brutes here, or nowhere. We're defending our homes now, and our families. They deserve every drop of blood and strength we possess. We can do this, and I know you won't let me down—or the king."

As he spoke Cenred caught and held many eyes around the tent, including Earic's. Then he gestured to a man waiting behind him. "Give it to them, Aylett."

The man stepped forward and extracted with precise fingers a single leaf of paper from a stack on Cenred's table. When this was laid atop the pile, Earic saw it was a hastily sketched map much like his own. But it was not his own: that one lay on his table in his tent. He edged closer for a better view but couldn't see through the press of bodies at the table.

Aylett cleared his throat and spoke quickly, walking his fingers across the map as he did. Most of what he said Earic knew already: the direct approach to the town and pass road would be protected by a shield wall. It would begin on the left—the east—with the Dweorg, and extend west below Suthgaet along a ridge of high ground Earic hadn't known was there.

Gods damn that scout!

The middle of the ridge and the right would be held by Human heavy infantry. And as Behrt had suggested to Earic, the distant right, beyond the western farmland, would be watched by the cat-sí company of Lady Zara, who would look for opportunities to strike the Orkhs as they arrived, harrying them. Earic was certain the aggressive Aelf would find that opportunity in every turn of the wind.

Aylett then scribed a broad circle on the map with a fingertip and looked up. "That leaves this gap here: the open farmland between the end of the shield wall on the ridge and Zara watching the far right. It's a problem. We don't have a quarter of the heavy companies needed to extend the shield wall out to cover that ground. As you may remember we discussed this at the last council with no decision taken."

The man stood straighter then, assuming an air of self-importance. "Since that time My Lord Cenred and I have worried at this problem, and we have a plan for it."

Earic pursed his lips. He hadn't heard of this new plan.

Aylett continued: "We need every little advantage we can get out there in the west. Everything will count for something. So what we—what Lord Cenred has decided is to gather up what's left after the ridge is covered, including all the reserves, and make them into two large formations that can cover ground quickly. Two legions, I suppose, as the oil-eaters once called them. They will defend that farmland."

"All the reserves?" a voice asked. "Is that wise?"

It was Cenred who replied to this. He stepped forward again. "Yes, Aldwin. All the reserves, plus whatever else we can pull up from the rear." A murmur rose then and Cenred held up a hand against it. "Yes, I know it's a risk, but there's too much ground to cover out there. If the Orkhs break through toward the town and the pass road, there'll be no stopping them, reserves or no reserves. These two legions will roam the field there, striking and retreating as they may, preventing the Orkhs from concentrating their forces. They will be centered around two core companies: Aethlwulf's Band and The King's Own."

Prickly heat washed over Earic and his belly tightened. He felt nauseous. *It can't be!* The King's Own was always held in reserve. That was its sole purpose. But now Cenred meant to drop The King's—and Aere—directly into the bloody cauldron that farmland was sure to be.

Earic realized suddenly he had cleared his throat.

"You have an observation?" Aylett said to him mildly.

Earic searched for something to say. "The King's wasn't meant for the front. Not like that."

"We're aware, sir. Nevertheless."

Earic addressed Cenred now. "The King's is better used as we intended, sir! As a ready reserve."

The Aetheling shook his head. "Not this time, Earic. That open land poses a special problem, which I'm sure you understand well. We must have quickness out there, for we have nothing else."

Earic flushed at this. He'd said a damned fool thing and Cenred knew it. The tent was very hot now and Earic scrubbed at the stubble on his face. His thoughts galloped. Was this new plan of Cenred's genius or foolishness? He didn't know, but it certainly seemed desperate. And what of Aere? How could he protect her? Nowhere was safe now. Everyone was being pushed up against the Orkhs.

Gods!

This had gone bad, and so suddenly.

Earic thought of the farmstead and its high wall. That place was important to this fight in the west, and he'd intended to recommend strongly it be taken and garrisoned against the enemy. But now he was utterly certain the King's Own, or some part of it, would be sent to take it. He would have done so himself: the company was made for such a lightning stroke.

But neither Cenred nor Aylett had mentioned that farmstead. *We need every little advantage we can get out there*, the aide had said, but then he hadn't breathed a word of the place. It was one hell of a little advantage.

The truth struck Earic then: they didn't know about the farmstead. It wasn't on their map.

"Are you content, Earic?" Cenred asked. "Or do you have something else? A brilliant suggestion, perhaps?" The man smiled, his face open and expectant, trusting.

Earic mopped his brow with a sleeve. No, he damned well wasn't content. Far from it. His mind warred against itself now: pulling him in two directions. In one, he struggled to think of a reason why Cenred might hold back the King's Own, or place it in the town, where Aere would be safer. But there was no reason, or none the man would accept.

In the other direction he anguished over his duty, and it was clear to him what that was: he should tell Cenred of the farmstead and its high wall. As Cenred's Master of Scouts, Earic's prime remit was to tell the man what he didn't know: to lead him from error, and so preserve lives that might be thrown away in ignorance. That was his duty and all Earic's career in the King's Service, indeed all his life as a noble, was given to doing his duty. It made him who he was.

Until now.

Earic tried to lick his lips but his tongue was thick and dry. He wanted water. No, he wanted to leave this place and its oppressive heat. But Cenred waited still: waited for something brilliant, something battle-winning, from his Master of Scouts. And the crowning folly of it all—the thing that made this seem an ill-conceived jest—was that Earic *did* have something brilliant: possession of this walled farmstead might turn the day in the west. He should open his mouth, now, and speak of it.

But he couldn't. He didn't know whether he loved Aere. This remained opaque to him. And he didn't know what he would do about this child. But he found, here in this tent, that he could not speak the words that would send Aere into that terrible danger.

"No, sir," he said at last, hiding his eyes by looking down at his hands. "I have no brilliant suggestion. Your plan seems to me as sound as may be."

His legs no longer wanted to support him. *Gods preserve me!*

Cenred let a moment pass before speaking to the group again. "Very well. One more thing. The king will arrive soon. In his own time, of course, but perhaps late tomorrow. So let's move the Fyrd down the road quickly and run these Orkhs back to their holes for him. I have every confidence we will. Get to work."

The others left the tent then, but Earic remained where he was, forcing himself to breath normally. His chest was tight and something had moved up to constrict his throat.

"Are you feeling well, my friend?" Cenred asked. He, too, hadn't moved.

Earic nodded but it was too quick, too jerky. He wondered if Cenred noticed. "Yes, sir," he said, pushing through the thickness in his throat. "It's been a long few days, sir, and there's more ahead."

"Indeed, there is," Cenred said, then he moved around the table to grasp Earic's shoulder with strong, friendly fingers. "We'll kill these bastards, Earic. A lot of them. And we'll drive them off. I know that. I know it because I have good men like you in my army."

Earic made no reply. Cenred was a fine war leader, and an even finer man: quick to praise, slow to blame, loyal to those he trusted. Earic had come to love him without reserve, but now he had betrayed him.

3

OF BERA

Bigan Heolfbera was a Half-Orkh, or 'half-bear' as his name was. But from the first his mother called him only Bera, and this was the name he knew. She was Human and she raised her only child alone in the high borderlands of the King's Dominion, where the soil was thin and stony and produced little. But those windy moors were also little-peopled, so there were few to see her dark son grow.

Of his father, Bera knew only that he was an Orkh, for his mother would say no more. But Bera knew from counting he'd been conceived and born during the Old War, the one before this one, at a time when Orkhs rampaged across the Dominion.

He knew also his father had survived that war, for as Bera grew toward his full stature, gifts came to their door, laid quietly on the stoop in the night. Gifts meant for a young Orkhish warrior, including the Orkh-wrought sword he carried at his hip now. Neither he nor his mother ever spied that giver of gifts, but Bera knew it could be none other than his own father, or one sent by him.

This pleased and saddened him both, for he wished to know his father and be known by him. But his mother stood duty for each as Bera grew into himself, and she loved her Half-Orkh son fiercely and raised him well.

But Bera had came to know others did not love him. When he emerged from those stony borderlands to make his way in the Human world, they saw only his towering height, his blacker than black skin, the curve of his canines as they emerged from his lower lip to crease the upper. They saw that his eyes were crimson as the dustiest sunset, and that his black hair stood from his head like the bristles of an old boar. So they gave him another name: *Heolfswin*, half-pig.

The ignorance of the slur goaded him. Did he not dress as a man? Did he not have two legs to march and two arms to wear a shield in the wall and work the sword? Did he not have the winning manners of a courtly man, learned at his mother's knee?

He could read and understand the Strictures of War, and he spoke the Common gently, altering its sounds by long care to blow soft and unthreatening around his teeth. And he learned to lower his head and pull in his shoulders to speak to those who called him *Heolfswin* behind his back, and to stand away from them a pace more than others might, so as not to overbear.

He did these things because he yearned for the acceptance of his mother's people, and for an honorable place among them.

But Bera's strong legs and good arms, his winning manners, his reading, and his habit of deference had carried him only to command of a guard company assigned to the provisions train of the king's Fyrd. Even this lowly station—as

Wulfric the Provisions Thegn had told Bera one cold day many months before—was granted to him solely by the grace of Bera's uncle, a warrior grazing now in pasture but hoarding still a career's worth of favors to call due.

The Thegn had left Bera no room for illusion that day: when the old man was dead, his body wouldn't be cold in the ground before the order came to send his Half-Orkh nephew to a quarter-pay post somewhere far, far away, where no one had to look at him.

But that day was yet to come. Bera still commanded that provisions guard company, and this morning he was arguing with his Second, a man named Dudda.

"You begged off your duty yesterday," Bera said to him. "To drink, I presume. And I suppose it's the same today, is it?"

Dudda was a small man, short and spare-limbed. He had a narrow, unwashed face and greasy hair thrusting from his head like a hummock of dark weeds. He was nearly lost in a oversized linen shirt with a ragged tail.

"There ain't no harm in it, sir," the man said. "Them other Orkhs, the bad ones, they ain't here yet. They're still down yonder." He flapped a hand in the direction of the pass road. "Any rate, sir, the troops know what to do. Dig the ditch, plant the 'batis, dig the privies. Every camp, every night. Don't need me to tell'em, do they?" He grinned at Bera. "Nor you either, sir."

This was not a new argument. Bera had heard it many times, and he was well aware the man would find a way to disappear into the camp's hooch tents regardless of permission. Bera could deny that permission, and by rights he should, but it wouldn't do to antagonize Dudda. Bera needed him. The Second had been with the company far longer than Bera had, and even in his present state of dissolution he could coax far more obedience from it than Bera the Half-Orkh ever could. So the man got away with far more than was right: a fact they both knew very well.

Even so, some token resistance must be offered. "Do you suppose," Bera said, "that other commanders allow their Seconds such liberties? Or permit their Seconds to shirk their duty to swill camp poison and roll in the mud like pigs?"

"Oh no, sir!" Dudda said. "I won't roll in no mud. On my honor!" He raised a hand but Bera could imagine no oath sticking to its dirt. "Any rate, sir, today I got on my best britches, or cleanest any ways."

Bera frowned. This man was truly the *heolfswin*. "Do not burn anything," he said, tiring of the dance. "Do not steal anything, unless we can use it. Do not get a washerwoman with child. Another of you is more than this world can hold."

Dudda lifted a hand to tug at his forelock. "Thank'ee, sir."

"This will be the last time," Bera added. "The line companies are already moving down the pass road. We will follow soon after. Tomorrow maybe. I want you sharp as a kite's whistle in the morning, Dudda. You'll have to work through the shakes."

The man was already turning away, licking his lips. "As you say, sir, as you say. You wouldn't have a coin or two on you, would you? Three?"

Bera nearly laughed at this. But he drew out his purse and passed the man three coppers. "So I'm taken in again," he said. "Now go, before I find my senses."

The little man did go, speeding away over the mud with

his shirt tail flapping behind him. Bera watched him go. He didn't wonder why he allowed this man such liberties, for he knew the reason: the Second was indispensable. Bera understood this and he'd made his peace with it.

What held him was the perennial question of himself. Was this worth it? Would that man, and the Humans around him, one day see him as more than a beast whose Orkhish nature might suddenly rise to slay them all? Would they come to consider his Orkhish blood only a misfortune of birth, as he did, rather than an indelible mark of savagery? Or was that hope only folly?

It couldn't be; for if it was, then what else was there to hope for?

These thoughts were interrupted by the sound of boots. Bera turned to it and saw Atul approaching. He, also, commanded a guard company in provisions, but his company was assigned to Thegn Wulfric's personal quarters. This was a post Atul regarded as far loftier than Bera's.

The man stopped well short of Bera and said, "Are your mule-switchers put to bed, Heolfbera? Can you come away? We need a fourth."

Bera had no taste for cards, and he was unable to read the small motions of his table mates that betrayed their minds. Yet a chance for goodwill with his peers was something he'd schooled himself not to avoid.

"Let me tuck them in," he said, galling himself by continuing the man's ill-mannered jest. "Then I'll be there directly."

"Don't be long, Heolfbera," Atul said. "I'm feeling lucky tonight."

The man turned away then and strode toward the common tent. It stood tall and wide-skirted in the distance, its canvas walls glowing with torchlight. A long pennant hung at the center pole, but the colors were dimmed to gray by the slow-lurking gloom of evening.

That same gloom cast a concealing cloak over the squalor and filth of camp that surrounded Bera; but it could do nothing for the smells. These were many and strong, and they were familiar to him now: damp canvas and woodsmoke, unwashed bodies of Humans and animals, the iron tang of smithy fires, and acres of dust mixed with piss and dung. They were the eternal scents of an army moving toward war.

Bera went to find where his company was working. He passed provisions wagons parked hub to hub, and long strings of mules and oxen picketed for the night. Teamsters sat at fires, drinking. They watched him pass and murmured low words in his wake. He ignored it.

He found a group from his company working at the eastern edge of camp. They were digging a ditch that would, if finished, protect the provisions train. In the trees beyond, others of his company chopped out branches and deadfall for the abattis works.

Dudda was right: they did know what to do. They'd done it a hundred times in a hundred camps. Whether they would do it well was another question. These were not the King's Finest. Given their heads, they would crawl into a jug to join Dudda.

"You there!" Bera said to the nearest. He struggled for the man's name. "Guncar, is it?"

The man spiked his spade into the mud and leaned on the

handle. "Which it is," he said, spitting through his teeth without turning his head.

Bera ignored this also. "Second Dudda is occupied elsewhere," he said and the man laughed. He knew: they all knew. Bera ignored this, too. "So here is your duty, warrior. You and these others will finish this section of the ditch and abattis. Then you will dig out the privies. When that's done, you may go to the Quartermaster for a dram each. I will tell him. This may be the last night we sleep easy. Do you understand?"

At the mention of liquor the man straightened from his slouch. "Aye. We finish this rot then we get a snort. The troops'll like to hear that."

Bera didn't doubt it. Those nearby had heard already and the sound of work took on a quicker rhythm. Guncar took up the spade again and resumed work without being dismissed. Bera let that go, too.

Perhaps they would complete the work here by full dark with this new incentive. It was an unusual one, but the company itself was unusual. It was long the rubbish pit into which line commanders dumped their undesirables: the lazy, the stupid, the ill-content, the craven. All were sent to guard the provisions train and Bera was sent to shepherd them, the most undesired of all.

He turned from the work and backtracked toward the common tent. Those who crossed his path in the light of the standing torches moved far around him, but he paid little notice. He was thinking of the game ahead. Atul would have two others with him: his own Second, a man named Egbert, and another of his company called Penda. These two ever trailed in their captain's wake, seeking favor by allowing him to win, or so Bera supposed. He took comfort in the thought he wasn't the only one looking for a place in the world.

At the common tent, he pushed past a dubious guard and stepped inside. The space was large and crowded with warriors. The floor had been grass once but now lanes of mud and puddling brown water snaked between tables crowded with card players, dicers, and drinkers, a great many of whom shouted to be heard. The air was warm and close, and the ceiling of the tent and the tops of its poles were concealed by a slowly tumbling cloud of gray smoke that rose from the torches.

Bera's skin prickled under his woolen sark: he didn't want to be here. The stale air, smelling of Human sweat, seemed to warn him of danger. But he swallowed his unease and moved deeper into the hot throng. Heads turned as he passed and voices fell, but he affected to ignore the attention.

He felt the shame of it even so. It was shame not for his heritage, but for his place in this tent of warriors. In truth, he had no place here. His work was not to fight, but to shepherd the unfit and to guard the train, far in the rear. He longed for glory on the field, and an honored place at these tables, but there was little hope for either.

He found Atul and the other two sitting at a table against the far wall of the tent, well away from the shouting knots of warriors. When he saw this, it occurred to Bera to wonder whether Atul himself might have as little place here as he did. He wondered if this galled Atul as much as it did him, and whether it galled the man still more to find himself no higher in the world than a Half-Orkh.

Perhaps, but he didn't look galled now. Atul had tilted his chair back on two legs and put his muddy boots on the tabletop by the only empty chair. His uniform coat was unbuttoned and it lay aslant on his chest. A wooden flagon sat on the table before him.

"Here you are," he said to Bera. "You've made us wait. Did the mules need an extra story for bed?"

Bera didn't reply, but gestured for Atul to remove his boots. Then he brushed mud from the table and sat, nodding to Egbert and Penda as he leaned to fish out his purse. It was plump with coin, for Bera had little use for money. He wanted other things more.

He set the purse on the table and did his best to look friendly. He knew a Human would have smiled here, but he knew also his own smile would bare his canines and have an ill effect.

"Let's play, gentlemen," he said, contenting himself with this.

Atul dropped the chair and scraped a deck of cards from the tabletop. "I like that!" he said. "This Orkh gets down to business."

Bera let the jibe pass unremarked and watched as three more purses were placed on the table. They anted the pot with a click of coin on wood.

"The game is five-and-queens," Atul said. "No three-draws, at least until I'm well into Heolfbera's purse." He brayed a laugh at this and shuffled the deck. Then he dealt, winning the first hand and looking arch as he raked the coins to himself. Bera wondered if the other two had underplayed their draws but he said nothing. His own hand had been poor.

"Wulfric tells us the move is tomorrow," Atul said. "I know you don't hear things down there in the mud."

Bera doubted very much the Provisions Thegn deigned to tell Atul anything at all. "My company will be ready," he said.

"Will it? I hear your Second would miss the ground if he fell. That'd never go in my company. There's a reason I'm with the Thegn, Heolfbera, and another reason why you're . . . wherever you are. Where are you?"

Bera kept his face mild. He'd come for companionship, but was finding abuse. Now he thought maybe something worse was coming. "I'm where I was ordered to be," he said. "Someone deal."

Atul shoved the deck at Bera. "That's you, Ceorl Heolfbera," he said. "Deal'em up." Then he reached between his legs and dragged the chair closer to the table until the flaps of his coat pressed against the edge, then he picked up the flagon and drank.

Bera took up the cards and shuffled. Egbert was pushing a coin around the tabletop as he waited and Penda stared silently at something over Bera's left shoulder. Neither of them had said a word, and now Bera felt uneasy about sitting with his back to so much of the tent. But he'd been given no choice, perhaps by design.

He dealt and Atul won again with two high courtiers. Half the pot had been Bera's. They played the next two hands in quick succession. One went to Penda, then another to Atul, who grinned at Bera over whatever was in the flagon.

"Mistress Fortune smiles on me tonight," the man said. "What do you Orkhs call her?"

Bera controlled his face. He was thinking of leaving now. "I wouldn't know," he said.

Atul clucked his tongue. "Tsk, Heolfbera, not knowing your own kind. I'm surprised. But I grow bored of these small stakes, don't you? Shall we play for something greater? Something to make the blood flow."

Bera leaned back in his chair. "What would that be?"

Atul ran a thumb over his chin. "How about that pretty sword of yours?" he said. "I'd wager there's not another like it in this army." He pointed then to the piles of coin in front of himself. "I'll push all this into the middle if you throw in that sword. You could win back your coin. Perhaps it's worth more than the sword."

Bera dropped a hand to his waist. The sword had been one of the gifts from his father. He ground his palm against its pommel absently.

"Yes," he said, "you're right. There's no other like it. Certainly not here. But I'll not wager it. It came from my father."

Atul darkened at this and his eyes went to the others, then he sat up straighter as if steeling himself. "Your Orkhish father, you mean," he said. "Maybe he's losing at cards also, even now, in whatever pig wallow the Orkhs call a war camp. Assuming he can count, of course."

Penda and Egbert laughed, but rage boiled up into Bera from that secret place where he kept it locked away. It flooded his mind with fire and closed his throat, choking off words. The rage didn't want words: they didn't suffice. It wanted action, and even now it screamed at Bera to fill his hand with the comforting weight of the sword and avenge the insult with spilled blood. For Bera knew in his heart his father was no ordinary Orkh, no ignorant beast who couldn't count. Nor was he a mindlessly violent brute, as other Orkhs were. Bera knew this was true of his father because it was true of himself.

He also knew this fiery rage that came to him, for it had been with him all his life. His mother had said it was his Orkhish blood rising to devil him, so he'd striven against it: seeking to build within himself some secure place to lock it away. For Bera was denied anger in this world of Humans: he was too big, too different, too Orkhish. Wreathed in rage he would appear what all believed he was in their hearts: a savage beast who would slay them. So he had fought the rage and denied it, and in time he did make deep within himself a place where he could shut it away.

But Atul's goad had loosed it in part, and now Bera willed his face not to betray him as he took up his rage and shoved it back into that deep place. It would do him no good here, or anywhere.

"I know nothing of my father," he said, when his throat was open again. He laid his hands on the table, away from the sword. They were long-fingered and sharp-knuckled, and his nails came to hard yellow points.

"You'd be a damned traitor if you did know your father," Atul said. "Throw in the sword, Heolfbera. Make this interesting."

"No. I will not lose it."

Atul smiled. It was a feral thing. "Maybe you will, but maybe you won't. That's where the thrill lies."

"I will surely lose it," Bera said. "Whatever you may say

about my father, I can count. And I believe you invited me here tonight to cheat me out of my pay, and my sword if you could get it. Tell me, did you sew the seam pockets into that tunic yourself? It was neatly done."

The three men at the table exchanged swift glances and Atul drew himself up straighter in the chair. Bera couldn't read the tells on the men's faces as they played, but his eyes were sharp and he'd watched Atul's hands and the coat pressed against the table edge; and soon he'd discovered that coat contained a ready reserve of high cards. The other two were surely party to the caper, doubtless expecting to be re-funded their losses later together with a cut of Bera's purse.

But now he'd spoken the words Bera wished he hadn't. A fight here would have many witnesses, and many participants: none of whom would take a Half-Orkh's side. He should have retrieved his lighter purse from the table and left without direct accusation. Perhaps not all the anger had been locked away.

So Bera put on the most agreeable expression he could find and said to Atul: "It was a jest, friend. On your uncommon good fortune. Allow me to buy you another round of whatever you're having."

Atul stared back at him. A cold, brittle look. "It was an ill jest," he said, "and I should demand honor be done to me. I truly should." Atul looked away then and shrugged carelessly. "But I'm a forgiving soul. Mercy dealt and all that." He picked up the flagon from the table and drained it, hiding his face, then wiped his lips on a sleeve without meeting Bera's eyes.

He's afraid of me.

This warmed Bera's blood again. In the man's heart, be-neath the crude bluster, he feared Bera. Yet he offered neither courtesy nor respect. Bera flexed his fingers on the table. He was strong, very strong: he could rip the man's head from his shoulders with a single wrench. But he wouldn't, because he wasn't a beast to be prodded to reckless self-destruction. He crushed the last shreds of his anger and calmed the twitching urges of his hands.

"Yes," he said to Atul, speaking quietly, "perhaps it was an ill jest."

"It was," the man replied but there was a undercurrent of disappointment in his tone. "But I do believe the game has lost its appeal, Ceorl Heolfbera. So I shall say good night to you." He raked coins into a large purse and drew the drawstring closed. "I wish I could say it's been a pleasure, but it hasn't."

Bera said nothing, but watched from his chair as Atul stood to move away from the table, followed by Penda and Egbert. They averted their eyes from Bera and he was certain now the three of them had conspired to lighten his purse and take his sword on the pretense of comradeship. If he protested it, they would set the crowd on him. He himself had played his own part in the ruse by falling for it in his loneliness.

He frowned sourly and gathered up the few coins remaining to him. He would retreat to his tent now, with its too short camp bed and its too small writing table, and console himself by composing a letter to his mother before he slept. One was long overdue.

But as Bera stood to leave a hand fell on his shoulder. It was heavy and the fingers of it gripped him strongly. Then a voice spoke in his ear: deep and confident, and drunk.

"This tent is for warriors," the voice said. "Fighters. That ain't you, Orkh. You should know better than to come here."

Bera pushed the hand away and turned. Standing behind him was a giant of a man, taller even than Bera himself: a rarity among Humans. The man's hands and arms were like two brawny pitchforks, and his left forearm wore the livid scarring of a thousand blows to his shield.

"I was invited," Bera said to him, and to the others who watched from behind him. "For cards," he added.

"Now you're uninvited," the man said. "Orkh." He pronounced the word distinctly in challenge.

Bera was a king's officer, but that counted for nothing here. If violence was done, it would be his word against everyone else's in the tent—every Human's. And anyway this great building of a man was right: Bera was no warrior, he was no fighter. Not as these here were. Despite the provocation the rage didn't come to him now. Instead he felt only deflated and ill-used.

He raised open hands to the man. "I'm on my way out, friend," he said. "I want no trouble."

The big man spit at Bera's boot. "Tomorrow I will blood my sword on black-skins like you," he growled. "Maybe one of them will be your cousin!" He turned to shout a laugh at the crowd and they laughed with him.

Bera said nothing more, but stepped around the man to walk toward the entryway and the cloaking night beyond.

"I was wrong!" the giant shouted after him. "You ain't no Orkh! But you ain't no man neither. I don't know what you are!"

The crowd muttered at this but no one hindered Bera's

way. Finally he pushed out through the tent flap into clean night air. He drew in a deep breath of it to purge himself of the staleness and tension of the tent, and thought of the man's parting shot.

I don't know what you are!

That was fair. Bera might have said the same of himself: he was Orkh but also Human, an officer but a pariah, a son but an orphan, hopeful but hopeless. There was nothing that he was a whole of. Nothing about which he could say, 'I am this.'

He walked through the torch-lit gloom of camp with his head down until he reached his tent where he sat at his writing desk. The chair cracked beneath him, as it always did. He leaned forward to gather to himself the quill and a clean leaf of paper, and his brass ink pot. But the letter to his mother wouldn't come. He sat instead in thought and solitude until sleep took him.

*　　*　　*

Wulfric was angry. "Ceorl Heolfbera," he said, "did you inspect your fortifications?"

Bera stood at attention in the man's tent. It was early, not yet dawn, and he'd been summoned from his bed.

"No, sir," he said. "I've not seen the final fortifications."

This was true but it was also damning: Bera should have inspected his company's work before retiring for the night. There were other things on his mind then, but certainly nothing the Thegn would understand.

"I should hope you haven't seen them!" Wulfric said. He was a hard man who came from an ancient military family. Even now, before his breakfast, he wore a scarred leather cuirass. "Because if you had, Ceorl Heolfbera, I would have cashiered you on the spot. And maybe taken that ugly head of yours in the bargain. What were you doing last night, if not your duty?"

Bera's face grew hot and a dozen false excuses occurred to him. But these would only dig his hole deeper. The truth would have to serve.

"I was playing cards, sir," he said. "In the common tent. I was invited. And this morning I was sleeping."

"Playing cards and sleeping," Wulfric said acidly. He jabbed a thin finger at the world beyond the tent. "That ditch is no ditch at all! And your abattis works wouldn't slow my mother! Worse, it has been reported to me your troops dropped their tools and went to the Quartermaster, demanding drink. Drink!"

Bera studied a dark stain on the far wall of the tent: it looked like wine. He'd been a fool to let Dudda leave, and a fool to trust Guncar. He'd been a still greater fool to believe Atul had anything but malice in his heart.

"Sir, I told them they could have—"

Wulfric interrupted. "It's very clear what you did, Ceorl! And you may hold your tongue." The man worked his mouth in anger. "The one reason—the only reason—your presence is tolerated here is your uncle is a very fine man, to whom I owe a debt of gratitude. He and his company pulled my family out of Hinxworth before it was taken in the last war."

"If I may, sir—"

"You may not. You may listen."

Bera shut his mouth and Wulfric leaned toward him. The ice in the man's voice chilled Bera's heart. "You are a favor, Ceorl Heolfbera. Nothing more. If you can't run a guard company competently, that favor will end. You will go home, or to the stockade, or worse. Am I plain?"

"Yes, sir."

The man stared at him. "This Fyrd is very nearly upon the enemy. Until today, you could get away with slipshod work. But that stops now." He emphasized the last word with another jab of his finger. "Tonight, shortly before sundown, wherever we are, here or down lower, I will inspect the outer defenses of the camp myself. And they will be perfect! There will be no more chances. Do you understand me?

"Yes, sir. I do."

"You may go."

Bera saluted the man and turned to leave. He yearned to argue his case, but the Thegn was right: he'd done less than his full duty, far less. He resolved this wouldn't happen again, and that he would be more careful still around others: speaking softer, stepping lighter, swallowing ever more, to gain their acceptance. The only other choice offered to him was to gather his things and slink from camp in the night, abandoning everything.

The rising sun hung in a notch between hills as Bera returned to his tent. He found Dudda there, waiting outside, slouched in his overlarge shirt like a man with a great deal to hide. He reeked of old sweat and the throat-scorching liquor favored by those who drank from need.

"What is it?" Bera snapped. He wanted only to disappear into the tent and lick his wounds in peace.

Dudda shifted his feet oddly. "It's the rumor wheel, sir," he said with diffidence. "It's been turnin' as you might say. You was with the Thegn, just now?"

Bera was astonished by the man's presumption; and astonished still more by his uncanny ear for something which had occurred only moments before.

"Yes, I was with him," Bera said. "What of it?"

"The word is . . . well, that His Lordness ain't happy. With us."

"No," Bera growled. "He ain't happy." He twitched the tent flap open and ducked his head to enter.

Dudda followed. Still more presumption. "It wasn't about—well, I mean, sir—you didn't—"

"No, Dudda, the discussion wasn't about you," Bera said, unbuttoning his tunic sleeves and wanting the man out. "Not directly. But I did lose my Second to the jug last night and apparently he's the only thing holding this mess of a company together."

The man's gaze sharpened at this. "Well, yes sir. I mean, me and them we been together a long while. A good long while now. That counts for a lot, you know."

And you're Human, Bera thought sourly. He threw his baldric and sword on the camp bed.

"His Lordness ain't wrong," Dudda continued. "I'll give him that. I seen it for myself this morning, that ditch. Piss poor job, you could say."

"He did say."

There was a pause, then Dudda said, "I can fix that for you, sir."

Bera rounded on him: the man had no shame. "For a price, you mean?" he said. "Is that it? I suppose your price is to look the other way every time you wish to shirk your duty as you like?"

Dudda took a step backward. "Well, I wouldn't put it quite so blunt, sir."

"No need," Bera said. "I understand you perfectly. Get out of my tent."

The man didn't move. Instead he stood staring at Bera, his head aslant, his eyes curious. It was clear he hadn't expected his Ceorl to resist, but to roll over as he had so many times before. But Bera had a bellyful of being walked on.

"Out!" he said, with a flick of long fingers toward the tent flap. "Attend to your duties, Second Dudda."

The man did leave now, closing the flap and stranding a sour smell in the tent. Bera went to his writing desk and sat heavily on the chair to put his head in his hands.

For the first time in a very long time he thought seriously of leaving. Of resigning his commission and walking away. He'd done everything right here, or most things, or enough anyway, but what would never be right was how he looked. He couldn't peel off his dark skin and don another, nor pluck out his red eyes and replace them. These were what he couldn't change, but they were the one thing that told above all else.

He surprised himself then by chasing a thought of going to the other side, wondering if his own Orkhish father, nameless and unknown, marched with that great army approaching the pass. Was he, even now, whetting his sword and thinking of this battle to come? Or had he died already in this new war? So many had, on both sides.

Bera scrubbed his face with his hands and looked over the papers on his desk. No, desertion wasn't the answer. Running from his duty wasn't the answer. What was the answer? He didn't know.

4

OF ZARA

Zara didn't know the tall grim-faced Human who stood before her, but he'd come with the dawn leading a legion of heavily armored Humans. These filed around Zara now, taking places on the ridge. This pleased her: now she could remount the *kansa* and be gone from here.

"The ground is yours," she said to the Human. "Ward it well."

"Aye, it is mine," the man muttered, giving Te'a a doubtful eye. "You're relieved, Aelf. Take your beast and get you gone."

Zara's hand fell to the knife at her waist but she didn't draw that keen blade. If she bared its steel now she was honor-bound to challenge the man and make him yield, or slay him if he didn't. But there would be no satisfaction in that victory: only disgust at the ease of it. Humans were weak of body and slow in mind, and the blade would open his flesh in a moment if she wished it. That was unworthy of the effort.

So Zara turned Te'a away from the man, dismissing him as beneath her notice. *This alliance will not survive the war,* she thought as she gathered the cat-sí's reins to herself. *It barely holds together even now, against a threat to us all.*

*

She rode west with her guard to find Salf. It was first light on the day after the ill-starred assault on the skirmishers. The van of the main body of Orkhs had arrived below the ridge in the night and it made its camp there on the fields. This was but the first part of that greater army to come, but even so it was a great host and from the ridge Zara had watched the fires of the Orkhs grow until they seemed to mirror in orange the stars above.

But now, as the sky lightened, the Orkhs could be seen arrayed for war on the plain below: three dark lines, one behind the other, each running far to the east and farther still to the west. And above them were lifted many standards of war, seeming overlarge and garishly colored to Zara's eye, and these tossed brazenly on an early wind as if promising ruin to any who opposed them. The flat bray of Orkhish war horns relayed commands across the fields.

Zara was grateful to be leaving. Her *kansa* would have been swept away by that great horde, had it come yesterday. But now the Humans were here. They were many also, and as they arrived they came together on the crest of the ridge to make a long shield wall, six ranks deep or more, to oppose the Orkhs. The battle here would begin soon, perhaps with the rising of the sun, and cavalry would have no place in it.

Salf came up on his cat-sí then, seeking orders.

"Make the *kansa* ready to ride," she said to him. "Our new station appointed by Cenred is under those foothills." Zara pointed far to the west where long well-wooded slopes reached down from high gray mountains. "We will wait in the trees there, hidden but watching for the chance to strike at the Orkhs when they come."

Salf nodded. "As you wish, my lady."

The tall Aelf's tone and his posture in the saddle were neutral, but Zara knew yesterday's events lay between them still. In his final report to her, delivered late in the evening, he'd taken care to enunciate distinctly the name of each rider and each cat-sí killed or wounded in the fighting. This had been a presumption but Zara took no outward notice: she wouldn't disrespect the naming of the dead, however much she might wish to reach across and strike the Aelf a chastening blow.

When Salf had ridden away, Zara reined Te'a around to stalk west along the ridge. She remained well behind the Humans now drawn up against the Orkhs. An animal stink rose from them, dark and musky; and they seemed not to notice the smoke and dust in the air about them, and the gray rain of ash from the fires they'd made. She twitched Te'a's reins to angle still farther down the back slope of the ridge, toward clearer air. Her guard followed.

At the west end of the ridge, where it began its fall toward the farmland below, she stopped to look back toward the wide saddle of the pass. Dark lines moved on the road there: more Humans coming down. A score of tall, bright banners rode over them. One of these lines curved westward as it came and it moved faster than the others: surely hurrying to take up position on the open farmland below her.

Turning forward again, Zara examined that ground from her vantage on the ridge. It was a checker of worked fields: a handful tawny still with uncut wheat, but most only stubble now, some of it burnt already. Here and there, among them, lay the varied greens of a field left fallow for the season. The whole was crossed by many double-rutted cart paths and fence rows made from stone or wood; and a few stream beds wound through it, narrow and brushy, together with narrow ditches of brown water dug to serve the fields.

These were obstacles, yes, but even so the place was a fine avenue for attack toward the pass. Especially where the only other choice open to the Orkhs was battering themselves against that Human shield wall on the ridge, or against the stubborn Dweorg on the left. Zara suspected the Orkhs drawn up below the ridge were meant only to fix the defenders there in place, and to draw in reserves, while the main effort would come here, later in the day or tomorrow.

As she waited for Salf and the *kansa* to come up, Zara looked further out, southwest, and saw there a stone structure lying between two wooded hills of the same shape. It was a building of perhaps three stories, surrounded by a wall that might be twice her own height mounted on Te'a. It lay well more than a mile distant from her, concealed in part by trees.

Zara frowned. That place hadn't been visible from the center of the ridge, or she hadn't seen it. It was surely the stead of some wealthy Human farmer of these fields. She drew out the grass and watched the place for a time, but saw no movement in the high windows of the building or at the wall.

The place troubled her. The Orkhs could surely use it as a base from which to attack across the flats of the farmland. The surrounding hills and the tree cover would conceal their movements until the very last moment, giving allied forces only a very short warning. This might be disastrous, especially if Cenred was forced to commit his reserves early to support the fighting on the ridge. Zara wondered why the man hadn't already sent a force to occupy the place. The need was obvious.

She pursed her lips: an idea moved in her, and she swung Te'a to face more south. The leftmost of the two hills hid much in that direction, but far off she could see Orkhs in column moving up from the southwest. This was the left wing of that army. She watched them for a time, pondering their speed. Perhaps there was time still to do something. Without turning her eyes from the Orkhs, Zara raised a hand to beckon Gar'an, the commander of her guard.

The Aelf rode nearer. "Lady?"

"Bring Salf to me, over there." He pointed further west along the ridge, where she might see the building and the wall better.

Gar'an acknowledged the order but he paused before leaving, letting Zara know he resented being used as a messenger. She smiled at this. It served her purposes to remind this imperious Aelf her father was not his only master.

She rode on and when Salf came up to her, he offered a salute she didn't return. "I have new orders for you," she said to him. "Halt the *kansa.*"

The Second looked wary at this, but offered no outward protest. He wheeled his cat-sí and made a sign to the horn-aelf. The call sounded and the columns of riders behind Salf drew to a halt, waiting. The heat of the day had grown and many brought out their water skins. None looked at Zara.

She addressed Salf. "Third Claw will take and hold that

stone building yonder, between the hills," she said, pointing to it. "It will be unoccupied. I will command the assault but you will go also, *Ritzar*. Then we will make a defense of that place until the Human foot soldiers can relieve us. Exactly as we did on this ridge. Send First and Second Claws to the wood as planned, and send a messenger to Cenred to inform him of our need for relief."

As Zara said this, the Second stood on his stirrups to study the building and the wall. Now he sat back again and frowned. Zara had come to hate that frown.

"One claw only, my lady?" he said. "Without support? Those are Orkhs over there, not too far beyond." He pointed southwest.

Zara didn't look. "I did not ask for your counsel, *Ritzar* Kve'ma. I have given my orders."

The tall Aelf eyed Zara, but she didn't see in his scarred face any desire to disobey her, as she'd feared. Instead there was something else, something equally intense, but she couldn't read it. Was it concern for the *kansa*, or anxiety, or his own loyalties warring within him? She didn't know, but she held Salf's gaze with iron resolve until he dropped his eyes.

He saluted her again. "As you wish it, my lady."

Yes, Salf, I do wish it. And I wish you far from me, also. I will not be thwarted by you.

As she waited for the Second to carry out her orders, Zara examined the building and its outwall again through the eyeglass. The view was better here, but still she saw no movement. She saw also no gate or door in the wall. If the place had been abandoned, it was likely the entry was unbarred, wherever it might be, and that was her way in.

She shifted the glass to study the high windows that looked out over the wall. She lingered on each, seeing no movement still. Then she swept left, studying the ground below the wall, and saw a sliver of narrow road or a cart path. It was well-churned, but anything could have done that: wagons, horses, stock driven away to safety. Zara decided then to take her riders left around the wall, toward that track. The gate would be there.

She swept the glass over the surrounding hills and stopped in surprise on a dense crowd of four-legged animals gathered on a hillside. They were sheep: at least a hundred of them and enclosed tightly in a paddock. So it seemed that not all this farmer's stock had been driven to safety, but this was no matter to her.

She glassed further south, looking beyond the hills. Salf was right: a large group of Orkhish infantry, several hundred, lay a mile or more south of the hills. She'd missed these before, and they were far closer than the ones she had seen. Even so, these new Orkhs didn't seem likely to move soon: the smoke of many fires, likely cook fires, rose from among them. It occurred to Zara she should drive off those sheep, to deny the Orkhs their feast.

She snapped the glass shut and turned to Salf, who had ridden near again. "Is all in readiness?" she said.

"It is, my lady."

"Then let us ride."

But the Second didn't stir. He was looking across the fields toward the wall and the building. His frown reached his scar now, turning it down like a second mouth.

"My lady—" he began, but then his courage seemed to fail and he stopped. He turned his gaze toward Zara and she expected to see resistance in his eyes: perhaps a new resolve to defy her will. She drew herself erect to stand against it, touching the knife at her belt to assure herself it lay ready.

But the tall Aelf's face wasn't hardened against her. Instead she saw indecision there. No, it was more than that: there was war on his face, as if he could find no middle ground between conflicting impulses.

"Damn you, Salf!" she said. "Must I give every order twice?

"No, my lady," he murmured. "You needn't. I heard you. But it is you who do not hear, or see. Many things." His gaze on her sharpened.

"Do you defy me?" she said. "Must I find another?"

He jerked at this and drew in a breath of surprise. "Nay!" he said. "I will do as you bid. As I said, I am here by my choice, even if I find the way hard."

He gave Zara a last look, as if meaning to say more, but only drew away to make a sign to the horn-aelf, who blew the forward ride.

Now, under Salf's direction, the *kansa* split itself into two parts. First and Second Claws went west, toward the trees, while the Third remained with Zara, following her down the last slope of the ridge and southwest toward the stone farmstead. The land below the ridge tilted south as it fell away from the mountains, giving Zara the pleasing feel of riding downhill. It was a good omen and she urged T'ea to greater speed. This work now was essential and it would not fail, and it would go far toward setting the balance right again.

When they were a half mile from the wall, the horn-aelf sent up a new call and the riders of the claw shifted from column into two assault lines, one behind the other. This was a precaution by Salf, as nothing moved ahead of them still. The wall remained a blank impassive face, and above it the windows of the building stared back at them, dark and empty.

At four hundred yards Zara lifted a hand to signal for a sweep left: they would ride around the wall toward the cart track and the gate that was surely there. But just then a small shape rose over the top of the wall. It was dark and round: surely a helm. Then more rose beside it, and now a score came up, peering at the Aelfs over the wall.

They were Orkhs.

Zara's hand trembled then but she scorned it, snatching it back down to strike it hard against the saddle. This was no time for either fear or doubt. Indeed this venture was better now: she would take that place with a fight, and the glory would be greater still when she presented it to Cenred as a prize of war.

She shouted to the horn-aelf and he blew the call to bare steel. Seven score sabers swept from their scabbards, and the riders of the claw yipped now, high and quick, as they rode over the grass. Zara untied her helm from the saddle and donned it; then she turned Te'a to ride a slanting course across the front of the onrushing Aelfs, drawing her own saber from her back. She lifted the blade in defiance and howled the *ritzan*. Their yodeling response fired her blood and cast all doubt from her mind.

Zara turned Te'a then to run straight for the wall. More Orkhs showed their heads there now, seeming to stand upon a catwalk or a platform placed high on the inner face of the wall. Some had brought up bows and now they loosed a ragged volley at the Aelfs. Zara twisted in the saddle to look back but saw no Aelf or cat-sí lying on the grass. The Orkhs had shot high.

She grinned and signed with her saber for the horn-aelf to sound full gallop. The strong note of the horn shivered the air and Te'a strides stretched out still more. Zara knew Gar'an and his riders followed her closely, but she could hear nothing over the war cries of the claw save the rub and jingle of her own tack.

Orkhs were in the windows now and a second volley was loosed from wall and window together. Arrows, thick and black-fletched, struck the turf near Zara with a sound like a fistful of stones hurled by a giant. Someone cried out and she twisted again to see an Aelf tumble from her cat-sí: her cuirass pierced deeply by a black arrow.

Zara galloped on and the claw followed, rolling over the last yards of green like a near-breaking wave. It rose gray and white, brown and black, and above it danced a white foam of sabers flashing like spindrift in sunlight.

Now the wall loomed high over Zara, tawny in the light, and Te'a's stride changed beneath her as the great cat gathered herself to leap. Zara leaned forward in the saddle, bracing herself against the kick, and the cat-sí pushed off with a mighty heave of her hind legs. Up and up they went; and Zara watched as the helmeted heads of the Orkhs rushed toward her then passed below and behind as Te'a cleared the wall.

Then came the rushing fall. A sudden wind was in Zara's ears and hard, sun-bright earth rose to meet her. She leaned back in the saddle now, balancing, and Te'a's front paws struck. The cat-sí stooped low as she hit, taking into herself the impact and sparing her rider.

Zara lifted her saber and crowed, calling a challenge to the Orkhs. She was here, and she would stay.

Te'a had come down, unharmed, on a pale, double-rutted roadway that crossed a wide grassy courtyard. The cat-sí rose to her full height now beneath Zara, and like her mistress before her roared defiance at the Orkhs. The sound was high and feral; and the cat's hair lifted tall about Zara.

But she gathered the reins, asserting control, and spun Te'a to watch the *kansa* come over the wall after her. Her own guard first, then the banner and horn Aelfs. They turned outward to ward her, and now the rest of her riders fell from the blue sky like mounted war-gods come to earth, until the space around Zara swirled with fur and bright steel. She knew they must strike fast and hard, while the Orkhs were surprised and disordered still.

The horn-aelf called for dismount and Zara slid from Te'a's back, then she tied the reins to the saddle. Around her, her guard did the same. In close quarters, the cat-sí fought more effectively without their riders. Freed of any burden, they could twist and leap and spin at will: raking Orkh-flesh with sharp claws, and seizing long limbs with wicked teeth. A rider on their backs would be a useless appendage, whipped helplessly about.

Zara peered around the courtyard. Several knots of fighting had formed already; and while all were fierce, none served any broader purpose. She decided the first task, the most important, was to secure the courtyard against relief by the Orkhs encamped to the south. She could see the gate now: two great wooden doors set into the south wall.

She reached to touch the horn-aelf's shoulder. "Sound follow the banner!"

The Aelf lifted the war horn to his lips. The call was high and clear, and lifted well over the cries of struggle and the clash of steel in the courtyard. Zara motioned for her guard and the banner-aelf to follow and she moved toward the doors. They were tall and arched at the top, and opened inward, though now firmly shut. Affixed to the wall on either side of the gate were two great wooden beams that could be pushed across the face of the doors to bar them.

Zara decided they would draw those beams and make a stand beneath the doors, where they would slowly whittle down the garrison until the stronghold belonged to her.

Twenty yards short of the doors, Zara called for her guard to turn in support of the others still coming. She put herself into the front rank and stepped within the guard of an unwary Orkh, cutting her saber across its neck. Black blood rained from the blade as it swung free.

"To me! To me!" she cried. And the horn-aelf winded the banner call again as if to shatter his horn.

Aelfs and cat-sí rushed over the courtyard, heeding her call. The Orkhs were close behind. The noise was great: many score of voices shouted in fury and elation, a hundred bright sabers rang against a hundred dark scimitars, and the war-clatter of shield and armor went on and on, like hail on a roof. The Aelfs of the claw yodeled their *ritzan* and the Orkhs began war songs, chanting them in unison: deep, slow, and frightening. Even the cat-sí screamed as they fought. Their dagger-like claws shredded hardened leather like silk, and the largest snatched up Orkhs in their jaws to shake them with bone-breaking violence.

Dead and wounded lay on the cart way now. Nearer the building, small knots of Aelfs and cat-sí were trapped, unable to reach the doors. Still most of the claw was gathered around Zara now and they fought beneath the doors. She stepped away from the fighting then to point up to the great beams with her saber.

"Bar the gate!" she cried. "Seal us in!"

A dozen of her guard sheathed their sabers and sprang to the bars. They moved first one then the other across the doors, securing the courtyard against attack from without.

Satisfied, Zara turned back to the fighting. But as she did her eye fell on two piles of coiled steel chain, brown with rust. They lay by the left door and they were enormous, half again the height of Zara herself, and the links were so great she couldn't conceive their purpose. For a moment she considered using that chain to secure the doors further, but it was plain its weight was far too great: the task would require more warriors than she could spare. The doors were well-secured in any event, and soon this stone fortress would be hers. All that remained was to remove these black vermin infesting it.

The Aelfs of Third Claw now formed a crescent around Zara and her guard: their backs to the doors and offering the Orkhs a wall of cold steel. The Orkhs met it with their own, and these ancient enemies warred beneath the high walls. The terror of it was close and intimate: body upon body, blade upon blade, striking and drawing apart to strike again. Aelf and Orkh each fought to live: to kill before being killed in that fearful melee.

Zara fought in the center of it, her eyes never leaving the blades before her as she slew their wielders. Each new blade that came sought to part her flesh with its keen edge, to spill her blood on the hard earth below the doors. But she followed precisely their paths, guessed their motions: deflecting a blow here, dodging another there, riposting with swift suddenness. Anything might keep that sharp steel from ending her.

She and her Aelfs slew many Orkhs under those doors; yet more came, throwing themselves at the claw and crying out in life and death in their hoarse, croaking tongue. The cat-sí had gathered at either flank, and they fought as whirling terrors; and a wall of bodies, more Orkh than Aelf, grew at the place where the foes met.

After some minutes—whether five or thirty Zara couldn't say—the press of enemies seemed finally to dwindle, and she felt the gods shifting their weights on The Great Scale, favoring her.

Now is the time to take the day in hand!

She pushed her way across the press of bodies to Salf and grabbed the neck of his cuirass. She meant to pull his ear close and order a counterattack. But before she could speak, a shout rose from the Orkhs and they seemed to gain new heart.

What deviltry is this?

She released Salf and moved toward the left door, where she climbed to stand on the lower beam and look over the fighting toward the courtyard. And when she did, the elation of victory died in her. The doors of the building were open now and a fresh company of Orkhs streamed forth like a black tide of filth uttered from bowels of stone.

There were too many of them in the courtyard now. Far too many. She had barred the wrong doors.

Zara knew then the fickle gods had shifted their weights again and now they laughed at her. Still the Claw might hold, with courage and skillful handling. Seeing that, the gods might favor her in the end.

But this hope, too, died when a great Trolle stepped from the darkness of the building into the sunlit courtyard. The creature was tall and long-armed, and its body was gnarled like the hoariest oak in the Woodland. And it clutched in one massive fist a great tree branch the length of a cat-sí.

Zara slammed her fist on the door behind her and howled at the heavens. *Damn this place! Damn it to The Six Hells!*

The Trolle moved across the courtyard toward the doors, kicking aside or crushing with the branch any Orkh standing in its path. Behind it, still more Orkhs poured from the mouth of the building. Panic licked at Zara now: a hot fire that closed her throat and weakened her resolve. She pushed it away and made a swift decision: there was no salvaging this fight. It was already lost.

They had to get out. Now.

But the only way out was the way they'd come in: over the wall. Zara shouted down to the horn-aelf, "Sound cat-sí to riders!" Then she leaped from the beam, calling for Te'a to come to her side as she did.

The warbling cry for assembly rose, and within moments the great cats began to land in a small area of open ground below the doors, searching for their riders. A handful of these were unharmed, but most were hampered by wounds. A few were slashed so cruelly the fur of their bellies dripped red lines of blood to the hardpan. One, a large gray near Zara, shook violently: the fur across a wide area of its chest had been burned away completely, exposing charred skin and pink flesh that oozed wetly. A clever Orkh had wielded a flaming brand against the beast.

The magnitude of her misjudgment fluttered at the edge of Zara's thoughts like a bird thinking to fly in though an open window. But she closed her mind against it and swung an arm to cuff the horn-aelf on the chest, venting her fury and anguish.

"Sound retreat, damn you!" she bellowed at him. "Retreat! Now!"

The Aelf fumbled with his horn then raised it to his lips and blew the dirge-like tones of retreat. Zara's gut turned cold at the sound: there would be a price to pay for this. She wanted to quit paying prices. She wanted to take what was rightfully hers: a high seat at the table to which she was born. But here, on this bright, bloody courtyard, that high seat seemed further from her than ever it was. She felt the darkness opening again to take her.

Around her riders who still had cat-sí mounted them. She shouted to them over the clamor of battle: "Get out! Over the wall!"

She slapped the haunches of a brown and black with the flat of her saber and it sprang away, carrying its rider over the tall doors.

That's one who will live.

More cat-sí leaped then, clearing the doors, but the fight raged hot and loud still as Orkhs from the building joined it. The Trolle was near now and it swept its heavy branch like a scythe, crushing Orkh and Aelf alike. Far behind it, near the building, a dozen Aelfs were trapped still and fighting back-to-back. They'd never reached the doors and now they made a hopeless last stand.

More Aelfs mounted their cat-sí around Zara. They were exhausted and their eyes on her were harried and frightened. She closed her mind to this also and turned until she found Te'a, who had come to stand nearby. The cat-sí appeared uninjured: only the black blood of Orkhs matted her fur.

Zara went to her and swung up into the saddle. From here she could see far too many Aelfs and cat-sí still under the doors, unable to disengage and flee. Something had to be done to buy them more time.

Zara guided Te'a to the *kansa's* scarlet and gray pennant and pulled its long pole from the banner-aelf's grasp. She turned the pole in her hand so the metal-shod butt spike pointed forward.

"Over the wall!" she shouted to Aelfs around her. "Over the wall! Don't follow me!"

She urged Te'a forward then, toward the Orkhs, catching a taste of fear from the cat-sí like a bite of cold iron. But Te'a obeyed Zara's heels and she shouldered toward the front of the melee. The Trolle was near now, tall and powerful, but Zara had seen that the flesh of its belly was warded only by a curtain of rusted mail. She centered the spike of the banner pole on that mail and spurred Te'a into a hard, charging leap.

The beast failed to see their approach, for it had thrown back its massive head and lifted the branch high to roar a challenge at the Aelfs. So the spear-like spike of the *kansa*'s standard pole went true: finding the Trolle's wide belly near its center. And the shaft drove half its length into the creature's vitals before Zara released her hold on it to guide the cat-sí past. The beast dropped its branch then and its hands fell to clutch the pole. It bellowed still, but now in pain and outrage.

Zara came to the center of the courtyard and she shouted to the Aelfs who were beleaguered near the building. But even as she did, she saw they would never escape: the horde that raged about them was far too great. She spoke a prayer for warriors going to their reward, then turned Te'a to look back at the doors.

She saw Salf there, staring at her from atop his cat-sí. His face was alight and his eyes shone over his scar like new-risen stars over dark and distant hills. The sight froze Zara. What was he about now? Did he mean to wrest the *kansa* from her after this? Her hand fell to the knife at her belt. Salf saw this and the light left his face, and it closed again into his habitual glare. He gestured for her to return to the doors and turned his cat-sí away.

The rest of the Aelfs disengaged and went over the wall then, including Salf. The Orkhs under the doors screamed frustration. Some went to the beams and began to draw them; others moved toward Zara. Te'a gathered herself then and leaped for the wall. But she misjudged the distance, perhaps in fatigue, and alighted atop it.

From here, Zara could see south through the notch between the hills that guarded this accursed place. The Orkhs she'd seen from the ridge were encamped still on the fields, far away and unmoving: there had been no need to bar the outer doors.

But she saw something else, also. In that narrow valley a flock of white sheep moved south through a long, open meadow. Herding them were a dozen Orkhs carrying spears longer than any Zara had seen. Nearer at hand, a short distance from the wall, lay the same pen of sheep she'd seen from the ridge. But now she saw there were two pens. The nearer was full as it may be, the further less so.

Then she heard a sound, unlike any she'd heard before. It was a vast, droning groan such as a war horn, but no horn could make such a great noise. Perhaps it was some new engine of war brought by the Orkhs. The creatures commonly brought their machines to battle: catapults, spear-throwers, bombs of fire. But none Zara knew of made such a sound.

It was surely a mystery, but she had no time to listen or

look more: she was exposed here, high on the wall, and an Orkh's arrow might find her back at any moment. She urged Te'a to the ground and as she did a terrible smell carried to her on a fresh breeze. It was sharp and putrid, like meat freshly rotting. She paused Te'a below the wall to look about again, but saw nothing save the sheep in their pens. Perhaps the creatures died there and the Orkhs left them to rot.

She set these questions aside and rode to where Salf had rallied the remnants of the claw, well beyond bow shot of the wall.

They fled north toward the foothills, where Zara could hide in the trees and lick her wounds. She sagged low in the saddle, her heart feeling tender and frail in her chest; and the fire of her will gone to embers. The darkness beckoned. Was this all she was? Would the gods not permit her to rise higher, however much she tried?

She felt a gentle tickle then: it was Te'a reaching out to touch her thoughts. It came as a warm, musky presence pressed against Zara's mind, like the scent of the cat-sí herself. But the creature didn't push, nor intrude; but lay against Zara like a pillow, warming her. And it came to Zara then the cat-sí sought to comfort her; and for a moment she allowed it. But then it came to seem a weakness, an undeserved indulgence among the ruin of her failure, and she pushed it away. The cat-sí receded without reproach and they ran north together.

5

OF BERA

Bera was brooding over his disastrous interview with the Provisions Thegn when Dudda shoved his head into the tent. A beam of strong early sunlight came behind it.

"The morning's news, sir," he said.

Bera was at his writing desk. He signed for the Second to enter, but did not bid him sit to linger. The man's tart odor had preceded him.

The 'morning's news' consisted entirely of rumors Dudda had heard in his hooch tent. Men who drink together have little to do but talk, and the camp's jug-vine could be counted on to have a rough estimate of events nearly anywhere almost as soon as they occurred.

Dudda's report this morning was that the allied center had been attacked by the Orkhs sooner than expected, and the fighting below was already in doubt. This was possible. Less likely were more breathless reports having that same center retreating back up the pass road in panic, and marauding bands of Orkhs a quarter-hour from the rear areas. The tranquil morning outside Bera's tent put the lie to this.

The hard nut Bera extracted from Dudda's report was that

the heavily armored Humans forming the shield wall of the center had been met by the Orkhs earlier than anticipated by Cenred, and the battle for the pass had begun. Orkhish aggressiveness should not have been a surprise, he reflected, and they were likely probing the line for weakness, indecision, or inexperience: in short, anything they could exploit later with greater force.

Bera imagined himself down there in the shield wall, meeting the Orkhs as they came. He yearned for that honor. He shouldn't be here, idling in the rear, straining to glean good information from boozy fourth-hand tales. He felt suddenly dispirited and ill-used.

"So that's the word," Dudda said when he was done, adding that he wasn't to be mistaken for any teller of tales.

"Your fine reputation is safe with me," Bera said. "Thank you for your news. No, Dudda, you may not return to your swill-den. You've had quite enough. I intend to go to Thegn Wulfric within the hour and tell him my company is ready to move to the new provisions camp. We both know that's not true, so go make it true. The gods know I need some good will with that man."

Dudda's face shifted to mulish recalcitrance. "Which it'll take a day at least to pack it all," he said. "Picks and shovels. Wheelbarrows, tents."

Bera shifted forward to survey the papers on his desk. He was looking for that unfinished order. "Then you'd better start now, hadn't you?"

When the man didn't move, Bera looked up again. "Yes?"

"They won't like it. We ain't a line company."

Bera sat back in his chair again. "I'm not asking them to be a line company, Dudda, or to like it. I'm asking them to be ready to move lower, to the new provisions camp. That's your job. If there's any grumbling, make them like it. That's why I keep you."

This seemed to sting the man and Bera regretted his sharpness: but it was true. Dudda was the friendly, less imposing hand Bera stretched toward the company to work his will. It had been that way from the first, and this division of labor had come to suit Bera. Dudda could pack the picks and shovels with the rest of the company while he sat here, at his desk, thinking on how the unpleasant Provisions Thegn might be massaged to order Ceorl Bera closer to the front, and so closer to acceptance as a warrior of the Dominion.

Dudda left and Bera watched him go with a frown. He was aware he should follow the man to speed the work along, but there seemed time yet to make a fair copy of his order of the day and to contemplate his approach to Wulfric. And also to finish the letter to his mother: he might not have a free moment to write for some days. He would omit his recent troubles, as he always did. They were his to bear, and he would have her blameless in his making.

He sat forward again and pulled closer his ink pot and the last leaf of the unfinished order. Morning had drawn on and it was no longer quiet in camp. He heard the jingle of stock waiting in harness and teamsters loading their wagons with the thousand sundries of war: barrels of salted beef and pork, fresher stuff in crates, boxes of dry bread stacked like bricks near his tent, wooden crates of weapons and armor, fodder for animals, tents for warriors, tools and gear of all description, even three entire smithies with workmen. The Fyrd pulled a train of staggering size behind it, and over the next day it would move down the pass road to support the line more closely. Bera's company would move with it to dig out fortifications in the new camp: fortifications Wulfric had threatened to inspect carefully.

Bera shook his head at his folly of the night before, with the men in the common tent. *I won't get fooled like that again.*

A voice outside the tent called his name, startling him. It wasn't Dudda or any other voice he knew: so it was a messenger, likely. Bera straightened in the chair and smoothed his tunic over his chest, striving to appear as if he had been doing exactly what his duty demanded of him in the moment.

"Enter!" he called.

A head of shaggy hair, limned brightly by sunlight, pushed past the tent flap: one of Wulfric's heralds. Bera couldn't recall the man's name.

"Beg pardon, sir," the man said cautiously. "The Thegn's regards and he requests your presence. Immediately, sir, if you please."

Bera frowned. The order and the letter would have to wait, again. "Understood," he said. "Inform Thegn Wulfric I will attend him directly."

The head of hair pulled back and the tent flap fell closed, and suddenly Bera was pleased: the Thegn wished to see him, and this had the happy result of sparing Bera the task of contriving a reason to see the Thegn. Better still, it might be Wulfric wished to say his earlier words to Bera had been too harsh by half, and he wished to make it up somehow. Bera laughed at this as he stood from the desk to check the buttons of his tunic. It was far more likely the man would have still worse to say.

He took in a long breath and blew it out slowly as he stepped from the tent into sunlight.

Five minutes later he was in Wulfric's tent, both surprised and disappointed to find he waited there with a large number of other Ceorls, each of whom Wulfric had also summoned. All were gathered now in a small space between the entry and the Thegn's work table. Even so, Bera found himself rather less cramped than others, because he'd been given, however covertly, an ample share of personal space. Indeed it was large enough to be insulting, had he chosen to take notice. But he wouldn't. It wasn't unexpected, and he'd long fortified himself against such slights. Instead, he maintained an unwavering composure and offered no sign of offense as he greeted others as politely as they greeted each other.

Bera looked around as he waited, over the heads of the others, and so far as he could see each of the men and women assembled here was the Ceorl of a support company still high on the pass road: quartermaster, provisions and supply, commissary, camp guards like Bera, armor and weapons smiths, healing and burial. Everyone, it seemed, not now down on the line. Whatever news Wulfric had to give, it affected them all.

The man himself appeared then, emerging from a screened off area and wearing full field armor. Behind him, three servants packed his personal quarters and quarreled quietly between themselves. Seeing this, Bera decided he hadn't given

Dudda enough credit: perhaps the Second had heard some-thing close to the truth in his hooch den.

When the last of the Ceorls appeared, bearing their apologies, Wulfric addressed the group.

"I'll get straight to the point," he said, "I've been ordered to send every spare sword I can down the road. No, I don't know what's going on down there. No more than what surely you've all heard. All I know for certain is I have my orders. I am to send down very spare sword." He looked around, measuring them. "That's you and yours, gods help us."

A gust of chatter blew across the tent and Wulfric held up a hand against it. "Every man and woman is a swords-man in this army. Here's what I need from each of you. Pull out every warm body not absolutely necessary to your work—and I mean not absolutely necessary. Send them to the smithies for weapon-take, if needed. I want them re-drilled in basic combat, and quickly. Then send them down to the forward muster post." He turned a cold gaze on Bera then. "As for you, I want your entire company. There are no Orkhs up here, short of a few scouts. We can do without you here."

Bera's heart thrilled in his chest and a great happiness fell over him: warm and wonderful. This was the chance to prove himself he'd long yearned for: to meet the Orkhs in battle, and to show himself worthy of trust, and to be accepted as an equal by these warriors assembled here.

"I understand, sir," he said, containing his sudden joy with an effort of will. "We'll be ready."

They would be, even if he had to sharpen every sword in

the company himself. A glorious gift had fallen unexpected out of a clear sky and he wouldn't let it hit the ground.

"However," Wulfric added, looking down at his papers, "your company will go down tomorrow. The pass road will be congested until then."

Bera wondered at this but nodded his understanding; and when the Thegn moved on to address others, he considered the work ahead of him. First and foremost, he would drill the company in shield wall order and discipline. That hadn't been done since he took over. Second, their weapons and armor were in a sad state of neglect, and surely a great deal of it would need hammering out, straightening, and sharpening. As for himself, he needed to draft a fresh set of orders to reflect their new purpose, and give deep thought to how to command a line company certain to be in hard fighting, whether it was tomorrow or the day after.

As Bera thought these wonderful, shining thoughts, he allowed himself a small smile of satisfaction. Perhaps things were turning his way at last.

He realized with a start the meeting had broken up around him, and now Wulfric gazed at him across the table. The man's craggy lean face was unreadable but his arms were crossed over the broad chest of his cuirass.

"Yes, do stay a moment, Ceorl Bera," he said. "I wish to speak with you."

The Thegn said this quietly, but Bera knew even so and with sinking heart that what was given publicly would now be snatched away in private. The joy left him and he mourned its going: the moment had been so sweet and so unexpected.

"Yes, sir?" he said.

Wulfric offered him a thin smile. "It seems I won't be inspecting your works later after all. You're relieved of that duty for now. But let's hope it improves in the future."

"Yes, sir. It will."

The man looked down at his table and shifted papers over it. "I'll be blunt," he said, "as a courtesy to both of us and because time presses. Your company will go down to the fighting tomorrow, and I have no doubt it will do its duty against the Orkhs such as it can. But you . . . well, your ultimate loyalties are less clear to me, Ceorl."

Bera jerked his head back and in the same moment the rage burst from its cage like a lean, starved animal. It rose swiftly, filling his chest with power and his mind with hunger. It desired to control him, to wear him like a skin, to use his hands and the sword to strike down this foul man, silencing him forever.

Do it! the rage raved at Bera. *Spill his blood!*

But he did not. He wouldn't permit the rage to claim him. He knew its ways well: the sudden rising flood of it, the scorching urgency, the demands it made. He knew also it wasn't the answer to any question he had or any problem he faced. It was a flaw, a failing: an unfortunate relic of his Orkhish blood he would carry forever.

And no one could know of it; so Bera marshaled his strength and wrestled with the rage. He took it firmly in hand and shoved it down and down, until it was put away again in that hidden cage, and only then did he dare open his mouth to utter protest.

But before he could speak Wulfric raised a hand to stop him. "Yes, I know. You've given me no reason to question you. But until now you've never faced your—" The man paused to frown. "You've never faced Orkhs, Ceorl. That makes it . . . well, there's doubt. My own and others." He forestalled Bera again. "No, I won't tell you who. It doesn't matter."

The rage pounded its cage door again but Bera bore down against it, controlling his voice. "I will fight, sir," he said. "I have no loyalty to the Orkhs. I promise you that. My company will be ready to fight, as will I."

The man looked away, irritation in his eyes now. "I have many problems, Ceorl Bera," he said. "You're not the only one. I'm seconding another officer to your company. You will remain in command for now, but this man"—Bera heard the stress on the word—"has experience in war. You do not. I expect you to listen to him carefully, and to take his counsel. Is that clear?"

It was clear. Perfectly so. He would not command his own company in battle, nor would he be permitted to command even his own fate. That gift seeming to fall from the heavens was only a cruel hoax, and for this Bera blamed himself in part: he'd allowed himself to be carried by joy to a place he did not live.

"Clear, sir," he said, for there was nothing else to say. Certainly nothing this man would hear.

The Thegn studied Bera from beneath long gray eyebrows. "I'll send him to you this afternoon," he said. "I will tell you plainly, Ceorl. I don't like you in my part of this army. You're an unknown I don't need. If you find yourself somewhere else and you like it better there"—the man's smile was wide and insincere—"you can stay there. I won't stand in your way. You may go."

Bera did go, returning to his tent to stand in its pale, muted light. The Thegn's words cut him deeply. More so because in a better world that man might have been a father-figure to Bera: lifting him up and smoothing his career, as he did for those he favored. Bera might have cursed his true father for leaving this empty hole, and for begetting a half-Orkh son into a heartless Human world. But that had never been his way: Bera's thoughts of his father were more tender, his imaginings more generous.

For he was utterly certain his father was no common Orkh. He was surely misfit among that brutish race: gentle and reasoning, thoughtful and tolerant, possessing of a softer soul. And so he had sent gifts to Bera—the sword he wore now and the other things—wishing to forge, if only from afar, a connection to his half-Orkh son. No, his father was no cruel savage and this gave Bera comfort.

He went to his desk then and sat, reflecting as he did that not all was lost, for Wulfric hadn't taken the company from him completely. The man possessed enough shame not to inflict that mortal wound. Bera opened his ink pot and fetched to himself a fresh leaf of paper. Not to continue the letter to his mother, for that had fallen far in importance, but to consider more fully what should be done to ready his company to fight. As he considered this, Bera doodled a long-tailed Dragon on a lower corner of the leaf; then he began to write.

*

He had worked a half hour or more when the tent flap shifted suddenly, allowing in a wash of yellow sunlight. Bera looked up at this, expecting to see Dudda's grubby face thrust in, eager to utter some ill-news. But it wasn't Dudda.

It was Atul.

Only then did Bera comprehend the full measure of Wulfric's perfidy. This was the officer he'd sent to supplant Bera: this blusterer, this drunk, this brazen cheat. It was a hard blow, harder even than the Thegn's open distrust; and Bera's heart, already low, fell to depths he'd never known.

Yet he held his face steady and they stared at each other across the tent until Bera said, "If you've come to take my company, Atul, I won't permit it."

The man stepped inside the tent without speaking and let the flap fall again. Gloom returned. When he did speak, standing by the center pole, his voice was cold and angry.

"My own company was taken from me," he said. "By Wulfric. Why, I don't know. And he's sent me here, to tutor you and your uncouth rabble." Atul spread his arms. "Look at me! Fallen to a station befitting only a bastard, unloved half-Orkh. Damn him, and you, to a thousand burning hells!"

"I see," Bera said. "Well, I am sorry you were— "

"Save your pity for yourself, Heolfbera. Where is this company of yours? I would introduce myself to them. It seems I have nothing better to do. Perhaps better leadership—Human leadership—will make something of them."

Bera stood: the rage rumbled in him now, pressing against the door of its prison. "It was the Thegn's word to me," he said, pushing the words past his canines without softening their sounds, "that I would remain in command. You are here only to advise me, nothing more."

"Careful, Heolfbera. Your true colors are showing. You will treat me with respect."

"Respect is earned."

"I would say the same," Atul said. "Do you truly believe you can keep them? You're an Orkh who thinks he's a man. You're fooling yourself, Heolfbera. They don't want you. No one wants you."

"Did the Thegn instruct you to take command of my company?"

"No, he did not," Atul replied. "I was surprised. He should have." He smiled a humorless smile. "They'll come to me anyway. You're no leader, and no fighter."

This stung Bera, especially since he knew its truth. But he would fight now to keep his company; and he could play a longer game at it than this bickering.

He crossed his arms over his chest. "Very well then, Ceorl Atul," he said. "You are here now. What is your first suggestion?"

The man looked surprised, then wary. Then he ignored the question. "Where's the company?" he asked again. "What are they doing?"

"They're on the edge still," Bera replied, sitting again and picking up the quill in a show of unconcern. "They're maintaining the abattis works under the not-so-watchful eye of my Second. I came here to compose new orders, and to make a plan for the day before informing the company of their new task." He tapped the papers on his desk with the point of the quill.

Atul shook his head at this. "You carry on with that, if you feel the need. What does this man, your Second, look like?"

"Dreadful," said Bera. "He has the skin-and-bones look of a man dedicated to his drink, a head of hair that last saw a comb at his mother's knee, and a look in his eye you wish you'd never seen. But I'll take you to him in a moment."

"No need," Atul said. "I'll find him." He turned then and left the tent.

Bera rose from the chair again. Despite his earlier pretense of unconcern, he knew he should follow Atul immediately, at least to keep him from making inroads on Dudda. Neither of them could be trusted an inch, and this was a war now for the soul of the company.

Ten minutes later he found Atul, who had found Dudda. The two stood together at the edge of camp by a poorly staked-in abattis works. Atul held his purse in his hand, surely feeding Dudda's habit. They drew apart as Bera approached: neither looking pleased to see him. Dudda's face in particular held a calculation Bera had seen before: a dog wondering whether it could get away with ignoring its master's will.

"Here are the company's new orders," Bera said, putting the draft into Dudda's hand and ignoring the man's blood-shot stare. He was well aware his Second couldn't read so much as a tavern sign, but he wanted the forms observed even so, if only to assert his right. "You will notice we've been relieved fortification duties," he continued, "and we will be moving down to the line tomorrow. The remainder of today will be taken up with inspection, weapon-take, and training."

"Will it then?" Dudda said, swiveling his eyes from Bera to Atul and back again.

"Certainly not," Atul said. "Second Dudda has his orders now."

"Indeed I do," Dudda said before Bera could open his mouth to speak. "I put'em already to their mending, over there." He pointed a group of warriors gathered in the shade of a spreading tree. "Their gear ain't hardly presentable, especially to be on line with them regulars. They'd get a good laugh at it."

The man offered his own hopeful chuckle at this, but a hint of doubt clung to his words as if he remained uncertain how the wind might settle in to blow.

"Mending?" Bera said, raising his eyebrows.

Dudda licked his lips and glanced at Atul. "Aye, sir. Mending."

Bera opened his mouth again to speak, but he hardly knew where to begin. Mending the company's soft gear—leather, boots, belts, packs—was perhaps the least important item on his list; and it was best done below, behind the line, while the company waited for orders. Both men knew this perfectly well. But mending was easy; and unlike drill and weapon-work under a hot sun, it could be done while sitting at ease in shade, socializing or even drinking. It seemed Atul had moved swiftly indeed to set his first hooks into the company.

Bera decided he needed to make a stand now. There was little holding the company to him, perhaps nothing at all; and in ten minutes more they might be gone forever.

"Absolutely not," he said then turned to stride with purpose toward the warriors working in the shade.

Dudda rushed to follow, the overlarge shirt flapping around him. "You won't find'em in any mood to listen, sir," he said. "They was real happy to be off diggin'."

Bera didn't slow. "I imagine they were. But I am Ceorl of this company. They will do as I say."

Dudda didn't reply to this. And when they came to the tree, Bera found the company's mood sullen and closed against him, making him wonder whether it was not already too late. He reminded himself to speak to them with quiet words and appeasing gestures, so as not to overbear.

"We have new orders," he said. "We are now a company of the shield wall, although held in reserve for now. This means no more digging ditches for every camp, and no more cutting stakes."

There was no reaction to this: they knew it already.

"The bad news," he continued, "is that we have a lot of work to do to get ready, and a very short time in which to do it. Less than a day, in fact. We're not ready for combat—not even close. I'd wager half my pay that most of you haven't seen the metal of your swords since we left Sternsham."

This last was meant as a jest, to break the tension; but it fell into a long, yawning silence in which Bera could hear leaves clattering over his head. Now Atul stepped forward into that silence, holding out his hands as if a sudden outcry of protest had risen against Bera.

"I hear you!" he said to the company, and then he smiled at them, something Bera couldn't do without looking bloodthirsty. "I'd make my own wager most of you have made it your purpose to be here, away from the fighting. Am I right?"

There was laughter at this and a few heads nodded agreement.

Atul stepped closer to them, edging ahead of Bera. "You needn't fear," he said. "The Thegn is a wise man and he knows your need, so he gave me to you. A strong hand, a new leader, a commander who knows war. Because he wants each of you to see your homes and your families again, and so do I."

Bera couldn't see Atul's face now, but he did see the many hard eyes turned on him, wishing him away. The rage rose then but he shoved it down. Dismay took its place. Had Wulfric ordered this treachery? Had there been in truth no plan at all to trust Bera with the company, but only to shame him so he would slink away under the burden of it? This seemed likely now; but Bera resolved not to go quietly, or at all.

He stepped forward, shouldering Atul aside. But when he opened his mouth to speak, he realized he didn't know what to say. Dudda had always spoken for him, because it was easier that way, and it came to Bera now this had been a great mistake. He wondered in what other ways he'd been a blundering fool.

"I want that also," he said to them, hearing and hating his own uncertainty. "For you to see your families again, I mean. But we have less than a day to remember how to be warriors again, and that means— "

"Remember how to be warriors again?" Atul cried. He turned up his hands and spread his arms wide, as if Bera's words made no sense to him. Then he punched the air. "I say bullshit! You're true warriors and let none tell you otherwise! I also know you're damned tired of digging ditches." He pumped the fist again. "To hell with digging ditches!"

They responded to this, some repeating the cry. And already there were far more smiles than Bera could ever hope to pull from them. He felt heartsick.

Atul kept the fist in the air, taunting Bera. "And to hell with Orkhs!" he shouted. "Without those black-hearted bastards we'd all be home in our beds squeezing something warm!"

They laughed at this. Some rose in response to Atul. "To hell with Orkhs!" they cried after him, and not a few stared now at Bera with undisguised dislike, something he'd never seen before.

His dismay turned to panic: they were slipping away from him. No, not slipping but yanked away. Bera understood now he'd depended far too much on Dudda. That had been an easy thing to do: a comfortable routine established in the beginning and never varied from. He wondered now at his own reticence but that was a meditation for another day: the problem couldn't be fixed in a moment, and it would certainly not be fixed in this moment. All he could do was fall back again on that same familiar, hoping it would work one more time.

He turned to Dudda, who'd watched this in silence.

"Assemble the company on the center ground," he said to the man. "Immediately except to do weapon-take as needed. Full armor, shield, and sword please. I intend to perform shield wall exercises within the hour and see where we are." This wouldn't be popular: shield drill was hard work and the day had grown hot.

Dudda stared back open-mouthed, the conflict plain on his face. He'd been given an order and his plain duty was to obey. But stepping so boldly to his Ceorl's side might cost him his long-held perch atop of the company, which seemed the only thing keeping him afloat in his dissolution.

Bera silently willed his Second to obedience. Atul watched also, confidence on his face.

Dudda looked up at the tree and cleared his throat, then again. "Well, I reckon, well, there's a reason—a fine reason, I'll warrant—why that Thegn sent this man to us—him." Dudda made a small gesture toward Atul, and Bera saw heads nodding agreement under the tree. "So I reckon he's—we can't be faulted none for giving him an ear, any rate. More, maybe, I reckon."

The speech was diffident and halting to a painful degree, but there was no mistaking that it was the final break: Dudda and the company with him had rid themselves of their unwanted half-Orkh Ceorl. Bera had held himself clenched against the blow, but even so it crushed him and he collapsed inside. He was finished: his time in the Fyrd was over.

"Well said, friend Dudda!" Atul crowed and he stepped forward to eclipse Bera again. "The company will finish its mending now, then go to mess. We shall do nothing more today on empty bellies!"

Dudda drew himself up, still not filling his oversize shirt, and he saluted Atul with a grimy hand.

"As you say, sir," he said.

Bera swatted aside the flap and ducked to enter his tent. He stripped off his baldric and sword, and threw them on the camp bed. They could lie there until they rotted, so far as he cared: he would never use that sword again and didn't deserve it anyway.

He crossed to his chair and fell into it. The litter on his desk—notes, letters, orders—seemed meaningless now and unimportant. He swept out a long arm and raked the desktop clean, knocking everything to ground. Leaves of paper scattered and the ink pot fell to leak a shiny black stain over the grass.

He had been pushed out. Worse, he had been pushed out and there was no one to hear his complaint. Certainly not the Thegn. Wulfric would look earnestly into Bera's face, feigning he had not set events into motion himself, and tell his half-Orkh Ceorl that if he couldn't command the loyalty of his troops he was unfit to command. Bera squirmed in his chair: there was no essential untruth in that.

Damn him!

He wondered what to do with himself now. Should he leave camp? Where would he go? Home to his mother? Gods no! What greater shame could there be? He needed some other way. He gazed down at the mess on the ground and saw the letter to his mother there. He should finish it, although he certainly wouldn't tell her of this fresh disgrace.

He had leaned forward to take up the ink pot when his attention was caught by a small movement to his right. He turned his head toward it, expecting to see a foraging rat.

But it wasn't a rat. Instead some small pale square object was entering the tent between the bottom edge of the canvas and the grass beneath. Bera rose from his chair and knelt to pull up the edge of the tent, but the heavy canvas was staked close to the earth and it moved no more three inches under his fingers.

"Who's there?" he called through the gap. "You there! Answer me!"

There was no reply. The pale object lay fully within the tent now, resting on the grass by his face, a small square. But Bera left it and ran for the tent door. He threw open the flap and sprinted around to the rear.

He saw there only a narrow strip of grass that lay empty between the tent and a warren of supply crates stacked high and close, blocking any long view across the camp. Bera investigated several of the larger alleys in that warren, but saw no one at all. He grunted, annoyed, and went back into the tent to examine this thing he'd been given.

He found it was only a single leaf of paper, folded artlessly into an uneven square. But surface was strangely mottled, and the fibers were large and crude, as if the paper had been made by someone only lightly schooled in the art.

Bera unfolded the leaf and saw it contained seven lines of script. The language of it was Common, but the hand was poor and unpracticed. Bera's eyes raced over the words:

Sashna,

You wish to be a great warrior. It must be so. You cannot be a warrior until the rage blooms hot within you. Come to the hanging tree and the angry rock, by the swift water east of the great way between mountains. At the dark of the moon's journey. This night. Alone. We will speak of your future with your true people.

It was unsigned. Bera stared at the words, a hundred questions crowding his mind. Who was this note meant for? Who was Sashna? He knew of no one by that name. Had this secretive messenger delivered the note to the wrong tent? Was there a spy at work in Cenred's camp?

He took a step toward the tent door, thinking to take the message to Wulfric. But then he stopped. This was a very dangerous thing for him to possess. Already he walked under an ever-following cloud of suspicion, which this cryptic, spying note would do nothing but confirm.

He returned to the desk and sat, smoothing out the leaf so he could study it more carefully. He examined the crooked folds of it and felt the rough surface with his fingertips. Then he read the words again.

Your true people.

Bera's gut trembled and he stared at the words, unseeing now.

Gods above! Could this be from my father?

The shock of it struck Bera like a sword blow. He jerked in the chair and struck the paper from the desktop as if it meant to poison him. It skated over the polished wood and fell to the ground among his other things. Bera's heart hammered in his chest like a call to arms.

My father?

Him?

Surely not!

Bera stared down at the paper. He bent to pick it up again to look at the scrawled words, considering the spiky aggression of the script. No, that messenger hadn't missed his mark. How could he? Bera was the only half-Orkh in the Fyrd.

His hand trembled. His father wanted to meet him. Would it be treason to go? Perhaps not if it was only to speak with him, nothing more. Or did Bera want more? He wondered now for the first time where his loyalties did lie. There was certainly no one here who was loyal to Bera himself. Not the company, not Dudda, not the Thegn.

Bera looked over the top of the paper to a wooden crate that lay under his camp bed. It wasn't quite hidden by the drape of his blankets. He'd hadn't opened that thing in years, but he knew exactly what lay inside. His mother had sent it, after he'd told her of his assignment to company command. Since then he'd carried the crate from camp to camp, never certain why he didn't toss it from a bridge as he passed. There was no profit in making such a show as to use what was in there. It would make him something he'd striven his whole life not to be.

He refolded the note and dropped it to his desk. He had much to think on now, and much to consider: for it seemed the Orkh who had sired him was somewhere in that great dark army approaching the pass. And he wanted to meet his son.

6

OF EARIC

Earic paced the dusty boards of the hayloft listening for the small sounds of Aere's arrival below. It was early afternoon of the day after his lie to Cenred and still he burned with the shame of it.

He was determined to say nothing of it to Aere, if indeed she came. She also was a creature of duty and she would insist he confess his perfidy to Cenred, and come to him what may. But the thought made Earic's hands tremble and his blood run cold. No, she could know nothing of that madness: the secret of it was too great. But he would certainly tell her that she was moving forward soon with the King's Own: to the right and hard fighting. This much she deserved to know.

Also, he held a frail, wan hope that luck would see him through to the end, and that damned place wasn't so important as he'd thought: making the lie only a white one. But this hope touched only his own plight, for Aere would be sent to those awful fields either way. He swung his fists at the air and cursed Cenred, and cursed this war. And cursed his own desire, which had led him to this folly. Then he wrapped his arms about his chest as he paced, to hold himself together against this slow crumbling ruin.

*

Soon a quiet voice called from below and he called back. The ladder rattled against the dry boards of the loft and Aere's scarred face came into view. She was smiling. It seemed the unpleasantness of their last tryst was forgotten, or maybe it was Aere would no longer let it to stand between them. He smiled back to her, uncertain still, and finding more crowding his throat than he'd expected.

"I'm glad you've come," he said.

"Are you truly?" she replied. She left the ladder to set the bow and her quiver by the wall, then she stood on the boards facing him. "I glory to hear it, Earic. But I fear I have only a moment for us. We're moving down soon. To the front they say, but I don't ken it. It's not our way to fight in the beginning."

He wasn't surprised she knew already: no secret kept long in an army camp. "It's true," he said, moving closer to her, "and yes, it's unexpected."

She stood her ground. "Why? What's happening?"

Earic stopped and drew breath, shifting his thoughts to war. "It's farmland where you're going: big, flat, open. Bad ground and we don't have the force to defend it properly. So Cenred is putting the King's there, with all the reserves. In two lumps." He held up his closed hands. "Like two fists, I guess. But there's a lot of ground to cover and it will be dangerous."

She thought about this. "All the reserves. So there's no help for us? If it goes badly."

Earic shook his head. "No, and the fight in the center goes badly already."

This seemed to shake her confidence. "So soon?"

"Yes, so soon. Cenred is calling up everyone from the rear who can be spared. This thing has not stepped off on the right foot."

"Perhaps so," she said, "but the gods will look after us, you and I. The three of us." She smiled again but not at him.

Earic took another step toward her, but still she stood unmoving by the ladder. He was suddenly very uncertain of his ground.

"I will tell you plainly, Aere," he said. "I don't have a good feeling about this fight. Cenred's planning has become desperate already, although he's put a brave face on it. The Orkhs are strong and they're moving very aggressively. Listen, I don't want you up there, Aere. Not in this fight." He held her eyes. "I can have you pulled out and put somewhere else, in the rear. But even that— "

She had stiffened and now she interrupted. "Don't you do that, Earic Eadwulfing! I'm not a plump-wife fearing the wolf at the door while her man's away. I'm a warrior-woman, sworn to my duty!"

"Yes, but— "

"I'll hear no buts from you, Earic! You leave me be!" She held his eye sternly, but when he didn't reply the steel seemed run from her. "I'm an archer-woman," she said. "I shan't cross swords with any Orkh, but woe betide it if I do."

Earic smiled at her again. He admired her plain courage and the fierce determination that drove her. These had drawn him to her in the beginning: she was the warrior he was not. But now it was different, more difficult. Complex knots lay between them.

"Very well," he said, knowing he would not sway her. "But promise me you'll go with care."

"Ever and always," she said. "But I haven't long to stay, Earic, as I said. Sit with me and let's eat this apple of mine." She produced a green apple from a leather pouch at her belt, then drew a dagger from somewhere Earic didn't see.

"I stole this from the Master of Horse," she said, waving the apple at him. "His damned animals eat higher than we do. A pox on him."

Earic laughed and they sat together in the hay, side by side, eating slivers she pared from the fruit. Her hair smelled of woodsmoke and camp soap.

"A fine apple," he said, "but a bit of beef would sit better."

She shook her head. "I can't lift meat to save the world," she said. "I've tried, you know, but the officers carry it away for their own bellies as quick as it shows." She cocked an eyebrow at Earic. "Ain't there meat in your mess, officer man?"

"Sometimes, but it's always mutton. Otherwise, it's beans and more beans, and old potatoes. We've eaten out what little forage there was here."

"I'd take a taste of mutton about now," she said. "The damned Orkhs are getting it."

Earic blinked at this. "What?"

She waved a dismissive hand at him and talked around the apple in her mouth. "It's nothing. I hear things. Some of it true, some not."

It did seem a trifling, but Earic carried still the habit of wishing to know all he could of any foe. "Tell me," he said.

She looked at him and laughed. "Truly, Earic? Mutton?"

He made a negligent gesture. "I'm curious."

Aere paused to swallow then spoke. "Fine. If you must know, I heard it from another, one who likes to talk, you know the kind, that the Aelf-folk with their big cats was doing something. Didn't say what it was. Then something bad happened to them. Didn't say what that was, either. Don't look at me that way, Earic! I'm not one of your scouts. Anyways, they was saying they—the Aelfs, I mean—found some sheep." She waved a hand at the world beyond the loft. "Out there. Somewhere. For the Orkhs to eat, I reckon." She was gnawing at the apple core now. "That's all. I was never much for sheep meat but I'd eat it with a will now."

Earic considered this information, but it seemed to have no importance and he set it aside. "Yes, it must be Orkh-fodder," he said. "The folks of the out-farms came to town days ago, or went over the pass. They surely took all their stock with them."

"Do you reckon they cook it? The sheep meat."

"Orkhs? Who knows, but please get enough for yourself, Aere. Next time I'll bring you something. Meat, if I can."

She looked pleased but shook her head. "No, you needn't look after me. I know a hundred ways to fill an empty belly in an army camp."

"Like stealing the Horse Master's apples?"

Aere smiled at Earic with genuine affection for what seemed the first time. "Aye," she said, "like pinching his horse apples." She gathered her legs under herself and stood to brush hay from her leggings. "I'll be going now. They'll miss me soon, and sure as the sun the Second will send someone to find me. He don't suffer defaulters."

Earic stood also and he reached out an arm to pull her

close. Her lean, bow-muscled body lay hard against his. "Tell me again you'll take care," he said.

"I shall," she replied then wagged a finger in his face. "Mind you, Earic, I mean it when I say you're not to pull me from my duty. Don't be thinking I'll forgive you later."

He nodded. "You have my word."

"Then all will be well."

She pushed herself up to give him a quick kiss and an uncertain glance that pierced him. But before he could respond, she broke away to collect her quiver and bow from the hay. Then she swung herself onto the ladder and climbed down without looking at him again.

Earic went back to his tent to vent the frustration of his heart on the derelict scout: writing a scathing order that transferred the man back to the line company from which he'd come. When this was done Earic pushed the paper from him and slumped low in his camp chair. He scrubbed a hand across his face: he needed a shave, but there was no will in him to rise and cross to the washbasin.

He reflected on how swiftly things had turned against him. It was only yesterday morning all had seemed so well, and he'd felt then a deep peace in his purpose and duty. Today that was gone, and all he felt now was very far out on a very rotten limb.

A loud voice pulled him from sleep. He pushed himself up in the chair, blinking. *Gods! I have far too much to do to be sleeping!*

He sat for a moment, gathering himself and studying the pale light filtering through the canvas walls: it was mid-afternoon. The voice came again: calling his name from outside the tent. Earic rose and crossed to the tent flap where he pushed his head through to squint against strong sunlight. Five paces from him stood a man in a gray woolen jerkin bearing the yellow and plum livery of Cenred's House. He was a messenger.

"The High Aetheling's compliments, sir," the man said, in a cool practiced voice. "And you are requested to attend him." The man's tone grew a fraction warmer. "Immediately, sir, I'm afraid."

Earic considered this. It could be nothing good. He wondered whether the situation in the center had taken still another turn for the worse. He nodded to the messenger and pulled back his head to straighten his tunic and comb his fingers through his hair. That shave seemed even more needful now, but Earic knew immediately meant precisely that to Cenred and not a moment longer. Still he went to the wash basin for a splash of cold water, banishing the last of his unwelcome sleep, and he dried his face with a dirty towel. It would have to do.

"Were you aware of this place?" Cenred asked. "This farm building, or whatever it is, with the stone wall?"

They were in the man's tent, alone. There had been no pleasantries when Earic arrived there, no easy greetings as was their long custom. There was only this question, posed with hard eyes and a finger stabbed at a map.

A new map, it seemed.

Earic stared at the back wall of the tent, considering how he lay squarely on the forks of a dilemma. It was one he had made for himself. If he admitted he knew of that place—that is, if he gave Cenred the truth of it—he would admit dereliction, and rouse suspicions of worse. For he should have certainly accounted for the place in his assessment of the field. Indeed, this had been his intent, before the man's new plan had emerged to wreck it.

But should he deny knowledge—and lie to the man again—it would admit dismal failure to scout the field, and so admit failure to do his essential work of protecting Cenred and the Fyrd itself.

There was no good answer to the Aetheling's question.

Worse still, if Cenred had the derelict scout's map, he would know any lie for what it was. That map was a poor thing, but it did show clearly the building and its outwall. It was also possible Cenred had spoken to Earic's own staff, and they would certainly give him the truth of it. The man was no fool, and even now he might be hiding in wait to pounce upon a lie.

So the truth would have to serve, or perhaps some slim part of it.

"I am aware of the place, yes sir," Earic said. "It was shown on a map made for me by one of my scouts."

Cenred drew his head back. "And you didn't think it was important? Lurking there on our most vulnerable front?" He lifted the finger from the map and pointed it to the world beyond the tent.

Earic knew he was finished, but still he needed to avoid the question of why he'd neglected to tell Cenred of the place— that damned place. The man would never accept, nor should he, that he and his Fyrd had been betrayed for the sake of a woman. Worse, a common woman whom Earic had carelessly gotten with child. It would likely mean the noose, for Cenred would regard the betrayal as an unforgivable crime against the Dominion itself, and the king.

So Earic listened with horror as he grew the lie greater still. "I didn't consider another farmstead significant—no, sir," he said. "It's cropland and those steads are thick on the ground. I take it, sir, this one is larger, or more important, than the scout's drawing suggested?"

Cenred slammed both fists down on his map table, rattling an ink pot on its tray. "You're damned right it's important! That's a fortress out there." He pointed again. "It's a stone building with a gods-damned stone wall, overlooking my front like a sword poked right at my face!" He turned the finger now jab it at that face, which was red now.

"Then let's take it, sir. I'll lead the attack."

For a time Cenred said nothing to this, striving even as Earic watched to master himself. When at last he spoke, his voice was carefully controlled.

"We cannot go take that place, Earic," he said, "because it's occupied already by a large force of Orkhs. An attempt was made to take it earlier today—unknown to me—and it failed miserably. That reckless fool of an Aelf who commands my cavalry lost a fair part of her company." The man's frown was bitter. "I will, however, give her credit for proper appreciation of military value."

There was nothing profitable to say to this, but it was followed by a long, tense silence Earic felt obliged to fill. "I see, sir," he said, knowing it was the wrong thing.

The words lit the Aetheling's passion again. "No, you don't see! Not at all! You fumbled this, Earic. You fumbled it badly. And now my already difficult right is exposed to machine fire. Yes, the Orkhs have pulled up engines. Worse, they have a short step-off to attack when it comes to that, and it certainly will. You can be damned sure of that!" The man now paced behind his table, flipping his hands about himself. "I'd thought my immediate problems were in the center, but now they're all over the place!"

"I apologize, sir."

The man stopped his pacing to turn on Earic. "What damned good does that do me? I need officers I can trust to do their jobs, Earic. I'm a busy man—godsdamned busy!—and I can't think of everything. I can't *do* everything!" He resumed his pacing. "You've put the Fyrd in a bad situation I don't know how to fix. Not yet."

Earic opened his mouth to respond, but a slashing finger stopped him short. "I'm certainly not taking suggestions from you," Cenred said coldly.

Earic closed his mouth and waited. *Here it comes . . .*

Cenred stopped again and drew himself up to face Earic. "You're relieved," he said. "You may keep your rank as a courtesy for your past service, but I'm putting you in provisions. A Ceorl's posting. Keep the beans cooking and my wagons rolling. You will report to Mordreth. He is expecting you."

Earic nearly wept at that. This great man, whom he'd come to consider a second and better father, had decided his fate even before dispatching the messenger to summon him.

"Yes, sir," he said. "I'm sorry, sir—again. You're right. It's not forgivable."

The man's fury seemed spent now and he went to a camp chair to sit. His movements were slow and careful, as if the troubles of high command had physically diminished him.

"You were one of my brilliant lights, Earic," he said, his voice quiet, tired. "Maybe the brightest. But I can't let this go. Too much is at stake. You're dismissed."

Earic bowed his head, shattered. But even so he knew he would have done the same in Cenred's shoes, and still the man didn't know the full extent of Earic's deceit. He knew nothing of Aere, or the child, or the lie. It would have to stay that way. Earic drew up to salute silently; and when he received nothing in return, he left the tent and Cenred brooding in his chair.

Earic wandered camp for a time, knowing his career in the King's Service was finished. Cenred had transferred him to Provisions but this was only a half-measure, he knew, and the man did no trade in half-measures. He would certainly ensure his former Master of Scouts was washed clear of the Fyrd in the great ebbing tide of conscripts returning to their homes for the Autumn harvest, when the campaigning season closed. Earic would return to his own home then: the Eadwulfing estates in the fertile east. His father would not be pleased by the news his third son bore, of the utter ruin of a promising military career.

"Sir?" a voice called to him from nearby. "Are you lost?"

Perilously close to it, Earic thought, stopping to turn toward the voice. It was an older warrior, likely some young Ceorl's gray-haired Second. His expression was polite but it was plain to Earic he'd wandered into an area of camp the man considered his own.

"No," Earic said, "but you can direct me to the Provisions tent." It was past time he reported to Mordreth, whom he knew in passing.

The man raised an arm to point east. "Over there, sir. The one with the peaked top. Aye, that's the one."

Earic nodded his thanks and moved away, still feeling the man's curious eyes on his back. Had rumor of his disgrace run ahead of him? That wouldn't surprise him: an army encampment was a perfectly tuned instrument for the transmission of gossip, both true and less so. One had only to touch its strings anywhere and the sound carried to every listening ear. No, he wouldn't outrun his new infamy for very long, and it even might be well for him to leave the Fyrd soon. Perhaps even before the fight below was done. None would stop his going.

Earic paused some yards short of the Provisions tent to draw a steel dagger from his belt. It had been a parting gift from his mother, a pale humorless woman who believed devotion to duty the highest of virtues. She would have disavowed entirely the use to which her son put that knife now.

With his fingertips Earic picked out and lifted the edge of an embroidered insignia sewn high on the chest of his tunic. This was—or it had been—the badge of his office, marking him as a privileged member of Cenred's inner circle. Doubtless this was what the curious Second had seen. Working with the point of the knife, Earic teased out and cut the threads holding the badge in place, until at last he could rip it free. It left behind a dark stain of unfaded fabric.

He looked down at the thing in his palm. He had been so proud of himself when Cenred gave it to him, years ago. He'd arrived then in a place he wanted very much to be. Now it seemed best simply to leave it on the mud and move on. But instead he pushed it deep into his belt pouch, telling himself he would dispose of it later, in a harder-eyed, less fragile moment. He made the last steps to the Provisions tent then and ducked through its wide flap to enter the gloom within.

But he found no work there. To be sure Mordreth welcomed Earic with a real and gratifying sincerity, but it didn't wholly conceal an undercurrent of bafflement at his presence. And in the end the man said he was sorry, very sorry indeed, but there was no command available in Provisions just now, even with the recent draw-down for the front.

And so Earic realized what Cenred had known very well: there was no place for him here. Rather he had been sent to Provisions to be stored away himself: out of sight and away from further trouble until he could be mustered firmly out. This pained Earic more than anything that had gone before: he was now without use to anyone, and nothing at all was expected of him.

So for the next hour Earic only sat in the tent and answered questions of others about the state of the engagement below. But that well of questions soon ran dry and those others excused themselves to duties, leaving Earic nearly alone in the great tent. He found he couldn't bear the stillness, nor the gloom, nor the uselessness, so he left to resume his lonely stalk across camp. Aere returned to his mind then, and he brooded over the dangers his own actions had set before her.

He thought also of their first meeting. It was at the spring weapon-take, near Brecca's Ferry where the Fyrd was gathering for war. Earic could write a fair hand so Cenred had set him to meeting the companies and war bands as they came; and he noted their names and leaders and the strength of their numbers in the pages of the King's Fyrd Book. Aere was among the band of Ealdorman Fenric then, and she stood near her liege, brandishing the burned cheek and the half-ear and her fierce gaze. Earic's eyes went to her often as he spoke with Fenric of his numbers and the state of his train.

But her own eyes were cool, later, when he found her at archery as if by chance. "I'm not what you might believe, my lord," she said to him.

"Nor am I," he replied. "I wish only to hear of the ear. That's surely a brave tale."

She was wary of him, but told the story even so as they sat in early spring grass beneath a spreading oak. It was indeed a brave tale: she'd lost that ear in service to her liege, warding his life against brigands. Now she stood among his guard.

"Do you wish to hear of the other," Aere asked, touching her cheek. "Do you hoard stories of wounds, sir?" Her tone was light now, nearly teasing.

"No," he said. "But I honor your wounds. I wear a sword"— he touched it—"but in truth I serve the king in other ways."

"Do you? I'm certain those ways are no less honorable, my lord."

This was true perhaps—Cenred would say it was—but Earic spoke little of his own work, preferring to hear her own tales of battles well-fought or narrowly escaped. He envied her this, even as he wished never to draw a sword in anger.

They lingered beneath the tree an hour, then more, until at

length she said, "Would you wish to join me in exercising on the targets, my lord?"

"It would be a pleasure," he said, although in truth he knew little of the bow, and still less of exercising on the targets with it. But he did know this warrior-woman had opened a door in answer to his knock, and he did not mean to linger long under the lintel.

And so they worked the bow until the light failed: she well, he far less so. And their first lovemaking was hurried and fumbling. When it was done, they spoke of themselves; and as they did, the vast gulf between their stations seemed to close to nothing. And soon Earic found he'd been taken utterly by her. For never had he known a woman in this way: coupling as equals, then speaking together frankly of many things without caution or reserve. It was a revelation that enraptured and dismayed him both.

He had been walking an hour or more, and finding no solace in it, when he came to the tent that housed the officers' mess. Its walls had been rolled up against the heat of the day, freeing upon the world clouds of blue woodsmoke and the unpleasant scent of burnt meat. Only a handful lingered here now, and all were engrossed in their eating, paying Earic no attention. He found a battered wooden table that stood apart from the rest and sat there, thinking he might eat also, if he could.

Hardly a minute's time passed before a tall Orkh entered the tent, ducking its head as it came. This was surely the half-Orkh Earic had heard so much of but never seen. The creature wore the rank stripes of a King's Officer—a company Ceorl—but it seemed uneasy to be here even so. It peered carefully about the mess as if expecting to see someone it hoped not to.

The Orkh's gaze fell finally on Earic, who lifted his chin in greeting. The Orkh nodded in return then looked away to examine the mess tubs: they held boiled potatoes, roasted turnips, and fly-blown stacks of mutton joints charred to black. The meat didn't surprise Earic: any army's Provisions train ate better than those they served. This was one of the immutable law of campaigning.

He watched as the Orkh picked over the joints and wondered if the creature ate anything but meat. It had been Earic's work to know the ways of Orkh-kind, but this hadn't extended to their eating habits. Earic surprised himself then by leaning forward to catch the Orkh's eye a second time and motioning for the creature to sit across from him.

The Orkh seemed to consider this, then it moved across the mess tent toward Earic on legs like young trees. It set a wooden trencher on the table with surprising delicacy then drew a chair across the dirt floor to sit. Earic saw the trencher held potatoes in addition to mutton, answering that question.

"To what to I owe this courtesy?" the creature asked. Its voice was deep and rough, as Earic imagined a bear might speak, but the words were clear and cultured.

"The honest answer?" Earic replied.

The Orkh took a mutton joint from the trencher and eyed it without interest. "Please," he said. "I so seldom hear honesty."

"I was curious," Earic said. "I've never met a half-Orkh, nor an all-Orkh. Well, except over a sword." Then thinking he might have wandered already onto dangerous ground, he added: "A few times. Long ago, of course." He waved a hand.

The Orkh eyed Earic over the mutton. "I am called Bera."

"I'm honored to meet you, Bera. I'm Earic. You're certainly bigger than any bear I've ever seen." Earic smiled to show it was a jest, but when the Orkh's face didn't change he pushed on. "So what do you do?"

"Nothing now, it seems," Bera said. "Until this morning I had a Provisions Guard company, but it seems tolerance for me doesn't run to fighting that company. It will go down the pass road without me, with a Human leading it."

"That's truly an injustice," Earic said, but it was a politeness. In truth he had no strong inclination either way, and he did wonder about the creature's ultimate loyalties.

Bera shrugged. "An injustice? Perhaps, perhaps not. Justice is what those who make it say it is. I can only accept it."

"Do you?" Earic said. "Have to accept it, I mean. Isn't it just in itself to rage against an unearned fate?"

"Spoken like a Human," Bera replied. "I have no such privilege. Complaint is only a shovel that digs me deeper." He took a small bite from the mutton and made a face. He returned the joint to the trencher and wiped his hands with a rag, turning his attention to the potatoes. They were gray with age.

"What will you do now?" Earic asked.

The Orkh studied him from beneath heavy brow ridges. "What is this to you?" he rumbled. "Did you call me here to stir the dirt over my grave?"

Earic lifted his hands. "No offense meant, friend! I came here to consider that question for my own part. Like you, I didn't expect to need an answer just now."

Bera ate potatoes as he listened. The metal spoon clicked against his canines. "Very well, friend Earic," he said, taking care to swallow first. "Tell me your sad story and I'll tell you mine."

Hearing this, Earic was surprised to find he did want to tell this tall half-Orkh his story. More, he wished to tell the whole truth of it. Until now he'd hoarded that truth to himself: parceling out a piece here and a piece there, telling one thing to one person and something else to another. The full truth was hard, but surely this creature lived in a world of hard truths: truths that couldn't be avoided, but only faced squarely and with courage. He might even understand.

So there, in that smoky mess tent, Earic told Bera everything. He told him about Aere and their child; and about the stone-walled building and his lies to Cenred; and about the danger to Aere in the west and his own promise to leave her there in that danger. And he spoke of his disgrace and his transfer to Provisions, which led him here, to this battered mess table far in the rear. And when it was done, it seemed to Earic some of the rubble had been cleared from his heart.

"You do not ask for judgment, friend," the Orkh said, "and I will not offer it. Perhaps I would have done the same in the same boots." He shrugged. "Who's to say? Too many have weighed me wrongly to take such weighing upon myself. So I will turn your own question back on you. What will you do now?"

Earic leaned back in the chair. He'd decided already he liked this creature. "I will follow my orders, I suppose. Do what I can. But mostly I'll worry. She's down there"—he gestured south—"or she will be soon, and now I have no way of knowing what's happening there."

A memory rose in Earic then and he gestured to the Orkh's joint, now pushed from the trencher to lie on the table top. "Do Orkhs like mutton—sheep meat?" he asked. "You seem not to."

Something unpleasant appeared in Bera's crimson eyes then: anger or annoyance. But even as Earic pulled back in surprise it was gone again, leaving behind only that studied mildness the Orkh seemed to cultivate.

"I cannot speak for the Orkhs," Bera said, his voice cool now. "I'm not one of them."

Earic put up his hands. "I didn't mean— "

"No, no one does," Bera said, "and yet they do." His gaze now went to the joint on the table. "I had thought to eat that, because my belly cried out for food. But it tastes of green grass to me, like eating turf, and I'm no horse. I want red meat if I can get it. Pork, if I can't. Potatoes, if I must."

"I see," Earic said absently, for his thoughts were again on the sheep Aere had mentioned. It was a strange place to find them: penned up between two warring armies. And now it seemed the Orkhs weren't eating them, or likely weren't. This was a puzzle indeed, and one to which Earic couldn't see even the beginnings of a solution. That bothered him.

Bera swept the trencher and the joint aside with a broad forearm. "But the food of Orkhs is not truly what's on your mind, friend Earic," he said. "What's on your mind is the same question I ask myself. What's keeping you here? Doing nothing, waiting for nothing. Who would miss you if you . . .

flew away?" The Orkh made a fluttering gesture with long, black-skinned fingers.

"Go to the front, you mean? To Aere?"

Bera shrugged his massive shoulders. "Your business is your business," he said, "and my business is not advice. But I would ask myself this, were I such a fool as you in such a foolish love."

Earic ignored the jibe and gazed past the Orkh's shoulder, thinking. Who *would* miss him if he were gone? He had no place here, no duties. Cenred wanted him unseen and unheard, so what was one step further in that same direction? Earic felt an unexpected sense of freedom then: he was his own man now in a way he hadn't been for a very long time.

He set this aside to consider later and turned his gaze back to Bera. "What about you?" he said. "What's your story?"

Those red eyes searched Earic now, and he noticed their pupils were subtly elongated, reminding him more a cat's eyes than a Human's. He wondered what it was like, being a lone half-Orkh in a world of Humans.

"My story is plain," Bera said. "It's written in my blood. I have the wrong kind. As I said before, tolerance of me runs only so far as digging ditches and watching wagons. When the time came for war another took my company and turned my warriors against me. It seems the Thegn—the Provisions Thegn—believes I will not raise my hand against an Orkh."

Earic crossed his arms over his chest. "That seems a fair question. Would you?"

That same strong emotion appeared in the Orkh's eyes again and Earic saw now it was anger. But once again it was snatched away as swiftly as it came.

Bera placed his hands on the table and laced his dark fingers together as if to tame them. "I understand why some might question my loyalties," he said after a time. "But I have always been a loyal soldier of the king. I always will be. What else can I be? Where else could I go? The other side wouldn't accept me even if I wished it."

The Orkh's voice carried conviction, but as he said this last his gaze shifted from Earic as if the eye of his mind had gone to something else.

"I believe you," Earic said, not certain that he did. "And you're right. No one would miss me. For a while at least."

"Then go find her," Bera said, "if that's where your heart leads you."

When Earic said nothing to this, the Orkh added: "Perhaps I will follow my own heart also." Then he pushed himself up to stand and touched a yellow-nailed fingertip to his chest. "I will keep your secrets safe, friend Earic. Fear not."

Earic nodded and the Orkh walked from the tent, looking neither left nor right at the Humans he passed. Watching him go, Earic returned to that spark of freedom he'd discovered before. It was still there, tempting him. He certainly wouldn't be missed if he left to find Aere, at least not for a long while. But—and it was a very great but—he might lose head for deserting his post, however meaningless it might be. Cenred had no tolerance for desertion and already Earic lingered perilously near the block.

And so he sat in the mess tent a very long time, bending his thoughts one way and then another: examining his heart and reckoning the cost of his choices. But in the end he faltered, finding himself unable to choose anything at all except to sleep on his questions. So in the early dark, before the coming of the moon, he rose from the table and went to his tent, where he flung himself into bed and slept a dreamless sleep.

7

OF BERA

era walked the camp toward his tent. He felt lit-tle sympathy for that love-sick Human: the fool had brought his troubles on himself. But he knew his own foolishness was greater still, for it wasn't the work of a week or a month, or even a campaigning season; but the ill-fruit of a lifetime spent imagining an illusion was truth.

At the tent he crossed to the desk to shift through his papers for the note: he wanted to read it again and ponder its meaning. But he didn't see it. He frowned and searched again, this time stacking his other papers out of the way in a corner.

But the note wasn't there.

He bent to look under the table, then under the chair. He dug his hands into his various pockets, but still nothing. He even searched the blankets of his cot, knowing it couldn't possibly be there. Then the truth swept over him, chilling his blood: someone had found the thing and taken it.

It was surely Atul. The man had been in his tent, rummaging in his things.

Bera moved to the tent pole and drew the sword from his baldric, but his hand shook. He understood now it had been a mistake to tell no one of the note. If it came to the Thegn from other hands, it would certainly paint Bera a spy—indeed, the very same spy many believed him to be already. The penalty for treason was death and there would be no trial: Wulfric would pronounce Bera's guilt with ill-concealed glee and he would lose his head within the hour.

Bera's heart thundered in his chest. Should he flee now, before the file of warriors arrived to take him to Wulfric? If he did, where would he go? To his mother? No, they would certainly find him there. Across the lines to the Orkhs? No, they also would slay him for a spy. He could go into exile in some far-off land, but Bera knew nothing of the wider world beyond the King's Dominion, and even there he would remain as he was: suspected and ever unwanted.

There was no escape.

Still, he couldn't remain here in the tent to be surrounded and trapped. He rushed outside, clutching the sword, but no file of warriors approached him. He stilled himself to listen for it but heard only the small sounds of camp: muffled talk from tents nearby, the hammer-ring of a smithy, hooves, iron wheels grinding over hard dirt. He heard no tramp of many boots, no jingle of weapons and armor; and he decided he might have time to gather his things before he fled.

Then a voice called out behind him. "Would you be looking for me, Heolfbera?" it said.

Bera spun, lifting the sword as he did. The voice was Atul's and the man wore an unpleasant smile. He wore a sword also, but for the moment his hands were empty.

"I saved you the trouble of finding me," he said. "Speaking

of trouble, put away that sword, Heolfbera, and let's step into your tent. Or shall we let everyone hear your song and dance of innocence? Surely it will be amusing."

Bera thought to slay the man where he stood, but murder in cold blood was far less ambiguous than a cryptic note. And it seemed possible now Atul hadn't taken the note to Wulfric—or hadn't yet. So he decided to hear the man out before deciding what to do. He gestured with the sword toward the tent flap.

Atul didn't move. "You first," he said.

Bera shrugged and pushed through, then turned to wait. Atul called for him to step back and Bera moved toward the rear of the tent, stationing himself behind the desk chair.

"I will not slay you," he called to the man, but not too loud. "I wish to talk also."

Atul pushed aside the flap cautiously to examine the interior of the tent from arm's length. Satisfied, he stepped inside and drew himself erect, then took from his belt a small thing that was surely the note.

"When I first found this," he said, waving the thing with a show of feigned disinterest, "I thought it was some little thing between lovers." He laughed, scornful. "Do you believe that, Heolfbera? What foolishness! No woman would touch you. But then—oh, then I read it more carefully." His tone grew cold now, dangerous. "Do you spy, Heolfswin?"

The accusation snapped across the tent and although Bera had expected it, it stung him keenly. But he drew himself up to his full height and set his feet firmly on the grass.

"You are the spy here, Ceorl Atul," he said, "and a thief!

Why were you in my tent and by what right do you take my papers? Give it to me at once!" Bera reached a hand for the note, the sword held still in the other.

Atul sneered. "What right have I?" he spat. "Every right, I say! Is this not the command tent of the Fourth Guards Company? Am I not an officer of that company? I am. But that's not the real question, is it?" He thrust a finger at Bera. "You, my dark friend, are the question. I ask again: do you spy?"

The rage came to Bera then, rising hot and seething in him, but he checked it firmly. It would surely reach for no tool but the sword in his hand, and cold steel would not answer here. The better course was to tell the truth, if only because Bera knew no better story to tell.

"I do not spy," he said. "I found that note on the grass, pushed under my tent." He gestured to the ground behind him. "It was folded as you have it now. I read it, but I don't know what it means. I left it here before going to my supper."

"I see," Atul said. "You just left it on the desk, did you? As you might if it was a daily strength request rather than an invitation to skulk, or perhaps to treason, arrived in secret. Why didn't you report this immediately?"

Bera searched for a good answer but Atul didn't wait. "I'll tell you why you didn't report it," he said. "Because you considered it! You *thought* about it. Maybe you even dreamed of being someone high and mighty—but for the Orkhs!"

"No!" Bera shouted. That wasn't it at all. Or was it? He was confused now, and wondered why he'd done what he did.

"I thought to take this to Wulfric," Atul said, "and see you hanged by your ugly neck. But then I thought what harm could you do, truly? You're not trusted with anything important. You can't hurt anyone but yourself. So you can have your little spy note, but I want something in return."

As he said this Atul's eyes fell to the sword in Bera's hand: the sword his father had given him, leaving it on the step in the night. Bera frowned. *Yes, of course. It was the sword, again.*

"This paper," Atul said, holding it out to Bera between two fingers, "and my silence for the sword. And stay away from my company. Soon we'll go down the road and I'll show my true worth to that bastard Wulfric, who thought to be rid of me. Cenred will give me a line company in time." The man smiled then without humor. "That's more than fair, Heolfbera. I get what I want, and you get to keep that ugly head on your shoulders."

Bera glared back, thinking. He needed the man's silence, but could he trust him? Might Atul take the sword and then decide a promise given to an Orkh wasn't binding? He might; and none would listen to Bera's explanation. Indeed he had no explanation, not a good one, no matter how or when the note got to Wulfric. He would have to take this chance and trust to Atul's silence, even if he couldn't.

So Bera flipped the sword in his hand and offered it to Atul over the desk. The man eyed him, wary, then drew near and reached for the handle, holding out the note with the other hand. When his fingers closed around the sword, Bera released it, reluctantly, and snatched away the note. He drew back again.

"I am no spy," he repeated. "But also I'm no fool, not in this. You have beaten me, for now."

Atul lifted the sword in his hand and smiled at it. "Indeed I have beaten you, Orkh," he said, "and don't you forget it." Then he turned, snatched the baldric and sheath from their place on the pole, and left the tent, saying no more.

Bera stood where he was, holding the note. His first thought was to burn it, and rid himself forever of its menace. But that might inflame suspicion against him still further, should Atul not keep his word.

Damn that man! He has my sword.

Bera sat at the desk and spread the note open again, smoothing its folds with a fingernail. Had his father truly written these words, or were they an enticement to betrayal crafted by someone in camp to test their half-Orkh's loyalties? This seemed possible. Wulfric in particular wouldn't be above such a ploy.

If it wasn't a ploy, who had pushed the paper under the tent? Not an Orkh surely, for no Orkh could sneak into the crowded provisions area. It seemed there was someone here in camp who could be bought to do anything at all. That might be worse than a lone Orkh on the loose.

Bera rubbed his forehead. He was unhappy and confused; and his heart remained heavy with Dudda's betrayal, and the loss of the company and now the sword. He sat long at his desk, thinking, until at last he came to a decision: he would follow the note, if he could. Perhaps he could make some good come of it, somehow. This was a forlorn hope, to be sure, but he saw no other to buoy him.

*

He took up the paper again and studied the words on it:

Sashna,

You wish to be a great warrior. It must be so. You cannot be a warrior until the rage blooms hot within you. Come to the hanging tree and the angry rock, by the swift water east of the great way between mountains. At the dark of the moon's journey. This night. Alone. We will speak of your future with your true people.

He considered the directions given. The time seemed easy enough: the dark of the moon's journey was surely the time between the setting of the sun and the first rising of the moon in the east: now the span of an hour or more. The place was less clear: a tree by swift water, and an angry rock. Was the 'hanging' tree a gallows? That made little sense to him, but so did an angry rock.

Bera pulled from within the corner pile a route map given to him a week ago, when the Fyrd first approached the pass. The map was rendered with only the simplest of lines, since its sole purpose had been to give commanders an essential understanding of the intended route. The area around the pass itself was rendered very sparsely indeed, and it showed no river or stream away to the east. Bera now realized he'd been remiss in not making his own map of the area, or at least augmenting this one. His task was to guard the Provisions train, yet he knew nearly nothing of what lay around its encampment here.

This was yet another failure. He seemed to have many now.

Then it occurred to him he could use this ignorance. Wandering the wildlands beyond camp might be thought strange in him, rousing the suspicion the guards; but not perhaps if he carried this map together with the story he was thinking of the camp's defense. He would do that now—and look for this place by the tree and the rock—while he had fresh courage to do it.

Bera bent to fumble in his travel case and found at the bottom a thin stick of black charcoal wrapped in a small cloth. He placed this in his belt pouch together with the note, then he left the tent with the map clutched in his hand. A wide lane between tents led to the camp's east gate, and as Bera walked this lane he seized a long-bladed spear from a stand of arms. He couldn't use the spear as well as the sword, but it would do for now.

The Provisions encampment lay midway down the south slope of the pass. Behind it, to the east, were heavily forested hills thrown out by the larger range. It would be easy for Bera to move into those hills and become cloaked by them, once he was clear of camp.

So he strode to the east gate with purpose, consulting the map ostentatiously as he did. But in the end the ruse seemed needless: he was allowed to pass with only a sour look. Still, to cover his tracks Bera remarked to the guard he was going south and down, to look for a place to site a sub-camp to provision the left wing. But the bored men seemed not to care what he did, nor where he might go to do it.

Bera did walk south for a time, until he could no longer see the gate guard, then he turned east and crossed a fortified ditch dug by his own company and passed into hilly woodland. Soon he came to a narrow stream that spilled down an overgrown slope in a series of lovely white falls bordered with small purple violets and muscular tangles of green rhododendron. When the water reached Bera's feet it turned to run east, passing into a wide hollow that ran in the same direction. This was the first moving water he'd seen and it was swift, so he followed it east into the cool of the trees.

He passed a long hour in that hollow, crashing through brush by the water and sweating in the chill air; but no feeling grew that he any closer to what he was looking for. He went to the stream and dropped to his belly to fill himself with cold water, wishing he'd thought in the tent to bring food. But his mind had been too tumbled then to consider hunger.

He moved to sit on a rock by the water. Evening drew near, and now that he rested he could hear small woodland sounds: the rustle of an animal foraging in leaf-litter, the hollow knock of a woodpecker, the creak of trees catching a late breeze in the canopy above. He could smell here fertility and decay together, as the wheel of life and death turned slowly in the long quiet here.

In time he stirred himself to consider what he might do now. The gorge of the stream ran straight here, as it had for a furlong or more, walled on its south bank by a steep-sided ridge laden with oak and white pine. The water wasn't deep here, perhaps no higher than Bera's knee even in its deepest wells, and he pondered whether to trade the heavy brush for cold wading. Undecided, he stood to gaze upstream. His eye fell then on an enormous fall of willow switches that drooped low over the water near the edge of sight.

Bera's heart stuttered. *The hanging tree . . .*

It was the only willow he'd seen, or so he thought. He stepped into the stream bed and waded forward eagerly. The bottom was treacherous with slick rocks and deadfall hidden beneath the surface, and cold water filled his boots to make his strides leaden.

But the willow drew him on, and in ten minutes he stood beneath it. It was a vast thing and ancient: a grandfather of trees that leaned sharply over the water, braced against falling by thick, knobby roots worn from the earth by the long gnaw of water. Yet the fall of its switches was green and youthful: thickly grown with many spear-bladed leaves.

Looking across to the opposite bank, Bera saw a tiny rill falling down the slope there. Before reaching the stream, the rill flowed across a wide face of stone made dark by water. Some way down that stone two round indentations forced the water to pause and reflect the light before moving on, and below this was a frowning ledge trailing green ribbons of some water-loving plant. Bera smiled to see these things, for together they formed the image of an angry face made from water and stone. And it seemed to him nearly Orkhish in appearance.

He had found the place. He was certain of it.

He waded across the stream and saw now to the left of that frowning stone a narrow path that ran straight up the slope: perhaps a hidden way from the south. An army couldn't pass here, but it was ideal for a spy or a squad of sappers bent on sabotage. And it had been used recently: small stones were pressed deep into the earth or knocked from their beds, surely by heavy boots.

Bera crossed back to the willow to wait for dark. He set the spear upright against the tree, ready to hand, and drank from the stream again, but the water sat cold and unsatisfying in his belly. He lowered himself to sit against the rough bole, concealed within the fall of switches, and allowed himself to sleep.

He woke at dusk. The air in the hollow was nearly cold now, and night insects sawed in the trees. Bera shifted on the ground, easing himself, and set watch the hillside, uncertain what he might see. But the weariness of the afternoon's march took him again and he fell back into sleep.

When he woke again he knew something had roused him this time. He held his breath and listened. Across the water, deadfall cracked and Bera could hear the leafy shiver of green branches and the scrape of boots on dry earth. He rose from the tree and took up the spear to peer across the water at the hillside. But it was full dark now beneath the trees and moonless yet: he could no longer see the stone face or the path beside it. Now he heard a voice muttering between footfalls.

Someone was coming down the slope.

Whoever it was carried no light, but seemed to be feeling his way down the steep, missing his footing often and cursing with a sharp hiss.

Bera called out: "Who's there? Show yourself!"

The noise stopped and Bera heard a great rush of sound like something large sliding over dry leaves. Then he heard a heavy splash as something—boots?—struck water. He gripped the spear and held it in front of himself.

There was a tiny metallic *tink*, barely heard, and a narrow ray of yellow light fell over the water: a lantern. The light swept over the surface, illuminating white riffles, as it came toward Bera, and behind it came a dark figure. Bera held the spear tightly, ready to strike, but allowed the figure to leave the water.

The yellow light swung up to shine into his eyes and he lifted a hand against it. "Father?" he said.

The figure laughed bitterly. "Fool of a boy! I am not he, no! I am to take you to him." The words were Common but they fell from an Orkhish tongue, harsh and awkward.

The light swung away from Bera and strong fingers closed around his arm. "Come, come!" the voice said. "Follow! The master is not patient. There will be whippings for lateness, yes."

Bera resisted the Orkh's pull, uncertain: he feared what lay ahead. He feared also what lay behind, if it became known he'd crossed this ridge to treat with the other side. But this chance to know his father would surely never come again, and his desire for that burned hot in him. So when the Orkh tugged his arm harder still, ungently, he allowed himself to be led into the water.

A half-moon appeared in the east as they climbed. The going was difficult for the little track was overgrown and nearly vertical in places. Bera used the spear to help himself along. Near the top of the ridge the way leveled, or nearly so, and left the trees to run across a wide stretch of open ground before disappearing into a narrow cleft between two tall cliff faces. Bera stopped here to rest. His legs burned and his breath sawed in his throat.

"How much further?" he said.

"Not far, no," the guide replied. He was small for an Orkh, perhaps hunch-backed, but the long climb seemed not to have winded him. Bera could see the Orkh in the moonlight pointing a long arm toward the cleft. "That way and down. Much down. But faster, the road is good, yes."

Bera nodded and they passed through the narrow defile, led now by the yellow light of the lantern. On the far side, they came out to a starry southern sky and a far wider track that switched back and forth as it drove down the south slope of the ridge. Bera followed the Orkh down the track until a gruff voice challenged them from the darkness. The little Orkh answered it with a single word and a wave of his hand, and soon he and Bera came to a great tent surrounded by a ring of torches.

Two Orkhs with long spears and clad in dark armor flanked the entryway: each was a head or more taller than Bera and more heavily built. Yet they made no move to bar his way, and the little Orkh ignored them altogether, grasping Bera's arm again to draw him into the tent. As they passed the guard, Bera wondered why he wasn't required to leave the spear outside. It seemed whoever lived in this tent feared little, or nothing.

The interior was lavish. Rugs of many colors were piled to make a soft floor, and the furnishings—among them a work table, a tall writing stand, and an Orkh-sized bedstead—were made from polished wood and they glowed gently in the light of oil lamps hung from the tent poles. But the light of those lamps could not reach the far corners of the tent and these were shrouded in shadow.

A deep voice spoke from that shadow. "You have come," it said.

That voice was Orkhish, yet it was quiet and composed, and it brayed less than the guide's: suggesting a greater refinement of manner, even a more spacious intellect. And so it was as Bera had known: his father was no ordinary Orkh. Perhaps he sought an end to this war, with the help of his son.

"I have come," Bera said, studying the shadows. "Show yourself."

There was a flicker of movement to his right and when he turned his eyes to it, he saw a massive Orkh step fully into the lamplight. He was taller than Bera by a head, his shoulders and chest were broader, and he wore a robe of shimmering gold cloth that fell below his knees. He glided over the rugs toward Bera with the grace of a predator.

"The young do not speak so to their elders," the great Orkh rumbled, then he twitched a long finger at the little guide, dismissing him.

Fear moved in Bera now, but he held his ground. "My mother didn't teach me your ways," he said. "Do you truly claim to be my father? How would I know it?"

The Orkh's gaze went to Bera's waist, then to the spear in his fist. "By the warrior's tokens I sent you, but you do not bear them," he said. "Where is the sword? Why do you not wear it proudly?"

Bera's free hand fell to his empty hip. The Orkh was his father indeed, if he knew of the gifts. "I left the sword behind," he said, but the words rang false even in his own ears.

The Orkh narrowed his red eyes. "The young also do not lie to their elders," he said. Then he stepped closer to loom over

Bera as none had before. "Speak the truth, *sashna*. Truth is power. Lies are weakness. Your *orkushna* knows this, or have you forsaken that, also?"

Bera bowed his head beneath the weight of the Orkh's presence. This wasn't what he'd expected. For all his trappings of wealth and refinement, this Orkh was no teacher or scholar. He was no gentleman of his kind. He was a warrior, and a mighty one. Suddenly Bera felt unequal to this meeting. He shouldn't have come.

"I gave the sword to another," he said. "It was the price he demanded for his silence concerning the note you sent me."

"A price demanded?" the Orkh roared. "You should have slain the dog where he stood! Did you not?"

Bera shook his head. "I didn't. It wouldn't have been . . . civilized. There would be punishment."

"Civilized?" the Orkh cried. "Am I not civilized?" He swept a gold-draped arm about himself, encompassing the luxuries of the tent. "But this is not a cage! It does not require me to be what I am not. I am Tsov-ar-kan, within this tent and without!"

The Orkh turned from Bera to stalk across the carpeted floor. "Your blood has been polluted by Human weakness, my son. It makes you cower before me. Worse, it makes you cower before men you allow to be stronger than yourself. This is not *orkushna*. It is slavery. Death would be better!"

Bera thought to say he had no choice, that the note made him appear a spy in a Human camp, and he couldn't murder others to achieve his ends. But he knew this Orkh—his father—would refuse to hear such excuses, for he lived in a world where power was valued above all else, and dominance the finest of virtues. More, it was plain the Orkh relished his world and lived fully within it.

So Bera stood in silence, mourning the loss of still another dream.

Hearing nothing, Tsov-ar-kan turned back to Bera and regarded him, then he gestured to a chair. Bera set the spear against a tent pole and moved to sit. The Orkh lowered himself to a broad divan, where he arranged the golden robe until it fell gracefully about his knees. He seemed to have put away his anger, and his manner now suggested a studied attempt at diplomacy.

"This," he said, gesturing to Bera with a great hand, "is my fault in some part. I lay with a Human female in the heat of my *orkushna,* heedless of what might come of it. And now I see before me an Orkh who does not know himself, or his own *orkushna.* So I will tell you of yourself, my son."

But before he spoke again the Orkh took up a small bell from nearby and rang it. Another Orkh entered, not Bera's guide but one equally small, bearing a silver platter with two drinking horns. He offered one of these to his master and the other he gave to Bera, who lifted the horn to his nose for a wary sniff.

"It is wine," his father said. "Nothing more."

Bera tasted it. It was wine: rich and very strong. He took a mouthful of it even as he knew he shouldn't let his guard slip away.

When the small Orkh was gone, Tsov-ar-kan leaned forward on the divan to bore his red eyes into Bera's. "Now I will tell you of your *orkushna.* It is in your blood, my son. It *is* your blood. It makes you strong." The Orkh brandished a fist.

His sharp knuckles flared like weapons. "It gives you power, *sashna*. Power over yourself, and power over others. Our *orkushna*—mine and yours—is strong, very strong. Am I not a leader of battle? Will I not soon lead this great army? I will."

Bera took another swallow of the wine. "I don't understand. What is this thing? *Orkushna*."

The Orkh shook his head fiercely. "No!" he cried. "It is not a thing for understanding! It is a thing for feeling. It comes from the blood and the belly. It rises." The great Orkh stopped to inhale strongly and he lifted his hands and shoulders together. "You have felt it, I know this. It cannot be otherwise, for you are Orkh. It is our strength. Our way and our birthright."

A rush of understanding flooded into Bera, and he leaned forward in the chair. *Orkushna* was the name for the rage that surged within him: the unwelcome fury that had frightened him as a child. It was the very thing he'd warred against all his life—pushing it down, locking it away—in his desire to be Human. Now this Orkh told him that seething rage was not an essential fault. It wasn't a shame to be concealed. It was instead strength: perhaps the very strength for which Bera had long yearned.

His hands trembled now and he set down the horn of wine. Suddenly his life was upside down.

"Yes!" the great Orkh hissed. "You know your *orkushna*. It has been with you always. But I see you have denied it. You have it, *sashna*, and it is strong."

Bera did have it and this new knowledge burned across his mind. Did that wild anger truly have a use? Could he control it? Even if he could, would it be wise to set it free upon the world, willingly? He could see now the faces in camp: dismayed and frightened, but also smug in knowing they'd been right all along and that Bera the Half-Orkh was only a wanton beast to be put down.

But still Bera felt as if a searching light had been shone brightly on his inward parts, showing him a new knowledge of himself he would be a long time coming to understand.

Tsov-ar-kan shifted forward on the divan. "Yes, you see the truth of it, *sashna*," he said. "That's good. You have hidden much from yourself. This is why you are a guard, not a warrior in battle. Yes, I know these things. I know many things. I knew where you were, and I found a weak one who would take a hand of gold to carry a message to you." He leaned forward toward Bera now. "It is time now to come to your kind, *sashna*. You will not be an honorless guard here, with me."

Bera had known this was coming and he feared to answer. If he refused, the Orkh might move to slay him and Bera had foolishly left the spear out of easy reach. But if he accepted, and went to his father's side, he would be a traitor to his mother's people, and to all he'd ever known.

"You hesitate," his father rumbled. "I understand this. Loyalty is not easily shed, and that is well. But I do not ask all of you now. You will return to your place there, and you will be my eyes and ears among the Humans. This has been my purpose for you from the beginning, *sashna*. And when we have slaughtered the Humans, and opened this door into their lands, you will come to my side and command with me. You are called by your blood at last, my son, and you will answer." The Orkh closed one great hand into a fist and he thrust it toward Bera. "Blood must be with blood. We will be *borkas* together, you and I."

Bera had read of this word, *borkas*, when he was younger at a time when he still had a desire to know his heritage. It was an Orkhish word for the sacred bond between warriors, born of oath-taking and shared battle. Each warrior swore to give his life for the others and to fall in battle only after taking many enemies first. It had stirred Bera then, but in the years since the word had fallen from his mind.

The word stirred him again now, but as he listened to his father speak, he was surprised to find in himself no temptation to go over to the Orkh. Certainly not after hearing him say he had groomed Bera to be a spy. This was surely the purpose for the costly gifts that had come over the years: the sword and the other things. This now tainted that giving.

But Bera also saw that the great Orkh was right: he *was* loyal, if to a people and an army that didn't deserve his loyalty. Perhaps this was the Human in him. The same Human the Orkh wished Bera to turn from, just as Bera had wished to turn from his Orkhishness. But Bera realized now he couldn't turn from either of his natures, Orkh or Human, not truly, because he was inalterably both.

So Bera found himself glad he had come, discovering here something important to him, but now it was time to go.

"No," he said to his father with a firmness of voice that surprised him. "My place is not here, or with you."

The Orkh surged from the divan. The golden robe rippled about him. His red eyes glared at Bera and he pointed a long, black finger. "You misunderstand, *sashna*! You may not refuse me, your father. I will permit you to speak again because you are my son and because you do not know our ways. Consider well your words now!"

Bera had stood when his father did, and now he stepped to the tent pole and took up the spear. His own rage had risen in response to his father's, but this time he didn't push it down. Instead, fearful but curious, he let it run free, seeing where it might go.

"I hear you," he said, "but I won't be your spy or do your bidding." The haft of the spear felt good in his hands and he keened to strike something with its blade, even if it was this Orkh who was his father.

Tsov-ar-kan reached behind himself and drew forth a naked scimitar. The blade of it was a hand-span in breadth, and the steel was blacker than the far shadows of the tent.

"If you will not come to me when I call," the Orkh rumbled, danger in his voice, "then you are my enemy. There is no other way."

The sight of the scimitar fanned the flame of Bera's rage like a high, keening wind. He yearned to work the spear and to leave this Orkh's black blood on the rugs of his own tent. The desire for violence came to him as a yawning emptiness: like a bone-deep hunger that could be sated only with the sight and smell of blood.

But even so Bera refused it. He knew well his rage, even in its new power, and he knew well the levers that would close himself against it. He'd spent a lifetime finding them. So he turned from that blood-rage and ran for the tent door, flinging himself through it and bulling into the left-most guard.

The Orkh stumbled from his post and fell under the weight of his armor some distance from the tent.

Before further thought came, Bera found himself standing over the Orkh, the spear raised to strike a death blow. The rage screamed for it, gibbering, while another part of him was horrified by the strength of his compulsion to kill. But even as he stood with the spear lifted, quivering between choices, his father came from the tent, slashing away the door flaps with the scimitar.

Bera knew he should flee, for he was only one against many here. Still he hungered to fight, as if only the contest of muscle and steel would ease his fractured soul. He drew back from the guard and turned to face his father in the torchlight. His feet moved without thought to the proper stance for the spear, and he stood balanced and waiting.

Tsov-ar-kan raised the scimitar and roared challenge. Then he came on, swinging the blade strongly. Bera knocked it away with the spear, then stepped forward to thrust the long leaf blade. But the Orkh dodged easily.

"Yes, *sashna*!" his father hissed, bringing the scimitar back to guard. "You want honor and respect. You hunger to take them. That is good. You can seize those things from others, here with me."

Yes, Bera did want respect, and he wanted honor and acceptance as well. But he wanted none of those things from his father, nor from any other Orkh. He would find what he wanted where it would mean more to him, and where the satisfaction in the finding would be far greater.

He drew back the spear to strike a blow, but now harsh

voices rose beyond the tent: Orkhs drawn to the sound of fighting.

It was time to go.

Bera flung away the spear and stood a last moment before his father. "Do not seek me out again," he said. "I will not listen. I am not who you think I am."

"Run then," the great Orkh growled. "But if we meet again, on the field of war, we will finish this."

Bera made no reply, but turned his back on his father and ran.

8

OF EARIC AND ZARA

When Earic woke, at dawn, he knew what he would do. He would find Aere, if he could, and do what he might there: even if it was only standing together with her when the fight came.

This seemed right to him, and he felt afire to do it, but he didn't stir from his bed immediately. Instead he lay in the pale light of his tent and listened to others, in their own tents, preparing themselves for the day. These were his fellow officers and Earic didn't want to see them or talk to them, or explain why he was carrying his kit as if to leave camp. Because he was leaving camp, and with no clearer plan than to walk down the road and turn west, toward those fields.

It was possible he wouldn't find her, and his search for her would be the last foolish act of a lost career. But he would try it even so, because it was the last worthy thing left to him. And because Aere had done so much for him in their brief time together.

For not only was she a greater warrior, but she was wiser as well. He'd known this since the time he brought to her his father's latest Testament. The old man made a new one every year, and every year Earic's grant was less, as the memory of his presence faded from his family's halls. A courier had brought it to Earic in mid-summer, and when he read it through he panicked.

"My things are packed," he said to Aere, when they sat a furlong from camp on a high bank of grass by a fall of clear water. "I haven't told Cenred yet. I hope he'll understand. I hope you understand. I must go or I'll have no place in my own home in a year's time. I'll be a stranger at my father's table!"

He'd grown to manhood at that table and in his father's hall; and no matter how far he'd wandered they remained the anchors of home. But now he felt cut away to drift by his father; and the sea of the world was vast, its winds strong and uncaring.

"What is there for you, there?" she asked, when he'd read her the Testament. "At your home."

He studied the falling water, searching for an answer. "It's where I'm from. I grew up there, on our Eadwulfing lands."

"Your father doesn't say our lands, in that." She pointed to the Testament. "He says his lands, and theirs. He doesn't respect you, Earic. Not as you deserve."

This struck him hard. He'd never shone such a stark light on his father's doings, or he'd never allowed himself to. In past years he'd made excuses: telling himself his father had many cares, and the matter of his absent son fell from his notice merely by inattention. That might be so even now, perhaps.

"Are you given respect here?" she asked, touching his arm.

"Yes, you know that. Cenred lifted me far higher than I dreamed possible. Higher than I deserve, maybe."

She smiled at that. "I don't believe it's more than you deserve. But go unpack your things, Earic, and remain here with me. No, let me speak. I would send you to your home, if I kenned it best for you. You're a good man and I wish you well. But it's not best for you."

Earic turned to look at her, surprised. She'd never before spoken to him so bluntly. He wondered now what this thing between them had become.

"Why?" he said. "They're my family."

Aere's mouth drew firm. "Family or no, you'd be a fool to go where you're not respected. Especially where there's a place here where you are. Cenred needs you. The Fyrd needs you. Your father does not need you, or want you. He has made that plain."

Earic knew in his heart this was true, though it wounded him greatly. He folded his arms over his chest: not against Aere, but against the pain of a well-loved past receding beyond recall. He would have to find a balm for that pain other than witless flight toward the very thing that caused it.

"You're right," he said, and she was. He did not go then, and the next time they were together he brought for her an undershirt of silk to wear beneath her jerkin. But even this seemed a paltry recompense for the benefit of her clear sight.

When the tents around him were silent, Earic rose from the bed and donned his baldric with the longsword he'd not practiced in a year. He hoped not to need it. He was never one to wear fine cloth, despite his station, so with the sword at his hip and the badge of his former office hidden away, he could pass well enough as a common soldier moving toward the fighting below. Or he would so long as he avoided any who might recognize him.

As he stepped from the tent, Earic heart thundered at his own boldness: he was deserting his post without leave. But he drew himself up against his fears and strode with purpose across the camp toward the pass road. As he walked he was surprised to find beneath his anxiety a real pleasure in moving, as if he were leaving an old and battered life for something new. This feeling buoyed him for a time as he descended the pass, walking on soft grass by the well-rutted road. But soon he met a train of wagons bringing up the dead and the wounded from below, moving over the road at the pace of tired oxen.

Earic didn't often see the human cost of war. In his remit he studied maps and pushed counters, and spoke of terrain and troop strengths, supply and forage. The horror he saw here sickened him. The wagons were heavily laden, and they stank of night soil and flesh-rot. And with them came an army of black flies to bedevil the living and the dead alike. The teamsters on their boards had swaddled their faces with cloth, so only their eyes could be see. Behind them, on the wagon beds, the wounded shrieked in protest and called for mothers and loved ones. The train was long and terrible to behold, and twice Earic veered away to vomit up what little he carried in his belly.

Still, he forced himself to study each wagon as it passed, fearing each time to see Aere's long dark hair and archer's right arm. The dread of it grew heavy on him. But none of those awful, shuddering wagons carried Aere and soon the train had passed beyond him.

Now he was low on the pass and his view south opened. He could see the peaked brown roofs of the town, Suthgaet, and the blunt spire of its central temple. Beyond these he saw, for the first time, the battlefield below.

The whole of it seemed too vast to comprehend. From east to west, and stretching far south toward the horizon, was a level plain that wore late summer greens. And all across that plain, below the town, played the countless motions of warring armies. Order was here but disorder there, starting here and stopping there, moving forward and doubling back, purpose and confusion alike. And it transpired beneath a hundred flags and war banners and pennons of every shape and color, all caught now on a morning breeze. And rising above it all, into a blue sky, were dark slanting columns of smoke so it seemed the armies met in a great leaning Cathedral of War.

Yet as Earic's gaze quartered that field, identifying and sorting its motions and parts, he began to see what he knew was there. Immediately below the town was the Human shield wall blocking the Orkhs' direct approach to the pass. That wall was made from companies of armored, shield-bearing warriors set close together to form a long, unbroken line of gray steel stretching far to the east and farther still to the west. It was five ranks deep, but Earic knew it should have been seven, or more. And so it seemed rumors of heavy fighting in the center were true, and Cenred had been forced to thin his line to cover the front. It was no wonder he had stripped his rear for anyone who could carry sword and shield.

Across from that shield wall, and separated from it by a broad lane of churned earth, was the Orkhs' own heavy infantry, drawn up in dense ranks. They stood on lower ground but their wall was thicker, and even now more Orkhs moved up to support it, crowding over the roads and the fields beside.

No, the battle here did not go well. Earic could see this already. The fight for the center was always a test of endurance and numbers: each side striving to outlast the other. It went on and on, sometimes for days, until one side lost the will, or the means, to continue and the rout began. But until that happened, the battle in the middle was a bloody mill of charge and counter-charge, thrust and parry. Thousands might be cut down in that lane of churned earth before the end came, or dragged from it, wounded, to die in the rear. The most feared fate was to fall amid the melee by some chance mishap, unharmed but unable to rise, and suffer a death by trampling under the ebb and flow of the struggle above.

Often, an army's will to continue in the center turned on its fortunes at the wings. On this field, no such battle-shaping event would emerge from the left, where Cenred had put the Dweorg, east of town. A large formation of Orkhs lay across from the Dweorg, but it sat idle in the fields without offering battle, fixing the Dweorg in place. It was a wily tactic of the Orkhish commander, who'd certainly judged the Human center a softer push than the left. Earic wasn't surprised by this cunning: no one who fought the Orkhs found them to be fools. As for the Dweorg themselves, he had no doubt they chaffed under the task of merely holding ground while others fought.

The right was another matter entirely. There, the town's farmlands spread west and southwest in a patchwork of fields, farm lanes, and tree-girdled ponds. From his vantage,

Earic could see dark lines of infantry and clusters of cavalry that were the dispositions of The King's Own and the other reserves Cenred had sent there. They looked too small in that vastness, too unavailing. But it was likely the Orkhs didn't possess sufficient numbers to cover that ground either. So when the fight came there, and it surely would, it would be a running, chaotic, ultimately ungovernable affair that would likely decide who controlled the pass at the end of the day.

And Aere would be in the middle of that chaos, fighting.

Frowning, Earic turned his gaze southwest to find the walled farmstead. It was partly concealed by flanking hills; and even as his eyes found it, a tiny, dark speck appeared over the near wall. It flew up and up, carving a high, arcing course through the sky before falling to raise a cloud of tawny dust some yards short of a low gray wall. A company of warriors sheltered behind it.

Earic was suddenly heartsick. *What have I done? Gods, what have I done?*

But he knew very well what he'd done. He'd given the Orkhs a stronghold, and they'd pulled up siege machines to garrison it. Trebuchets, it seemed. He watched more dark specks rise, and more puffs of dust spring up, some closer now to the defenders as the Orkhs worked to find the range.

To the south of the farmstead, dark columns of infantry moved into concealment between the twin hills: Orkhs assembling for the first sally across the fields, toward Aere. Seeing this, Earic cried out in dismay and struck his head with his fists: wishing with all his heart he could undo what he'd done, and that he wasn't now an outcast, alone and effectless. But he was, and he knew he must do what little he could to right this wrong. He took an unsteady breath then, and another, settling himself, and he resumed his descent toward the town.

When the road entered Suthgaet it widened into an intricately rutted and dung-spotted street that drove straight south between two rows of weary buildings. Here the noise of battle was loud, echoing between the walls. He heard the endless clatter of metal, the calls of many war-horns, and the steady drone of a thousand voices. He passed south between the buildings, finding on their far side a ridge of high ground, the one Cenred had spoken of; and between the last buildings and that high ground lay a wide, grassy swale.

On it was a vast panoply of war: hundreds of supply crates stacked head-high, piles of arms and armor stripped from the dead, long open-sided tents for the Healers, who did little more than remove injured limbs and plug wounds with lint. And there were a great number of people here, attending to the vast business of war: officers, messengers, food-bearers and water-carriers, the lightly wounded waiting to return to the line, and a grim parade of stretcher-bearers leaving their charges on the grass in neat rows.

Earic looked west along the swale, toward the right wing. He meant to go that way, but threading through that vast, intricate snarl would be slow and painstaking. Worse, there was a strong chance he would be pressed to service by an officer for some urgent task, or even recognized.

His gaze fell now on an enormous cat-sí. It was tall and gray-furred, and it bore a saddle on its long back. Standing beside it was an Aelf-woman who was bent low to work at the beast's girth cinch. She had long silver hair tied back fiercely, and she wore a cuirass of forest-green leather. A curved cavalry saber lay across her back.

It was uncommon to see Aelfs outside their own realms. They were skillful warriors and bold, especially when paired with their warrior mounts; but only the greatest of needs stirred them to leave their lands and to make common cause with others. Cenred had counted himself fortunate to receive just a single company of Aelfin cat-cavalry—or he had until word came back to him its commander, The Lady Zara, was overly aggressive and took disturbing losses. But this was no matter to Earic: he knew Cenred had assigned the Aelfs to the right, and that's where he was going.

He moved to stand a respectful distance from the Aelf, then he placed his right hand on his chest with the fingers spread.

"*Ali-ja noesh, i'at!*" he said, speaking loud enough to be heard over the noise about them.

The Aelf straightened and turned to face him. She was lovely but in a cold, remote way such as the Moon was. Her features were finely cut, almost delicate; but the set of her face was forbidding, speaking of willfulness or arrogance.

"What do you wish of me, Human?" she replied to him in the Common, her mouth twisting the sounds of it strangely.

"Your pardon, noble captain," Earic said, bowing, for the marks of her rank were visible now on her cuirass. She was an officer, perhaps even Lady Zara herself, or her Second. "I'm bound for The King's Own, yonder," he said, pointing west. "Can you tell me an easier way, lady?"

The Aelf's eyes weighed him. "You are bold for a

commonling," she said. "Tell me first how you came to know the words of greeting."

"My home is in Eathwald," Earic said. "Near Lord Mon-thal's Great Wood. I learned from his people a little of your speech." He bowed again and said, *"Ngha fensah á the phansh."* This was a compliment of parentage two strangers might exchange upon first meeting.

The Aelf's wariness receded but didn't wholly disappear. "I think you are more than you appear, Human," she said, "or perhaps more than you choose to reveal. But I have neither the time nor the mind for idle mysteries now. I am in haste."

"As am I, lady."

The Aelf turned back to the girth cinch. "Since you have charmed me with some of my own speech," she said, "and because you do not smell as bad as you might, you may ride west with me for some little while. I am Lady Zara Thu'sem. I command the *kansa* of my people here."

"I'm honored to know you, Lady Zara," he said. "I am Earic." He eyed the tall cat-sí then. "Will he . . . or she bear me?"

"Te'a will do as I wish. But you should greet her."

Earic considered this a moment then shifted so he could meet the cat-sí's great yellow eyes. Then he bowed low to it, then lower still, not knowing the beast's temperament. Perhaps it was disagreeable and would rip his head from his shoulders if he moved or spoke wrongly.

"I'm deeply honored to know you as well, Lady Te'a," Earic said to the cat-sí, thinking this could not possibly go awry. "And I beg from you the favor of bearing me for a time."

The cat-sí blinked slowly, then stepped forward to bump her wide head against Earic's chest, knocking him back a step. He found himself charmed.

"She honors you in return," Zara said. Then she leaped nimbly up the saddle and reached down a gloved hand for Earic. "Quickly now, Human. My duty calls."

Earic took her hand and swung himself up to sit on the broad yoke of the cat-sí's saddle bags. Dense gray fur rose about him, radiating a pleasant dry heat. Zara clucked and used her heels to urge Te'a west, through the vast tumble of war gathered on the back side of the ridge.

As they rode, Earic studied what he could see of this Aelf. She carried, in addition to the saber on her back, a curious knife at her waist. It had no great length and curved slightly, as if to echo the saber. The handle was pale, polished white, perhaps bone, and it bore an inset of gold lettering wrought too fine for Earic to read. It was a beautiful object and Earic thought to ask Zara about it later, if he felt bold enough. For now he was content to be moving west, toward Aere, with the swiftness of four legs.

And swift they were. The cat-sí wound through the chaos of the swale with speed and grace that astonished Earic; and soon they'd left all of it behind to move across a broad, grassy hillside toward the farmlands.

By now Earic had decided to trust this Aelf, despite her reputation: she had chosen to help him when she might have dismissed him out of hand, and he could use an ally, if he could get one. So he took the insignia of rank from his belt and held it forward for Zara to see.

"Your judgment was keen, lady," he said. "In truth, I am an officer of the Fyrd, formerly of Cenred's council."

The Aelf looked down at the badge then back up to their way. "Formerly?" she said. "It seems mine is not the only hard story on the field today."

"Perhaps so," Earic said, thinking that whatever ills had befallen her were surely of her own making. But he was eager to bring the Aelf to his cause. "Shall we share our stories as we ride?" he said.

Zara considered the question for so long Earic thought she hadn't heard, but at last she said: "Very well, Human. I will go first, since you have shown manners to which I am not accustomed from your kind. As I have said, I am called Zara Thu'sem of the clan . . . you would say cat-rider or beast-rider in your speech. I am kin, though distant, to Lord Mon-thal, whose Wood you say is near to your own home. My father is our king. But I am only his daughter and the sixth, so I am sent to war."

"I hear no hard story there," Earic said. "All here not common have war as their trade. My father is Earl of Eadwulfing and I, also, am late-born. The youngest of all."

"Then I shall call you Lord Earic," she said. "As for my hard story . . ." She gestured roughly. "It is no secret I wear disgrace. Indeed, all here seem to know of it. I seek a return to honor, Lord Earic, but my designs go awry."

She told him then, in a brittle tone, of an ill-advised charge at Orkhs below the ridge, and of a failed assault on the walled farmstead. Earic recalled Cenred mentioning this to him.

"I know that place," he said, looking across the fields at it as he spoke. "My own troubles are bound up with it. But in battle the hazards of fate are many, lady. Your time may come yet."

Zara shook her head. "Not so, Lord Earic. When we met I was just come from your prince, Lord Cenred. That Human was bold enough to instruct me not to return to my *kansa*. He believes he has taken it from me, to give to my Second. But he has no right and I would not yield to him if he did. So this is my haste, Lord Earic: I must reach my *kansa* and retire from the field before knowledge of this comes to my Second. We will return to my father's realm where I will think on other ways for myself."

Earic was disappointed by this. He'd hoped for the Aelf's help, but now it seemed she was bent on leaving the field. It seemed also he had come, unknowing, far too near Cenred's new headquarters behind the line. Had he been recognized there, he would have lost far more than just his high office. Earic looked over his shoulder, determined to be more vigilant.

"That is my hard story," Zara said. "What do others seek to take from you unjustly, friend Lord Earic?"

"Nothing I didn't deserve to lose," he said.

"Indeed? Then yours must be a hard story indeed. Tell me of it."

He did tell her, unburdening himself as he had to the tormented half-Orkh; and when it was done he found himself feeling a kinship he didn't expect with this star-crossed Aelf. Perhaps she wouldn't judge him so harshly as he judged himself.

"That accursed place!" she snarled. "That foul den of Orkhs! You and I were fated to fall with it, I fear." She made a noise. "When I return to my father, with this war unfinished, he may send me to the cat-sí pens and forget he sired me."

Earic laughed bitterly. "I might say the same, lady. My father is a hard man. But I wish only for Aere's safety now."

Zara nodded. "Yes, that at least we may do. With haste. Where is your lady?"

Earic pointed to where a line of bright standards flapped above a gray stone wall. "We can begin there, by that wall," he said. "I will know the banner of the King's Own."

As Zara guided Te'a toward the stone wall, it seemed to Earic the world had finally bent his way in a small part. His thoughts now turned to his empty belly.

"Your pardon, lady," he said, "but do you have anything to eat in these bags. I've eaten little since yesterday." *And I lost even that*, he thought, remembering the wagons of dead.

"No," she said without turning, "but surely there is food for us in your lady's camp. I am hungry as a Dragon, also, though there may be nothing there to suit my taste."

Earic started at this. For a thought now blazed across his mind. It was hard, clear, and bright, and left him breathless and unbelieving.

A Dragon.

He twisted in the saddle to look south, toward the twin hills that cradled the stone building and its outwall. The sheep there were a distant daub of dirty white on green.

Is that it? Is that what they're for?

He grasped Zara's shoulder and shouted in her ear: "Stop! Stop!"

The Aelf flinched in surprise and rounded on him, but

Earic rode over her protest. "We must go back to Cenred!" he said, shouting still. He jabbed a finger back toward the ridge. "Turn around!"

Zara halted Te'a, then half-turned on the saddle. Anger was plain on her sharp face. "Do not shout, Human. Return to Cenred? Whatever for?"

Earic lifted a finger to focus his thoughts. "There's a . . . I think . . . there's maybe . . ." He stopped: the thought seemed too big, too exigent, to utter aloud. "Great Gods!" he cried. "Surely it can't be!"

Zara laid a hand on the white knife. "What can't be? Have you lost your wits, Human? Perhaps I called you friend too soon."

Earic closed his eyes and breathed, summoning calm. Then he pointed south, toward the hills. "See those pens? Those sheep?"

"Of course. I saw them the morning of yesterday, when— yes, why?"

"Yes, exactly. Why? Why are they there? Why were they not taken away by the people who lived in that place? Or if they belong to the Orkhs, why are they there? Why are they not far in their rear, in their provisions camp? And why—"

"What does this matter?" Zara said. "Orkhs eat sheep, surely."

"No!" Earic said. "Or at least they don't if they can get something else." He thought of the half-Orkh in the mess tent, shoving away the mutton joint. "But even if they are eating the sheep, where's the butcher? It would be right there, next to the pens." Earic jabbed a finger at the hills. "There's not one."

The Aelf growled. "I have no time for this madness, Human. Be plain."

"And why are the Orkhs not pressing hard here? This is the easier way to the pass, but they're just lobbing stones now."

"That is not plainness and I know not the answer! Perhaps they perceive no need for now. I'm told the center goes poorly."

"They're waiting," Earic said.

"Waiting? This is no great insight! Yes, surely more Orkhs will come in time. We see them south of the hills now." She pointed there.

"No, lady, they're not waiting for more troops. They're waiting for a Dragon or waiting to use a Dragon. Maybe. One that must be sated to be controlled."

"You *are* mad."

Earic held up the finger again, this time to stop her. "Consider for a moment, lady! Yes, it may not be true, but it may be. Enough that Cenred must be warned against it. If a Dragon does come and we're not wary . . ." He stopped, waiting for her to catch him.

But Zara's frown was deep with misgiving. She turned her eyes toward the hills and the sheep pens. Te'a pranced beneath them and Earic felt a tickle of fear that seemed not his own. He wondered if it came from the cat-sí. He'd heard of a bond between mount and rider.

"Do the Orkhs truly dislike the meat of sheep?" Zara asked at last.

"So I've heard," Earic replied. Then he told her of the half-Orkh.

Zara considered this. "I did see chains," she said. "Great

chains within those walls. But I was hard-pressed then, and there was no time to wonder at their purpose. And I saw Orkhs between the hills, driving sheep south from their pens."

"You did? South?"

"Yes. And I heard a noise also. A great sound I did not know. I supposed then it was another of the Orkh's cunning machines." She pointed to the stone building. "You can see them working now."

"A sound," Earic said.

"Yes. Like a horn, but louder, different. And a smell. It was terrible, unlike any other I know. It puzzled me." The Aelf stopped then and swung her gaze toward the town. "The pass would be lost."

"It would," Earic said, "and much beyond it. But perhaps not if we're prepared. Would the chains you saw hold a Dragon?"

Zara shrugged. "Perhaps. The beasts are said to be unwarlike. One might be overcome by shackles, with enough strength of Orkhs. But perhaps not. I know little of what I speak."

"Shackled and enslaved," Earic said, turning his gaze to the southern horizon as if he might see even now a great beast come to sweep the field clear. "And fed sheep to keep it sated and governable. But why hasn't the thing been brought up already? Why do they wait?"

Zara said nothing. Her gaze moved around the fields.

"I must tell Cenred," Earic said. "I may be wrong, but if I am, I am. What more could I lose?" His head, perhaps, but that might be a fair price: if a Dragon did come, unwarned, Aere surely would be consumed by it. Panic quickened his blood.

Zara turned Te'a to face the ridge. "I am not wholly convinced, Lord Earic," she said, "and this may be a fool's errand, as you Humans say, and my own need presses me. But I will take you to that man to say what you must, though I swore never again to cross words with him. In truth I think you are misled by a chance meeting of circumstances, but I concede the hazard remains, however small. The danger of such a beast—should it come—would be dire beyond measure."

"Thank you, lady."

Zara urged Te'a toward the ridge. "I have known you but an hour, Lord Earic," she said, "and already you lead me astray, to trouble I need no more of. My own purpose may be delayed beyond recall."

Earic placed a hand on her shoulder. "We're already far astray, you and I," he said. "What's a mile more?"

Zara laughed at this but it was bitter. "What indeed, Human. Fly, Te'a!"

They sprang up the hillside again, back toward the tumult of war they'd left behind. As they did Earic considered what he knew of Dragonkind. They were said to be numerous once, in a time long past, possessing wit beyond that of common beasts and so having dealings with other races of the Earth. But the Orkhs warred upon them long ago, for reasons unknown to Earic; and in time the race of Dragons fled to mountain heights at the edge of the world. Or so it was said.

It was also said they were taller than the tallest tree and wore hide hard like tempered steel, turning aside sword and spear alike. Their jaws held teeth a clothyard long; their breath might melt a warrior from his armor; and their gaze could beguile even the wisest.

These tales had perhaps grown in long telling, but if half such a creature came now, from the south, it would send a great terror over the fields before it. Even those who ran from it might be hunted down and slain before the beast's fury dimmed.

Unless we're ready, Earic thought, and he steeled himself against this coming interview with Cenred.

Zara directed Te'a along the back side of the ridge, behind the shield wall. "I know where Cenred's tent lies as well as anyone," she said sourly. "I had hoped never to see it again, or the man himself."

"I do not ask you to," Earic said. "In truth, I think it best I go alone. One anger will make my task difficult enough. The weight of two would close his ears against anything I might say."

Zara nodded. "This is wisdom. I will wait out of sight. Perhaps I will find food for us while you suffer." She smiled but with slight humor.

Earic felt a warm rush of encouragement now from that alien presence which had intruded on his thoughts before. "Does she speak to you?" he asked Zara then. "Te'a."

The Aelf's smile fell away and she seemed discomfited, as if Earic had trod unknowing on a secret. "Does Te'a speak to me?" she said. "No, but there is a . . . connection. She makes her feelings known to me from time to time."

"This is a great gift," he said, caressing the cat-sí's tall fur around him. "She must be a wise counselor."

Zara's face now suggested offense. "Seek Te'a's advice? You are mistaken, Lord Earic. Cat-sí are to be ridden, not consulted—as a Human rides a horse. The troopers I command have their superstitions, but what is this to me?"

Earic now felt disapproval from that presence, then sadness or grief coming behind. He looked to Zara but saw no hint the Aelf had felt it too.

"Your pardon," he murmured. "I would have thought it a great advantage. Perhaps I am mistaken."

Zara said nothing to this, but only nudged the cat-sí to greater speed.

Thirty yards short of the command tent Earic slid from Te'a's back. He knew he was taking a terrible risk, but he owed Cenred: he'd failed to warn the man of a danger of which he was unaware. It had been a great mistake, done in greater foolishness, and Earic would not repeat it now.

He stroked the great cat's fur as he spoke up to Zara. "I will meet you here in half an hour."

"No longer," she said. "I fear I have already given you more time than I possess. Go and return quickly. I will be here."

Earic nodded and turned to move toward the Aetheling's tent. It was mid-morning now: fortuitously, a time between the man's scheduled war councils. Perhaps he would be alone, and of a mind to hear news.

As Earic approached the tent he brought out the staff insignia and showed it to the spear-woman standing sentry. She glanced at it then studied his face doubtfully; but when Earic said he had important news, she let him pass.

He pushed aside the heavy canvas flap and stepped into

the pale light of the tent. As he'd hoped Cenred was alone, glowering down at a map table with his arms folded over his chest. He looked up when Earic entered and scowled.

"What are you doing here?" he said, his voice a whip. "Why are you not at your post? If you've come to plead mercy, Earic, I'll not change my mind."

Earic spread his hands in placation, and so the man wouldn't think he'd come with a knife in hand for vengeance. "I've not come to plead my own cause, sir," he said.

"Explain yourself then. Why are you here? You have five seconds before I call the guard."

Five seconds was all Earic needed. "A Dragon is coming, sir! We must prepare for it!"

There was a moment of silence now in which the sounds of distant combat could be heard. Cenred's mouth had become a hard line. "You've lost your wits," he said. "Guard!"

Earic took a step toward the map table. "Hear me out, sir! Have you wondered about the sheep?"

The spear-woman entered the tent but Cenred said nothing to her, not yet. His eyes remained on Earic. "What about those sheep?" he said.

"You've seen them?"

"I know of them, yes. Why?"

"Think about it, sir! Why are the Orkhs so passive on our right?" He pointed west. "They're just throwing rocks right now. Why don't they attack there, instead of pushing here in the center? I know you've asked yourself that question, sir."

"What of it?"

"Those sheep are the key, sir."

"The key?" Cenred said. "To what? They're just food."

"Well, yes, they are food. But not for the Orkhs. Orkhs don't eat mutton. They're food for something else. Something that eats a lot." Earic extended his hands to Cenred, as if to physically pass understanding to the man. "And there are great chains in that farmstead. Zara—the Aelf commander— she saw them. And she heard a sound also, a loud sound, near the stone building."

Cenred stared back at Earic. His eyes were hard and cold. "You were once a good officer, Earic," he said. "One of my best. But now you're only mad. Guard, get this man out of my tent! He's under arrest for absenting himself from his post without my leave."

The woman's fingers closed around Earic's arm. Her pull was strong and insistent, but he resisted it.

"Sir!" he cried. "I lied about that place! It wasn't a blunder. I wasn't careless." Maybe if he admitted everything the man would bend. "There's a woman! And a child. My child! She's an archer in the King's Own. I wanted to protect her. It was wrong, sir. I was wrong. But I'm not wrong about this!"

Cenred moved around the table to stand with his face inches from Earic's. "Have you taken leave of your wits?" he shouted. "You admit you lied to me before, and now you want me to believe a cock-and-bull story about a Dragon? A Dragon!"

The man put a finger in Earic's face. "Do you take me for a fool? I am not! Aside from how preposterous it is, there hasn't been a Dragon seen north of the Orkh Ranges since my great-grandfather's great-grandfather carried a sword! I don't have time for this . . . whatever it is! Guard, take this man out and bind him to the horse rail. I'll deal with him later. If my center hasn't collapsed around me and an Orkh hasn't stirred my vitals with a spear!"

The woman's fingers pulled more strongly at Earic's arm, but he twisted it violently, breaking her grip. He couldn't be arrested. Not now, not with Aere and their child in the path of terrible danger. He must go to them.

He bulled past the guard toward the entryway.

Cenred bellowed after him: "Stop that man!" And Earic heard the quick metallic ring of a sword snatched from its sheath.

Gods! how has it come to this?

He punched the tent flap aside and burst back into bright morning sunlight. Then he turned left, toward the place where Zara had left him, and he ran toward it. But nowhere near a half-hour had passed yet and the Aelf surely searched for food still. He would have to go west on his own this time. He heard shouts of pursuit behind him, but only dimly above the rasp of his breath and the pounding of his heart in his ears.

The swale was thick with wagons, provisions, and stacked arms, and Earic weaved a wild way between them. And as he made a quick turn around the tall wheel of a parked wagon, his left boot slipped on a pot of mud below a water barrel. The boot skated wide on the mud, carrying the leg with it, and his ankle turned outward. Then he fell, his weight bearing down strongly on the leg, and it stretched until a sharp pain in his thigh made him cry out.

Striking the ground, he rolled to his back and clutched at the leg. It burned with fierce heat.

No, this can't happen! They need me!

He twisted around to his belly and dragged himself over the

ground with his elbows until he could grasp the long spokes of the wagon wheel. He pulled himself up on the spokes to stand again. Waves of agony made his head light, but he shoved off from the wheel to limp on, every footfall a stroke of lightning.

Earic berated himself as he went. He shouldn't have returned to Cenred, even with this news. It was another mistake, even if well meant, and now he was both crippled and a fugitive from his own army.

9

OF BERA

Bera ran from his father into darkness.

Almost immediately he lost the switchback path up the ridge, so he ran straight up the slope. It was steep and brushy, and his legs were heavy. Undergrowth grabbed his tunic and whipped thin, burning fingers against his face. Trees emerged from the darkness to deflect him from his way. It seemed as if the life of the wood now rose to slow him, doing his father's bidding.

But shame drove him, and anger. Shame that he'd walked open-eyed into his father's trap, and anger that the Orkh had thought his son so craven and rudderless he would betray his mother's people, and spy upon them, simply for the asking.

He wasn't an Orkh trapped in a Human world, as his father believed. He didn't think of himself that way, despite his troubles. So Bera's easy refusal must have surprised the Orkh, and he'd responded to it not with suasion or gentle persistence, but with a rage that drove him to threaten his own son with death. That alone was enough to drive far from Bera any doubt his choice had been the right one.

But that did not settle all. There was this other thing: the thing he'd known nothing of. This *orkushna*. It was not so easily rejected.

Bera stopped to bend and put his hands on his knees. His throat was cruelly dry and his legs shook, but his thoughts were on that core of anger clenched within him. It was an old enemy and he could hear it now, urging him to go back, to take up the spear again and cross it with that black scimitar.

Was this—this rage, this dark desire—truly the *orkushna* his father had spoken of? Surely it was.

He straightened and listened for pursuit over the sound of his own breathing. But he heard only the night sounds of the forest. He went on then, walking now on leaden legs; and when he reached the top of the ridge he moved quickly through the narrow cleft between cliff faces. But when he came out its far side he couldn't find the little track down to the stream, even in the light of a half moon; so he thrashed down the slope, pushing a way through brush by the waning strength of his body.

As he went, he began to see the truth of his life and it struck him the hardest blow he'd ever known. That truth was he'd misspent his time, seeking to be something he was not. He'd sought to act as a Human, to speak as a Human, and even to feel as a Human. All in service to a Great Lie he believed to be Truth: that one day, if he only tried hard enough, and wished for it passionately enough, he would be accepted by the Human world.

He'd cherished that hope for so very long. But it was a false hope: a mirage born of desire and loneliness. He would be forever the same tall, dark, angry presence his father was: a red-eyed, long-toothed beast to be feared.

Rage spouted in him like the warning flares of a volcano. It wasn't fair! He'd put his life force into that Great Lie, and he'd convinced himself utterly of its truth. All that long dreaming, all that fervent hope: only a waste.

A great, gods-damned waste!

Bera pounded down the slope, snarling and battering branches from his way, until he came to one too thick to move. He stopped to grasp it with both hands and slip the chains from his rage. It fell to the task with glee: giving strength to Bera's limbs and iron to his will. The branch came free with a heavy crack, and he broke it over his knee and flung the pieces at the ground. He stared down at them there, wanting to take them up again and shatter them to flinders, then grind those flinders into the ground with the heel of his boot, punishing the Earth itself.

I've been a fool! Such a gods-damned fool!

He lashed out with a bare fist to strike the trunk of the tree itself: again and again. Then with the other fist. But the bark was hard and sharp under his knuckles, and the pain of it brought him up short.

He let his hands fall to his sides and stood in moonlit darkness, breathing heavily. He could feel the power of his rage still in the fire of his mind and the greedy flex of his fingers. A wild beast did live within him, truly, and long had he run from it, believing it a fault of his dark blood.

Was it instead his essential strength? Was it, more deeply, who he *was*? This frightened him, as if he saw not himself in a mirror but someone he didn't know. But he refused to be cowed, or controlled: he drew back the rage, confining it, yet he left a small flame of it burning. He allowed this to give him strength without consuming him.

He moved down the slope again, finding as he did his feet struck the earth with greater purpose and the eye of his mind looked ahead to the future with keener glance. This pleased him. But he felt also, remote like the cry of a distant horn, an emptiness in his right hand that longed to be filled, and a disturbing desire—nay, the need—to exert his mastery over others. This pleased him less.

In camp he would find Atul and reclaim the sword, by force if need be. He had allowed himself to be worsted by that man and disarmed, and the shame of it must be erased. Then he would reassert command over the company—his company—and lead them into battle against the Orkhs. This would be the more difficult task, but Bera was carried now by a conviction that he knew, for the first time, who he truly was.

Still, he dared not approach the gate guard in darkness. So he sat against the bole of a great tree, a hundred yards from the east gate, and stretched his weary legs on the ground to wait for first light. He slept for a time, and when he woke the sky was pale with dawn. Bera rose and moved toward the gate.

But found himself walking with his shoulders hunched and his head held low, an ancient habit. *The time for that is past!* he thought and he raised his head and shook out his shoulders until his strides were loose and confident.

Soon he was challenged and he called back the countersign without slowing. Even so two warriors stepped out from behind a broad tree to bar his way with long spears. This was the dawn picket thrown out by the gate guard and Bera recognized them immediately: two of the most hardheaded of his own company. He wondered why they were here instead of preparing for the move down the pass road. It was more failure he would soon correct.

He stood over them, repeating the countersign but making no attempt to ingratiate himself as he might have before.

"That's yesterday's word, in'it?" the left one said. The other nodded agreement. Neither shifted the blade of his spear from Bera's chest.

The anger grew from that little flame. Both these men knew him well and they should have allowed him to pass without question. But they had been emboldened to insolence by Atul's perfidy against Bera. He reached out suddenly with long arms to snatch the spears from their grasp. Each cried out in surprise but Bera only dropped the weapons and took a step toward them, to loom taller still. They blanched from him, but he didn't care now how he appeared.

"I do not have today's word," he said. "But your problems are larger than that. If I'd been the enemy and disarmed you so easily, you would be dead now."

Neither answered this. Bera bent to pick up the spears and he returned them, knocking each man back a step as he did.

"I will pass now," he said to them. "And you will drill with the spear. How to hold it properly, how to use it, how not to be disarmed by an unarmed Orkh. And you will have pride in being warriors, even if I have to beat it into you with a mace. Am I clear?"

The guards stared back, slow calculation moving behind

their eyes. Bera stepped closer still, commanding their attention with his physical presence.

"Am I clear, warriors?" he repeated.

"Aye . . . sir. Yes, sir. Clear."

"Yes, sir."

"Good. We'll be in this fight soon but we have a great deal of work to do before then. I will tell the Gate Master you're to return to your company immediately. Do so."

Saying this, Bera pushed his way between the men to stride toward the gate. When no spear blade thrust into his back, he smiled. He had found the way.

Dawn had brought the Fyrd from its tents. Bera walked among them, stretched to his full height. He knew exactly where he was going—Atul's tent—and he made as straight a way toward it as he could find. That odious man was surely abed still, sleeping off his night of cards and drink. It made a poor example for the company, but Bera knew he'd been no shining totem of virtue either: slinking about camp trying to be Human and a leader but failing at both.

He stopped ten paces short of Atul's tent. The flap was tied shut and so it seemed he was right: the man did linger long in his bed. But as Bera stood searching for the right words to say, old habits rose to threaten his resolve: visions of flight to the comfort of his own bed, unquestioning deference to a fate on him imposed by others. That would be easier now, causing no fuss in camp, no harsh judgment. These were the habits of a lifetime and they were not easily shed.

But then a hot flame of rage kindled in him, and steadied him. He placed his feet firmly on the ground and drew himself up, ready to fan that flame into a blaze of rage. He wondered whether he could control it once loosed. He might bring the entire camp down on himself.

Still he pressed on against his fears. "Ceorl Atul!" he called. "Come out! And bring the sword in your keeping. It is not yours!"

There was no response from within.

"Come out!" he shouted again. "I will have the sword!"

Others stopped to watch, drawn by the challenge. Bera ignored them and called a third time, and now the tent flap jerked as its stays were untied from within. Then Atul himself came out to stand before Bera, clad in a long linen shirt belted at the waist. Bera's baldric and the sword were slung over his shoulder, but he made no move to offer them.

Instead he glanced mildly at the morning and stretched himself in a show of unconcern. "Why do you disturb me, Heolfbera?" he said.

Bera put out hand. "Give me the sword."

Atul gestured to the watching warriors. "Shall I tell these here how I came to have it? What would your ugly head be worth then?"

"That sword came from my father!" Bera said in a loud voice so all could hear. "An Orkh! And I went to him."

Atul crowed at this. "So you admit your treachery, do you?" He drew the sword then. The grip was overlarge for his hand. "All of you here now witness me slay this Orkhish traitor!"

Bera didn't move. "I'm no traitor," he said, speaking still at all. "My father is Tsov-ar-kan, a mighty Orkh and Commander in that army. Yes, he would've made me a traitor, and a spy, but I refused him. My mother is Darah, a Human, and her people are mine. Give me my sword, Ceorl Atul. It is not yours to keep."

As Bera said this, the rage of his heritage rose hot and clean in him. His limbs flushed with strength and the desire to do violence raved at the edges of his mind. But he knew control: it came to him easily after a lifetime's denial. So he banked the fire of his rage until it fed him only what he needed. He would not kill this man, but he would reclaim what was his.

He took a step forward.

Atul was not a courageous man at heart, and Bera saw the horse-shy in his eyes even now, but the habit of bullying ran strong in him.

"You look like a big pile of trouble," he said to Bera, "but I know you ain't. You're soft. Always making yourself small and agreeable, like you want to be Human. But you ain't Human and you never will be. You don't belong here, Orkh!"

Bera expected mutters of agreement from the crowd, but there was only silence. Encouraged by this, he took three long strides toward Atul, swift and sudden, and intending to snatch the sword from the man's hand as he'd taken the spears from the guards.

But Atul stepped back, leaving Bera short. Then he drew the sword and lunged with it. Bera turned to avoid the blade even as he reached out to catch the man's wrist. The bones of it seemed thin and fragile, easily crushed, but Bera squeezed only until the man's hand opened and the sword fell from it. Bera caught the pommel before it struck the ground and he drew the sword away.

"You are right in one thing," he said, holding Atul's wrist

still. "I'm no Human, not wholly. But you were wrong in another. I do belong here, in this Fyrd. You are relieved of your duties with my company, Ceorl. Do not let me see you again."

Atul stared at Bera, seeming now a ridiculous figure with his bare legs under the long shirt. Then his gaze shifted to the watching crowd and something passed behind his eyes, something Bera couldn't read. Then the man's free hand went to his belt, swift and sharp, and a bright flash of steel swung at Bera's side.

But he was swifter: he brought up the sword to knock the dagger from Atul's grasp with the flat of it. The blade spun away, flickering in the morning light, and Atul cried out in pain.

Bera used his grip on the man's wrist to pull him closer, then he stripped away the baldric and its sheath, ungently. He could smell the man's alcohol-stink now: sour and stale. Repelled by it, Bera drew back the fist that held the sword and punched the man in the chest. The blow was tempered but Atul collapsed beneath its weight, stumbling backward until he fell though the tent flap and out of sight, too stunned to cry out.

The crowd was silent through this and now Bera turned to it: the sword in one hand and the baldric in the other. It had felt good to strike a blow, and his *orkushna* called stridently for more. But he slipped the leash over its head again.

"Is there another," he called, "who wishes to question my right?"

No one spoke.

Dudda was precisely where Bera expected to find him: sleeping on a pile of rotten straw in a vile hooch-tent on the outskirts of camp. The place stank of unwashed clothes and old sweat, and dissipation pursued as a calling. The man lay wrapped in a darkly stained horsehair blanket, snoring.

Bera prodded him with a toe. "Wake up! The day, and war, calls!"

The man rolled from the toe, toward the wall of the tent. He worked his mouth and grumbled, "Lee'me alone."

Bera stripped away the blanket and bent to grab Dudda's shirt. It was stiff with mud and what might be old food. He dragged the Second into bright morning sunlight and dropped him.

Dudda shrank away, covering his eyes. "What the hell? Leave me be, damn you!"

Bera's rage would have solved this problem of Dudda by slaying him where he lay. But that wouldn't answer: he needed the man. Bera took another grip on his shirt and dragged him to a half-barrel of horse water that stood nearby. Lifting the little man with the strength of his arms, he dropped him in, head-first.

The splash was tremendous and Dudda came up instantly, sputtering water. He glared at Bera. "You go too far!" he cried, his voice strained and phlegmy. "Ceorl Atul will hear of this! And that Thegn! Atul will have the company for good and all now. Yes, he will!"

"You'll not be seeing Ceorl Atul again, I think," Bera said. "He's been reassigned."

Dudda scowled. Water dripped from his brows. "You lie."

Bera pushed him under again. The rage stirred, rumbling darkly and demanding he hold the odious man down until his struggles ceased. But he took away his hand instead and stepped back.

Dudda came up in an explosion of water: he raised his dripping face to the morning sky, mouth wide, and wheezed a long, warbling breath. He looked frightened now.

Good. Maybe he'll listen.

"Sober yet?" Bera said. "Or do you need more?"

Dudda coughed violently, then sobbed in another long breath and said: "What do you want?"

Bera let the rage bleed power into his words. "I want a company that can fight," he said. "I want a Second who executes my orders instead of wandering off to fall into the jug. And I may want you to die in battle, Dudda. Valorously, if possible."

The man pressed a nostril with a finger and blew water from the other. "I done my time in the ranks," he said sourly. "I'm a Provisions man now. Dyin' ain't on my list. Leave me be."

Bera hadn't known this. "You were in the ranks?"

"Aye. And I had a belly full of it, too, don't you know. Don't want this battle of yours. You can stuff it."

"Surely you can—"

"No, I can't!" Dudda snapped. He fixed Bera with a rheumy eye before receding to sit on his haunches in the water and mutter. "Why do you think I drink, you great fool?" he said. "The line ruined me, that's why. I'm not the man I was. Not a bit. Look at me! Ten years. Ten years on the line and now a ruined man."

Bera studied his face. It was deeply lined and filthy still despite the ducking. "You could—"

Dudda jerked and threw back his head. "Ten years!" he shouted. "Thirty years in the army all told and not a pot to piss in!" He peered up at Bera. "Why do you think I'm here rotting in Provisions with ten years service on the line, Ceorl Bera? Hmm? Why do you think that is?"

Bera said nothing, waiting.

The man pointed a finger. "I'll tell you why. I'm no good to fight. Not no more. I seen too much. Too much for a man to bear up." He rubbed his forehead with a palm. "It's the screaming what don't leave me. I hear'em calling out, sometimes to me. Friends, some. All gone to their graves, or laying in a hole in the ground with a thousand others, all chopped up. Meat at the end. We're just hot meat, that's all, waitin' to cool."

"I'm sorry, my friend," Bera said, and he was.

Dudda flipped a hand. "Save your pity. You don't know nothing, do you? Thank your gods you don't know. The gods-damned army is all I know. I ain't a farmer, and I won't break my back in a field anyways, not like some thrice-damned plow horse." The man snuffled water, avoiding Bera's eye now. "No, I ain't a warrior no more. I'm just stuck here, that's all. Stuck here with a gods-damned half-Orkh what don't know nothing. The gods have mercy on my weary soul."

Bera's anger cooled at this, and he considered the man afresh. In truth Dudda was not so different: trapped in his own skin and by own demons. And like Bera he'd chosen the wrong way out, finding himself trapped in a dead end.

It was a revelation and Bera found his heart going out to the little man. He stepped back and stretched down a hand to Dudda, silently. The Second grumbled but accepted it, and Bera helped him from the barrel. Then he held the man until he stood on his own, sluicing water.

"The company needs you," Bera said, knowing now how he might lead Dudda to another way. "I need you. I know you don't want more war, but war is on us. Go to your tent—your duty tent, not this pit—and clean up. I want you and the company on the center ground, ready to work, in half an hour. We have a great deal to do and I need your help. I can't do it without you."

Dudda didn't meet Bera's eye but he muttered something that might have been agreement before gathering himself to move off. When he was gone, Bera closed his eyes and drew in a long breath. It was a struggle to master the rage, and he'd been shocked by its demand he kill Dudda outright. He couldn't do that. He wouldn't do that. Yet he'd felt the need in his fingers like a deep itch that could be eased only by violence.

So he now had a new fear for himself: that he might do harm to those around him. This new way between Human and Orkh was a knife's edge, and he must find his balance on it quickly, before someone who shouldn't fell beneath his hand.

You will feed in time, Bera told his rage. *But on the blood of Orkhs.*

He walked toward his tent, giving thought to how he might address the company. His mind moved first, as he knew it would, to old habits: to speaking in the manner of a man, to smiling and jesting, and using the rough speech of camp to win their affections with false comradeship. But he knew this was not the way. He could not pull from these warriors something they would not give to him freely.

So he would instead require them to remember who they were: warriors sworn to king and country. They might not fight for him, but they would fight for their homes and their families, and for each other. They might also fight for a sip of the glory that comes with victory.

Glory and victory. Bera's blood quickened at the words.

In his tent he knelt before the bed to drag out the wooden crate. It was long and heavy, and came forward only reluctantly. Bera pried away the lid with a knife and set it aside. He'd never thought to do this, but now it seemed needful.

Within that crate, protected by a layer of thick black cloth, was a leather cuirass. He swept aside the cloth and took the cuirass in his hands to lift it free. It was Orkh-make and black as a moonless night except for its scarlet bindings. The chest was broad, tapering to a narrow waist, and the tall arch of each shoulder was made so it curved upward like a flaring wing.

But its greatest wonder was the design across its front. It was made from red gemstone inlaid in fine lines to evoke, by cunning art, the torso of a great Dragon. And the leather was wrought with the same skill to suggest the scales of the Dragon, so the wearer might seem to his foes a great armored beast, fearful and dire.

His father had chosen the gift well.

Bera stood and put the cuirass about himself, and he tightened its scarlet fittings so the thing gripped him snugly. Then he bent to lift two black greaves from the crate. These were hard black leather also, and they mirrored the cuirass's make and style except the lines of red gemstone made the feet and claws of the Dragon. Bera pulled the greaves over his calves and tightened their buckles, then drew from the crate two black gauntlets and donned them. These fit him well, and their design completed the Dragon: long claws that would flash red in the sun. The cuffs of the gauntlets were long, to ward his forearms, and their knuckles were reinforced with heavy black steel.

He left in the crate the great black helm and the tall shield emblazoned with a hundred intricate scrollings of red Dragon's-fire. He wouldn't don that helm, nor put his left arm into that shield, until he stood in the face of the enemy. Then and only then would he allow the fire of his rage to rise and possess him fully.

As Bera armored himself in these gifts, given long ago, a part of him shied still from his new purpose. He wondered if surrendering to his *orkushna* for all to see, even on the field of battle, would break the last weak bonds holding him to Human society. Would he be cast out, finally and forever, as a rampaging beast? Would he wander the Earth, spurned by both his kindred? He didn't know, and this frightened him even as he stood in the tent arrayed in that black armor.

But he did know one thing and he knew it with utter certainty: he couldn't go on as he had. That way was a false road, a glamor, enticing him but leading nowhere. He'd found the true road in his father's tent, or so he believed, and he would walk it as he may.

The company grew quiet as Bera approached them wearing the black armor and the sword; and already this was more respect than he'd received before. But he was angered to find they stood on the field in huddles of their own choosing, for Dudda hadn't deigned to dress them into ranks.

The man stood apart from the company and he studied Bera, taking in the armor. His expression was bland and un-readable: perhaps he was in his cups again. Woe betide him, if he was.

"Here they are," Dudda muttered as Bera drew up. "As you wanted."

Bera stopped to look up at the company's standard, held aloft on its long pole by the banner-woman. It was a dull brown thing with the uninspiring heraldry of a square crenel-ated bastion with an arched gate.

"As I ordered," Bera said mildly.

"Aye," Dudda grunted. "As you ordered."

Only then did Bera affect to notice the company, turning himself toward it. "What is this mob?" he said. "This is a com-pany of war, not a town fair! Do your duty, Second Dudda, and form up the company properly!"

"But you didn't—"

"Do it now," said Bera.

Dudda took a step back from his captain and wobbled, but only slightly. Then he turned to face the company, his gaze lingering on Bera from the corner of his eye.

Then he drew breath and called "Company in ranks!" but his voice was high and thin, weakened by years of drink.

There was some attempt among the company to form ranks, but it was more of a general circulation and soon even this faded with little improvement that Bera could see. There was simply no will to do better. He knew this was his fault at bottom: he'd been self-absorbed and hadn't given them enough of himself.

Bera looked around and saw a heavy wooden crate that had once held iron ingots for the smiths. He dragged this by its rope handle until it sat centered on the company's front. He stepped up to stand high on the lid. From here, he could see many faces he'd once coaxed and cajoled to do their duty.

He would no more.

"Warriors of the Fourth Guards Company!" he began, in a voice that carried far across the assembly ground. The rage simmered in him still, giving his words a keen edge. "I will tell you plainly the battle below does not go well. The enemy presses hard, very hard, and we have been called forward to help."

He paused, catching a few eyes as he could and hoping. "So we have a choice, you and I! How do we wish to be remembered?" He gestured to them with a gauntleted hand. "Will you be this sad rabble, staggering to swift and effectless deaths?" He clenched the same hand into a hard fist. "Or will you be warriors who answered the call to glory and rushed forward to turn defeat into victory?"

He threw the last word at them and stopped to examine his handiwork. A few eager faces looked back, perhaps driven more by curiosity at the novelty of his appearance than by any true inspiration. He pressed on.

"I know I look like your enemy—*our* enemy," he said. "More so now than ever before!" He slapped a gauntlet against the Dragon cuirass. This made a warlike sound that pleased him. "But I am not your enemy!"

Before, he might have added that he was Human too, like

them. But this was not true and he'd resolved to deal henceforth only in truths. "I am not your enemy, but I am not your friend either. I am your Ceorl. Your captain. And I will lead you to glory and victory!"

This sounded good to Bera's ears and he'd hoped for more reaction. A precious handful looked ready to follow him, and a few more stirred restlessly as if they could be swayed in time. But most simply stared back at him, or looked away to other things as if he'd spoken in a foreign tongue.

So he decided to shift the ground beneath them. It was an idea on which Bera had meditated since returning from his father; and while its possibilities thrilled him, he was deeply uncertain of its reception. It might be what finally turned the company against him, but he wouldn't know until he'd tried. What he did know was that the scale of his fate was balanced very finely here, and to swing it his way he must throw all he had upon its pans.

"Second Dudda!" he called, gazing down at the man. "This company has a new name."

Dudda stared back, then shook his head. "A new name? You can't—"

"Bera's *Borkas*."

The man let a beat of considering silence pass, then he said, "Bore . . . kass?"

"Boor-kass."

Dudda shook his head again. "That ain't even—"

"No, it's not," Bera said. "It's an Orkhish word." He shifted over on the crate and pointed down to the space he'd made. "Stand up here, Dudda. Just here, beside me."

The man hesitated then shrugged and climbed onto the crate to stand next to Bera. But his face remained uncertain, as if he wished not to be so closely associated with his Ceorl.

Bera addressed the company again. "We are now Bera's *Borkas*!" he said. "Yes, it's an Orkhish word. It means war family, or battle band. It's a sacred word for a sacred bond! It's the bond between warriors who go to war together, who swear to die defending each other." As he spoke he hoped this was yet another of his father's gifts, this one unknowing.

Dudda make a noise. "I ain't no Orkh," he said, "and I don't aim to be."

"No, you're not," Bera replied. "But I am."

The words took his breath away. He was not Human, and he would never be. Not fully, nor even in the largest part. These here had known this all along, but he hadn't. He'd denied it. He'd fought it, tooth and claw. But now he understood who he was, and he would embrace it for good or ill.

"We must go to this war below," he called to them, "whether we wish it or not. So we will go as *borkas*! Proud and strong fighters for each other!" He drew the sword his father had given him—his sword—and he lifted it.

"I swear I will fight for you!" he said. "If my death will preserve you I will gather death to myself with open arms!" He stretched the free hand toward them: its fingers open and grasping. "I swear it to you!"

He looked down at Dudda then and in the same moment the little man's eyes came up to meet his. There was a keenness there Bera hadn't seen before. This surprised him at first; but then he understood, with the brilliant clarity of sudden-revealed truth, that this man might follow a strong leader. Indeed, he might follow *only* a strong leader, and that was exactly what Bera had never been.

"Swear with me!" he roared to the company. "Swear the *borkas* with me! We must be together to fight! We must be one, for war comes to us!"

And so he stood upon that crate, waiting and hoping: the sword held high. And at last they began to respond.

The first was Dudda. The man lifted his filthy head as if remembering past strength and he drew his own sword. The steel of it was stained and pitted with old rust, but he held it aloft with more pride than Bera had seen him bring to anything.

"I swear—" Dudda began but stumbled and cleared his throat. Then he spoke with more force so his words carried to the company. "I swear it!" he said. "I swear the—the *borkas*! My life for yours!"

Bera nearly laughed aloud with delight: the little man had found some small part of his lost fire. Bera wondered what else was lost that could be found again.

They stood a mismatched pair on the crate: tall and short, dark and light, Orkh and Human. And their words hung still in the air, waiting. Bera swept his gaze across the company, silently willing them to remember the duty they'd shirked and the honor they'd forgotten.

And soon they did.

Here and there across the field a blade rose into the air. They wavered in the beginning, uncertain, but grew firmer as more rose to join them. Then swords rose more quickly, coming up by twos and threes. Then quicker still, until finally a forest of steel stood over the field, flashing in the sun.

The sight thrilled Bera. "Swear it!" he shouted to them.

Now eight score voices called to him, swearing, in a sudden rush of sound that grew in eagerness. Bera knew this was only the first lick of flame coaxed from kindling, yet it was a beginning where before a beginning had seemed impossible.

He would breath upon that little lick of flame and give it life.

10

OF EARIC AND ZARA

Earic hobbled west, toward Aere, as fast as his injured leg could carry him. It swung stiff at his side and the boot slapped the earth, making him grunt with every stride. What he needed now was a horse, but nearly every mount that could bear a rider was with the cavalry on the right wing: exactly where Earic was going. He pushed harder, hopping on the good leg and dragging the other behind. But this was far too slow and he tired quickly.

Boots came up behind him now and a voice cried out, "Halt!" It was deep and commanding: not Zara.

No!

Earic hopped faster. Pain scourged him and his vision grayed. Then he stumbled on nothing and cried aloud as he fell hard across a rutted wagon track. He lay there stunned and unmoving, waiting to be taken up by Cenred's guard and raging against his own uselessness.

This should not have been his fate.

He and Aere had spoken of fate, in one of the many twilit hours they'd found for each other. Had it brought them together? she wondered. He had no answer to this, or none he would speak, for he knew in his heart it couldn't be so.

"I like it not," she said. "This fate. I will take you by my own choice, not another's."

He laughed. "You will take me, will you?"

"Aye. Did you think to be driving this cart, my lord?"

He bridled. "I came to find you at your archery, did I not?"

"And I very nearly sent you about your business! Far too many men have thought to 'find me at my archery' then sought to take the bow from me. But not you."

"I like your strength."

"That makes you different. Especially in an army, where the only measure men seem to ken is their own strength."

"Strength is important, yes," he said. "But more so is perseverance in duty. Strength has no purpose without it. Or so I see it."

She smiled at him. "You do, and I know this of you. You're a good man, Earic Eadwulfing, and you will make a worthy husband. Fate is cruel to me, if truly it did bring us together."

Earic's heart sank then. It was he who'd first brought them together, not fate, and it saddened him to know this caused her pain.

Aere seemed to see his distress and she touched his arm. "No, Earic," she said, "I am glad you found me at my archery, truly." Her smile now was frank and uncomplicated. "I'd rather have this than not, for however long we have it. And I will go freely when the time comes, don't worry. But I will hope fate sends me another like you."

They had lain together on the grass that day, and on many bright days that long mid-summer before the cares of war and duty grew to consume him. Their future had seemed then no more distant, nor more burdensome, than the next afternoon.

But when this child came and Aere's gaze upon Earic grew heavier, the future stretched out from the next day to encompass years. And so war came also to Earic's heart: war between who he was and how he felt, between his duty to Cenred and his duty to her. It seemed fate was cruel indeed, and like Atul it threw high cards on the table at every round.

A strong hand closed around his shoulder and shook him. Then it turned him on the ground until he could see above him a face, dim against the sky. It was a Dweorg face, broad and flat. And hanging below it was a silver pendant in the shape of a tall-antlered stag frozen in mid-leap. That face spoke to him now but Earic didn't understand its words. He stared back, confused and uncomprehending, until another voice came.

"My lord asks if you require a healer," it said.

Earic did need a healer but there was no time for that: he pushed himself up, gingerly, to sit on his knees and saw now there were four Dweorg standing over him. The nearest, wearing the stag pendant, looked older and his garb was richer. The others stood a pace behind him clad in plain plate and carrying spears: surely the older Dweorg's guard.

"I must go west," Earic said. "To the right wing. Can you help me?"

The older Dweorg turned a questioning eye on the smallest of his guard and these spoke in Dweorgish before the guard said to Earic: "My lord says he has business of his own, Human. But he asks again whether you require a healer."

Earic lunged to grab the older Dweorg's arm. His leg screamed. "Help me!" he cried. "There's a Dragon coming and Cenred doesn't believe me. I need your help to go west! Please!"

The Dweorg snatched his arm from Earic's grasp and moved away; then he turned toward his translator to utter a long, rumbling sentence while pointing a finger at Earic.

But the younger Dweorg seemed not to hear his master. He was looking elsewhere in thought. "I know not this word," he said to Earic. "*Drah-goun*. What is its meaning?"

Earic described a Dragon to the Dweorg, pantomiming as he did the flapping of great wings. The little Dweorg's eyebrows lifted at this and he muttered a word that sounded like *cresh-nag*. Then he spoke at length to the older Dweorg, who considered Earic as he listened. Then he spoke.

"My lord wishes know why you believe this," the guard said. "It is most unlikely."

Slowly, one sentence at a time, Earic told the older Dweorg of the sheep, and the chain Zara had seen at the farmstead, and the great sound she'd heard there. And as he did, he was surprised to find the older Dweorg listening attentively, although his blunt face remained impassive. When Earic was done, the Dweorg asked him whether the Aelf had noticed a smell.

Earic sat up, surprised: Zara *had* spoken of a smell, but he'd forgotten. His heart thundered in his chest, making his leg ache.

"Yes!" he said. "It was like no other she knew. Terrible, rotten."

This was translated for the older Dweorg and he turned his gaze west, although the line of the ridge blocked any very long view in that direction. Then he made a long, rumbling speech filled with growls and hollow clicks.

In a quieter voice the younger Dweorg said to Earic, "My lord does not speak to you directly, but he says he is unpleased with the purpose we Dweorg have been given. And a *cresh-nag*—a drah-goon—would be a worthy foe for we Dweorg, if what you say is true, although it surely isn't. I would add my lord came here to protest our lot to Cenred. But that Human's ears are stone and we were sent away without satisfaction."

Earic nearly laughed. The man's ears were indeed stone. "I, too, was sent away by Cenred," he said. "He did not believe me. Still I must go west swiftly, to do what I can if the Dragon comes."

This was translated for the older Dweorg but he seemed not to hear it. His thoughts were elsewhere and something new was in his eye: cunning perhaps, but also amusement. But this disappeared when he turned toward a cat-sí drawing near them. It was Te'a, and Zara rode her.

"Lord Earic!" Zara called, ignoring the Dweorg. "Why are you there on the ground? Rise! We must leave!"

"Thank the gods!" Earic cried. "It went poorly with Cenred. He refused to listen and he set his guard on me."

"So I guessed," Zara replied. "I saw hunters who are surely on your track. We must go now."

Gingerly and with great effort, Earic pushed himself up to stand, choosing as he did to ignore the Aelf's surprised questioning. Then he leaned forward to stagger toward the cat-sí. The translator moved to help and Earic thanked him, adding: "Prepare yourselves."

"We have heard you, Human," the Dweorg replied as he pushed Earic up to sit behind Zara.

Earic settled himself on the bags and then let his head fall to his chest to close his eyes, for he was weary and sick with pain. He heard Zara say in a cold voice: "You are far from your station, Dweorg." To which the voice of the translator responded: "My lord will hear no scolding from the disgraced, lady."

She made no reply to this, but clucked at Te'a and the cat-sí sprang away beneath them, leaving the Dweorg behind.

Soon they were crossing the same grassy, wagon-rutted hillside from which they'd turned back a long hour before. Earic turned to look for pursuit but saw none. Indeed he doubted anything running on foot or hoof could keep pace with the swift cat-sí beneath them.

"Thank you," he said to Zara, after explaining his injury. "I was nearing the end of my rope."

"We may both come to know the end of a rope yet," she said. She raised a hand then, pointing toward a small company of Human warriors waiting a quarter-mile distant. "I will leave you with them, Lord Earic, to continue your errand. For my part, I must return swiftly to my *kansa* and depart the field. If indeed Cenred's ill-news has not reached my Second already."

Earic stiffened: he needed this Aelf, desperately, and the cat-sí as well. He gripped the shoulder of Zara's cuirass. "Don't leave me there! Please! I can barely walk and I won't find Aere without you!"

"Root and crown!" Zara cried. "You ask too much of me,

Lord Earic. Were you not noble born I would throw you from Te'a's back here and now!"

Earic ignored this. He pointed past the warriors to a long wall of gray field stone, still more distant. Many companies of foot were set behind it.

"Take me there," he said, "and ride along that wall. It's only a little from your way and I can look for Aere as we go."

Zara growled. "Very well. But in haste. Very great haste."

She guided Te'a closer to the wall and they passed west along its length, riding behind the ranks of waiting warriors. Many faces turned to mark their passage, but Earic ignored them. He was peering past Zara's shoulder to study the war banners ahead.

"The King's Own is a golden lion on white," he said to her, and even as he did he saw that banner lift into sight on a quickening breeze. His heart thrilled.

"There!" he cried, pointing. "See it?"

Zara made no reply but urged Te'a onward. Some distance short of the banner they came to a cluster of archers resting on a wide sward of grass. Earic studied them as he passed, looking for Aere's dark hair and slim form. But only strange faces stared back to him, wondering at the sight of an Aelf and a Human riding together on a cat-sí. Earic shouted Aere's name but there was no answering cry or wave.

Then a tall, broadly built warrior stepped out from the wall to place himself in their path. He raised his hands high and wide, and Zara halted Te'a before him, muttering darkly in her own tongue.

"Easy there," the man said, eying Te'a warily. He was

heavily bearded and his brow was sun-darkened and scarred by pox, and on his cuirass he wore the twin chevrons of a Second of infantry. "Who might you be?" he asked them. "And why are you troubling my people so?"

Zara gestured back to Earic, who slid to the ground, balancing his weight on the good leg. "I'm looking for Aere," he said. "She's an archer, here in the King's Own."

The Second considered this silently, then squinted up at Zara. It was plain he suspected mischief. "And what would the two of you be wantin' with little Aere? She's not but a common bow."

Earic decided it was no time to hold back. He dug into his belt pouch and pulled out the staff insignia. He limped closer to the man and held it out.

"I am Lord Earic Eadwulfing," he said, pushing brisk efficiency past his pain. "Cenred's Master of Scouts. I need Aere for an errand of great urgency. She's an able scout and trustworthy. I've used her before." That was a lie, but a story about a coming Dragon would surely go nowhere with this hard-faced Second.

The man eyed the insignia with doubt but stood a fraction straighter. Suspicion didn't leave his face. "She ain't no scout, sir," he said.

"She is now. Bring her to me."

The man made no reply to this, but moved his gaze between Earic and Zara, plainly searching for some clue to this mystery now before him. Zara made an impatient noise then and Earic raised an arm to point toward the ridge, now far distant.

"Things aren't going well up there," he said. "I expect

you've heard that. So Cenred sent me to find something—anything—to help them. You can't help. You have your own problems." He gestured to the farmstead. "So I need every scout I can get, right now, surveying that army." He pointed south now, toward the Orkhs.

This appeal did noting to soften the Second's gaze, but the man had spent a great deal of his life obeying orders; and it was certainly this, and this alone, which moved him now.

"Well, I guess little Aere ain't but one bow," he said, frowning deeply. "But I know damned well there's foolery at work here. And Ceorl Hengar will hear of it directly—or as directly as may be, as he's off somewhere getting his skin full." The frown grew deeper still and he spit through his teeth.

Relief flooded Earic, but he willed his voice to remain cool and detached. "That's your business, Second," he said. "For now, you will attend to mine and fetch me Aere. Quickly now, and with a horse."

The man laughed now. "A horse, too, is it? Next you'll be wantin' my balls!"

"You may keep those," Earic replied. "And yes, a horse. What good is a scout without a horse?"

The poxed Second offered no reply to this, but instead beckoned to another who stood nearby. They spoke briefly and the other hurried away. Then Earic and Zara suffered under a last glare of disapproval, surely meant to wither them for good, before the Second turned his own back on them to stalk away.

Zara leaned down from the saddle and spoke to Earic with urgency. "I must leave," she said. "I cannot wait longer."

Earic said nothing to this but remained where he stood, watching for Aere's approach. It seemed a long age since he'd seen her last. But here she was now: riding toward him on a tall, black-maned bay. The lines of her were so familiar to him: that archer's frame broad and square, her hair lying dark on her shoulders, the great bow long across her back. She rode well, sitting tall in the saddle, and Earic's heart lifted to see her.

"There she is!" he cried, pointing.

He hobbled to meet her, swinging the bad leg wide but caring nothing for its pain. When Aere drew nearer, he saw she seemed well. Her skin was ruddy with sun and her eyes were bright, and they rested on Earic now. But her face wore a frown.

"Are you certain of this, Lord Earic?" Zara called to him. She was following on Te'a. "The lady seems ill-pleased."

Earic hardly marked her words, for he had no thought except to greet Aere. He stumbled toward her, gasping, until at last agony overcame even his ardor and he stopped to sway awkwardly on the grass, waiting.

"It's good to see you, Aere!" he cried as she came up to him. He stepped toward the bay and took the bridle in his hand.

But still she frowned. "Why are you here, Earic?" she said. "This is not your place and I've been taken from my own. And you're hurt! What happened to you?"

"There's much to tell," he said, "but not now. Come, ride with us to Lady Zara's company"—Earic gestured to the Aelf—"and I'll tell you there. But we must go quickly. She's in haste for her own reasons."

Aere glanced to Zara and cocked an eyebrow, curious. But still she spoke to Earic. "Why must I go with you? My place is here, with my bow clan. Shouldn't you be at your own duty, Earic? Why aren't you?"

He shook his head: he couldn't answer that. Not now, not without telling her everything he'd done. Not without also baring to her the shame of it. He might later, perhaps, if he found the courage to do it.

"Aere," he said. "We have to leave here now." He paused to take himself in hand and speak calmly. "There may be a Dragon coming. Yes, a Dragon. Yes, I know it sounds mad. But I want you and the baby in a safer place, in case I'm right."

Aere's frown deepened at this, and her eyes shifted from confused to wary. "That's witless, Earic! And even were it true, my rightful place would be here with my clan."

Earic glanced around them, looking for eyes that watched from afar. Aere's resistance had become unseeming, even suspicious: no common warrior would speak to an officer so. But no one watched them, or none did so openly. Still he drew himself up to harden his face against her, mourning as he did the loss of his joy at their meeting.

"Warrior!" he said to her. "Follow me. Now."

Then he turned to hobble back toward Zara and the cat-sí, striving to move as if he expected Aere to follow him without question. But he heard no hollow thump of the bay's hooves coming behind.

Reaching Te'a, Earic steadied himself against the cat-sí and looked up at Zara. "Tell me," he said, "does she bend her bow to put an arrow in my back?"

The Aelf looked amused by this. "No," she said, "but I

do believe she is considering it. Come now, Lord Earic, and mount. It is my belief she will follow you."

Zara reached down to help Earic up. The task of mounting Te'a had gotten no easier, and there was no helpful Dweorg to push now; but Earic managed all the same, climbing Te'a's flank like a giant louse.

But as he hauled himself up to sit straight on the bags, a voice cried "Hold!" and his heart sank.

No! We're so close now!

Zara turned Te'a toward the voice and Earic saw approaching them a short, soft-featured man wearing on his chest the insignia of a Ceorl. This was surely Hengar, Aere's commander, prodded to action by his pox-faced Second. The Second himself now walked close behind his commander's shoulder, perhaps pushing him forward with a knuckle. They stopped fifteen feet short of Te'a.

"I am in great haste, Ceorl," Earic said, finding his official voice. "I cannot be delayed."

"Who are you?" Hengar asked. "And why are you taking one of my archers? And Great Gods!" he added before Earic could reply. "What *is* that smell?" He turned his head to the Second. "Is that your foul odor, Oswald? You really must bathe!"

A terrible reek came to Earic then, riding on a weak breeze. It was ripe and rotten, like the fur-smell of a dog new-rolled in a carcass.

Could it be?

His heart pounding, Earic straightened to peer south but he saw nothing not there before. Even so he felt a fresh rush of certainty and this bolstered him as he turned back to the drunken Ceorl.

"I am Earic, Cenred's Master of Scouts," he said. "This warrior is now seconded to me as a scout."

The man laughed. "Seconded? By whose order? Not mine!"

It occurred to Earic then the man should be warned, whether he believed that warning or not. He and his warriors didn't deserve to be forsaken utterly in this place.

"By my order, Ceorl," Earic replied. "And you must prepare your company for the coming of a Dragon—from there." He pointed to the twin hills. "Warn the others on the wall."

Hengar stared back at Earic, surprised, then he uttered a wet laugh. "Ha, ha! A Dragon? Great Gods, man, what do you take me for—a fool? Or is this some game of yours? I tell you, sir, it's not the least amusing. I was taken from my table!"

Earic opened his mouth to say more to the man, but he checked himself when Zara lifted an arm to point east, back toward the ridge. Two riders came from there, crossing a far field on black horses. They were no more than a mile distant.

"They come for you, Lord Earic," Zara said to him, "or carrying Cenred's messages for my Second. Either way we must leave, now."

Earic nodded. He turned to Aere and cried to her: "Follow us!" And in the same moment Te'a sprang away beneath him, carrying her riders west toward the green wood.

Aere came behind, galloping the bay, bent low over its long neck as if pursued by swift arrows. But the Ceorl sent only shouts after them and soon even these fell away, and all they heard were the quick hoofbeats of the bay, for Te'a ran soundless over the grass.

*

They ran west, toward the wooded foothills hiding Zara's company from sight. Earic thought much of Aere as they went, and of himself, and how he might rebuild his world again now that it was turned upside down and shaken out.

Until Aere came into his life, he'd been a solitary creature, devoted to his duty. There were few friends and fewer women; his roving life in the Fyrd had pulled each away in time. He saw now there'd been no check on him: no one he knew long enough to trust to rein in his excesses. So he'd become as a child: impulsive and unthinking, giving no thought to aftermaths. He could see this now in a clearer light, for the evidence lay before him as plain as any map he'd studied to move armies. He flushed with the shame of it.

He'd lied to Cenred, his friend and mentor. Yes, it had been right and worthy to wish to protect Aere and the child, but not with a heedless lie. It could—no, it surely would—cost the lives of warriors waiting in these fields. Then he'd lied to Cenred a second time, hiding Aere from him. He regretted now the lie, but not the reason for it. He knew he would fall into Aere's arms again and be glad of it. It came to him he'd never told her this, and so put doubt in her, together with the fear of raising an unexpected child alone.

He was responsible for that also, and it hurt his heart.

So he must make a choice, before he could build again. For he knew he could no longer divide his life into one part and another, the two never meeting. That was a lie he'd told himself. Worse, it was a lie he'd told Aere, if only in the doing. So he must choose. He must either end the lie, or he must make Aere his truth.

He turned gingerly to watch her over his shoulder. She rode the bay easily with her back straight and her heels down, moving with the rhythm of the horse's gait. She met his eye boldly but offered him no smile, and this pained him. Still he knew Aere's new reserve was just: for he had drawn her in, and taken her from her place, and given her a child, while withholding from her any reason to see a future that included him. He would have felt the same, regardless of their separate stations.

Then, as Earic watched her, his decision came to him: he would wed Aere, if she would have him.

This resolve made him dizzy, for it came to him without debate or calculation, as if it lay long in wait for the proper time to rise and take him. He would have thought it yet another hasty decision, taken without reflection or judgment, but his gut told him otherwise. It was warm with approval, and he knew he'd neglected its wise counsel for too long.

Ever more the fool!

He did love her and he would marry her, or so he hoped. Even if this meant, as it surely would, exile to a cot in the flinty hills of his father's up-country. But there, with Aere's help, he could remake himself into a man they might both trust. He looked forward to that time; and as he turned to face the wood ahead, he smiled: both for himself and for Aere, although she did not know it.

In time they came to a dense wood that lay like a green blanket over the foothills cast down by the larger range. The edge of the wood was straight here, Human-made, and in the marge between tree and field ran a low wall of piled gray field stone marking the boundary between wild and tended. Te'a leaped the wall, followed by the bay, and Zara guided them into the trees. Soon they reached a broad, sunlit meadow spread with green grass and delicate yellow wildflowers.

A large company of dismounted Aelfin cavalry was assembled in the meadow; and standing over it was a scarlet and green swallowtail pennon affixed to a pole that seemed to Earic freshly made from a green sapling. As he watched that pennon rose and rippled once on a breath of breeze before falling limp again, as if its welcome of him was only half-hearted.

The company's cat-sí were far more welcoming. Several bounded over the grass to rub their broad flanks against Te'a, jostling Earic's leg cruelly. There were many score of the beasts in the meadow, together with what seemed an equal number of Aelfin troopers. These sat in huddles: talking, eating, or sleeping as they wished. The scene was strangely peaceful, as if no war lay beyond the wood.

They drew up to a younger Aelf who was brushing his mount, and Zara spoke to him in their own tongue. The Aelf replied stiffly before pointing deeper into the meadow. Zara urged Te'a on and Aere followed on the bay, saying nothing. They passed through the meadow until Zara stopped near a group of four Aelfs gathered by an ancient gray stump. Zara dropped from Te'a's back then and she signaled for Earic to do the same.

But she didn't wait for him, instead striding with authority toward the four Aelfs, who watched her coming with an air of wariness. Their dress differed little from the other Aelfs here, but their manner suggested to Earic they were officers or Seconds. One sat on the stump and as Zara approached he rose to bow. This Aelf was tall and lean, and his movements were graceful, but his face seemed marred in some way.

Earic slid from Te'a's back, holding her her fur until his good leg stood firmly on the grass; then he turned to Aere, thinking to speak to her. But he found her gazing over the meadow with a distracted smile, perhaps amused by the gamboling of the cat-sí. Zara called for Earic then and he hobbled over the grass to stand with her, opposite the four Aelfs at the stump.

"We will speak the Common," Zara said to all, "so the Human may understand. He is Earic, a Human lord and an officer of Cenred's High Council."

She turned to Earic then and gestured to the tall Aelf, who bore a brutal scar across his face. "Lord Earic, this is *Ritzar* Salf Kve-ma, Second of my *kansa*. These others are no matter."

"My hearth is yours," Salf said, inclining his head to Earic.

The Aelf's accent was thick with the Forest and the scar made him seem bloodthirsty despite his native grace. He carried a saber on his back, and wore at his waist a white-handled knife much as Zara's. His manner was polite now, even deferential, but it seemed contrary to the set of his mouth and the wary caution of his eyes.

So it was before another word was spoken here that Earic guessed two things about this meeting by the stump: first, the tall Second was ill-pleased to find his commander returned, and second, word of her relief had yet to reach him here. Earic wondered how Zara would tread that uncertain ground.

Salf turned his attention back to her. "Is there news, my lady?"

"There is news," she said, "but not as you would like. This Human believes a greater foe approaches even now. A Dragon."

The four Aelfs grew still at this, and Salf swept a glance over the others, as if to divine their support for something. "Do you believe this also, my lady?" he said. "It seems . . . most unlikely."

Zara stepped closer the Second, placing herself subtly between him and the others. "I believe we should prepare against the chance of it," she said, "so we are not wrong-footed if it does come to pass. The first task is to shift the *kansa*, to be better positioned."

And to keep Cenred's dispatch riders guessing, Earic thought. This wary Second might not hesitate to take command.

Salf gestured to the meadow around them. "My lady, we are well-placed here against surprise."

Zara stepped closer to him. She was shorter than the Aelf, and slighter, yet her words scourged him. "You have heard my wishes, *Ritzar* Kve'ma!" she said. "Your place is not to question them, or me. I want the *kansa* mounted and ready to move in ten minutes."

The Second dipped his head in acknowledgment, but Earic noticed the tall Aelf had stood his ground. Whatever lay between them, it wasn't settled.

"Where shall we go now, my lady?" Salf asked quietly.

Zara pointed south. "A half-mile, no more. Remain well inside the trees."

"As you command it."

"But give the task to another," she said, "and come to me at the wall. We will hold a council of war there."

Salf raised a eyebrow at this, but he said nothing more before departing. The other Aelfs followed in his wake, their eyes carefully averted from Zara.

She watched them go. "Those four plot treason against me," she said, her voice cold and dire.

Earic wondered why this was so, but said nothing. Instead, he turned his attention back to Aere. She sat astride the bay still, and she was regarding him now with the same wariness Salf had directed at Zara. A fresh worry now rose to trouble Earic: whether all these wounded and doubtful souls about him could come together and fight as one before the Orkhs, or a Dragon, came to devour them all.

He limped back to stand under the bay and look up at Aere. "We're moving to the edge of the wood," he said. "To that wall, to decide what to do. I'll tell you everything as we go."

Aere nodded silently and he took the reins to lead her and the bay from the meadow. He'd decided to walk as he could, rather than ride behind her, hoping the pain of it would remind him to be honest: carrying away that vanity and that ill-chosing, and that heedless frivolity, which marked him as an unserious and untrustworthy man.

So they moved among the high trees, he and Aere. Through cool shade and spangles of sunlight—he walking the bay, she riding upon it—and he told her everything. He told her of his lie to Cenred and the reason for it; of his reassignment to Provisions and his leaving there to find her; of his suspicions about a Dragon and his going back to Cenred to warn him; and that he was now a fugitive from his own army. In this telling, he felt anew the shame of it.

One thing only did he hold back: he did not tell her of his resolve to wed her. When it came to that, after confessing his untrusty foolishness and his long fall from grace, he felt unworthy of the asking. For he could not lay claim of marriage upon her in weakness and despair. There should be joy in the asking, and a joining of strength with strength. So this secret Earic kept for himself.

And when Aere had heard him, she was quiet for a time, swaying silently on the horse as Earic led them between the trees. There was no trace of war here in the wood, save a tang of woodsmoke that might be some farmer's hearth. The air was dusty and warm.

"You did these things for me?" she said to him at last.

He nodded. "Yes. For you, and for our child."

"Then what a fool you are, Earic Eadwulfing!" she cried. "You have ruined yourself! Now whatever will you do? Whatever shall *I* do?"

Her vehemence stung him. He'd cherished secretly a hope she would be pleased with him, and glad of her importance to him. But what he hadn't told her remained a chasm between them, and she saw him still in the same light as before: unwilling and unattainable. Now, hearing his confession, she feared even the little support he might have given her was gone. Instead of giving her gladness, Earic had sunk her heart deeper.

Will I ever stop being the fool?

But still he did not speak his secret. Not yet, not here. It would be ill-received. "I don't know what I'll do," he said in answer to her question. This was both true and not: his life now would turn on whether she would have him, when the time came for asking.

If the time came.

In the silence that followed, Earic felt Aere's measuring eyes on his back. "I wish to return to my bow clan," she said. "My duty is there, not here. You were wrong to take me away. I was wrong to follow."

Earic considered this. He wished above all else to keep her here with him, safe for now. But if she pulled the bay from his grasp and galloped away, he couldn't stop her. He wouldn't stop her. She could make her own choice, as he'd made his.

"Grant me this," he said. "Hear out this council of war, and only then make your decision."

She made no answer to this. But also he did not pull the bay from his grasp and gallop it away.

They were gathered now by the gray fieldstone wall at the fringe of the wood. Earic and Aere stood together under the bay, while Salf and Zara each stood on the stones of the wall, somewhat apart. She was studying the fields with a looking glass, while the tall Aelf waited in silence with his arms folded over his cuirass. Zara's guard remained at a discreet distance.

Earic moved to the wall and climbed up carefully. He needed to see, but the effort to lift his injured leg made his lips tremble and brought sweat to his brow. Atop the wall, he saw they were now far closer to the twin hills and the farmstead, and the gray-white stains of the sheep pens stood out clearly against the green. He strained to study them. Were the flocks smaller now? It seemed so, but it might be a trick of his mind. He remarked on this to Zara, and she turned her glass on the pens.

"I do not know," she said finally, "but I did not attend to the creatures before, not closely. Certainly the pens are not so full as they might be." She brought the glass down then and closed it. "But let us speak now of the future. What are we to do about this great foe you believe is coming?"

"We do nothing," Salf replied before Earic could speak. "Until we are called to do our part. You know this very well, my lady."

Earic expected a hard response to this, but Zara's thoughts had gone elsewhere. "What do you know of Dragons, Salf Kve-ma?" she said. "You account yourself learned above others."

The tall Aelf's scarred face remained closed and reluctant, but he turned his eyes away in thought. "Very little, my lady. Maybe nothing true." He shrugged. "They are supposed to secret themselves in heights far to the south. Nearer to the Orkhish realms than others, but still greatly far. They are said to have wit, but somewhat less than you or I, and wisdom that comes with long life. They are peaceable, it is said, and do not relish battle."

"Peaceable," Earic said. He felt that chill of doubt again. "Lady Zara said this before. Could it be one truly comes?"

Salf sneered at this. "None but you speak such nonsense, Human. Yes, they are said to be beings of peace. Uninterested in war or conquest, or the doings of other races. If this is true, then the beast's violence need be compelled. Even so, it would be a most formidable foe."

Earic studied the twin hills. *Compelled*? What could compel such a creature? And could it be slain? He realized now he'd given no thought to the how of slaying a Dragon. Perhaps it couldn't be done, or not by them. Perhaps they would do naught here but ride to their doom on these green fields.

"We cannot aim to kill the beast!" Aere cried into the silence on the wall. "If it is wise, and not a fiend. It wouldn't be fitting."

Zara turned to her. "Not slay it? What would you—"

Earic held up a hand to stop her. "Aere might have the answer. Perhaps we can turn the creature on its tormentors."

Salf spun his hands in an odd Aelfin gesture. "Free it?" he said. "You plan like children at play, imagining what you wish!" He pointed to the companies in the fields. "We should be out there among those yonder, gathering what strength we may against the Orkhs! Orkhs, not Dragons."

Zara stirred at this, but didn't rebuke her Second. She frowned at the twin hills and Earic sensed her slipping away from him.

"*Acgh!*" she muttered. "This grows more a fancy all the time. Perhaps I have been drawn overmuch into this foolishness. They are only sheep, after all, and Orkhs grow hungry too."

"Yes, my lady," Salf said. "You have been beguiled. But I am no such fool. Let us go into the fields." The Aelf clucked to his cat-sí then as if this had been decided, but then he peered north, frowning.

Earic followed his gaze and saw the two riders from before, now approaching along the wall, guiding their black horses around brush and trees. Surely tipped to where the *kansa* lay now by one of Salf's silent three.

Zara gave a shout and she leaped from the wall onto Te'a's back. But whether to flee or to charge the riders, Earic didn't know. Salf scowled at her and opened his mouth to speak. But what he said was lost beneath a great noise that came from the south. It was a long, honking note that carried far over the fields to echo back, little diminished, from the foothills in the north.

Salf whipped his scarred face around to look south now, and again Earic's gaze followed his: but he saw nothing there that might make that terrible noise. Then it came again: a great blast coming close on the heels of the first, even before its echoes faded. The note of it was mournful and keening now, as if the thing that uttered it wished to purge itself of a long ill it could no longer bear. It was a greater noise than Earic thought possible and the air shuddered under its blow.

Then a massive beast loomed over the trees between the hills. It had a long, sinuous neck that ended in a blunt head probing forward as it came. And coming behind was a great arched back that pushed through the treetops, cracking branches and shaking the high canopy like a storm.

And above it rose two skeletal frames, unfurling to the sky, and these swayed over the great back like leafless trees buffeted by a winter wind. These were wings once, Earic saw, but now only long sheets of torn flesh hung from their empty frames. The great beast had been made flightless in a cruelty that spoke to his heart, even as he considered how he was right, and how the great beast might be brought down.

But even as the Dragon cleared the wood between the hills and stepped into the flats, a second pair of skeletal wings lifted above the trees to sway in a rhythm all their own.

There were two Dragons.

11

OF BERA

In the end Bera had only three hours to exercise the company in sword and shield before the order arrived to move down the pass road. The order had been addressed to Atul, making no mention of Bera; and he'd sent back an acknowledgment making no mention of Atul and with his own name signed in the same spiky aggressive script he'd seen on his father's note. There had been no reply and this pleased him.

The exercise had pleased him far less, being in its beginning a shambles of forgotten footwork and fumbled equipment: a discreditable effort altogether that sent Bera into private despair. But by the end, after a great deal of instruction in the rudiments of the shield wall, and a liberal application of the flat of his blade, he had worked the company into a rough and ready shape that, if not ideal, would have to do.

That was then. Now, it was noon or near enough, and Bera and his company waited on the crest of a low, grassy ridge that abutted a shabby farm town. Below them, but still high on the south slope of the ridge, was the main shield wall of the allied army. It ran east and west nearly as far as Bera could see. Across from it, on lower ground, was the Orkhs' own wall. It had been repulsed only moments before, and now the two armies faced each other, quiescent again, across a broad lane of darkly churned earth.

That lane was a terrible place: littered beyond counting with splintered weapons, smashed armor, the dead, and pieces of the dead. There were many wounded also, and runners came out from both sides to drag them away, clearing the ground for the next attempt.

Below Bera the warriors of the Human wall were spent: they leaned over their shields and against one another, pushed by war beyond what mortal flesh could endure. Water-bearers moved among them, carrying skins to sluice gore from armor and dust and gall from throats. And blood was everywhere, red and black, soaking the dust and smearing what little grass that remained with terrible, slick stains. Bera had never seen a field so fearful and dire.

But it was the noise of it that brought him to the highest pitch of dread. Ten thousand voices—Orkh and Human together—rose to form a single, discordant note that filled the world. It ebbed and flowed around the armies like the roar of breakers on a beach; and above it, like shrieking seabirds wheeling over the same beach, were the cries of the wounded and the dying, calling for aid or the mercy of the sword.

It appalled Bera. And a part of him wished to flee this place and never hear that terrible sound again. But another part responded to it: emerging eagerly to hear the horror, as if it lived for nothing else. That part was what his father had awakened in him, and Bera feared it still.

The sound of Orkhish horns rose, flat and bleating. It began in the center, near Bera, then spread down the line, east and west, until an echoing skirl of many horns rose to the heavens.

The Orkhs were coming again.

On the slope below Bera, the shield wall rippled with a thousand motions. Warriors who had moved from their places in the line to eat or drink, or relieve themselves, now rushed back to their places, shoving through others already dressed in their own ranks. The standard-bearers lifted their pennons high; and in the front rank shield was set against shield in a long clatter like cold rain on a metal roof.

Then all motion ceased, or nearly so, and there was only stillness and waiting as men and women counted their charges received, and weighed the odds of surviving the next. Bera's duty lay in bolstering any part of the wall that buckled under pressure.

He spun to find Dudda, who stood nearby. "Get them up and formed!" he shouted. "I want you over there, on the right. Watch for any trouble below and send a runner if you see it. We're the bung to plug any hole!"

The little man grinned at this, knowing much of bungs, but his eyes told a different story: he was afraid. Bera understood. This was war now, and some of the company would die today. He looked for his own fear and found it: a sickness of dread lurking in his gut. He was glad for it. It would balance the wild urgency of his rage, and make him prudent in the moments to come, and chary of spending the lives of his warriors.

When the Orkhs came up the slope again it was with the discipline of battle-hardened troops. Each held aloft his tall shield to cover himself and the right shoulder of the warrior to his left. And through the narrow gaps between their shields they thrust short spears with cruel barbed blades to form a spiked hedge of steel. And as they moved they chanted in time with their steps: *Lo-ho! Lo-ho! Lo-ho!* Deep and steady as a drumbeat. The whole of them seemed to Bera like a great moving rampart, not of cold stone but dull, battered steel.

Below him the Human wall waited, their own shields set together. He wondered how many charges they'd endured. Surely many. Death seemed inevitable here. If not now, then the next time the Orkhs came, or the next. Close-order battle was an ever-grinding mill of death that given enough time would grind them all away.

The horns of the Orkhs brayed again, a different note, colorless and sour, and the pace of the shield wall quickened. Their chants came faster now, louder: a great crumbling cliff of sound. Shield rattled on shield, a thousand footfalls struck the tortured earth, and Human and Orkh cried out alike in fear and challenge. The waiting wall below Bera now swayed forward as the warriors in the second and third ranks leaned to place their shields against the backs of those before them. In this way did the wall mass its strength against the coming collision.

The wall came on. The sounds of voices rose higher. Armor and weapons rattled. Horns brayed. Standards leaned as if to lend their own strength. Ranks closed, leaned, waited.

Then the walls met.

It was the loudest sound Bera had ever heard. In the span of a single breath thousands of shields slammed together, shocking the air. It was a calamitous thing, profoundly violent, and the noise of it echoed back from the mountains above. Bera wondered how any in the front rank could survive that collision.

Yet they did.

They swayed backward under the impact, like a field of grain bent by a sudden gust. But then they returned: stiffened by resolve and by the press of ranks behind them. Now shield ground on shield, making an earthquake of sound that rose into Bera's legs. Sword and spear were brought up to search for gaps between the shields, or thrust low to pierce thighs or cut hamstrings.

All the valley thundered with battle, and Bera was dismayed by it.

It also spoke to him: the Orkhish rage fed on the noise and the sight of battle. The flame bloomed hot, and he drew the sword only to feel its cold deadly weight in his hand.

"Ceorl!" a voice shouted and he turned to it. It was one of his warriors. She gestured over her shoulder. "Second Dudda wants you! Back there!"

Bera looked there and he saw Dudda point with an urgent

finger toward a place to the right of the company where the shield wall now curved back sharply, making a bow in the line. Bera knew this was a weak point: the seam between Ceorl Aculf's company and Twicga's band on Aculf's right. The warriors of both companies were exhausted, and a dark wedge of Orkhs had pushed between them behind their shields. The Humans retreated, a small step at a time.

Bera signed for the banner-woman to follow him and ran west across his own company's front, sword in hand. "Dudda!" he shouted. "Shift them right! Quickly!"

The man drew breath to shout orders but Bera didn't wait. He tugged the pole from the banner-woman's grasp and ran with it to a place squarely behind the parting seam. There, he thrust the spike of the staff into the ground and turned to see the company filing toward him.

"Bera's *Borkas*!" he shouted, lifting the sword. "On me! Form on me!"

The Orkhs had forced their way higher now and Aculf and Twicga's sharp-pressed warriors withdrew in poor order, making the line here weaker still. Bera saw panic in their tired eyes and many cast their weapons aside and dropped their shields as they fled. Bera knew his moment had come at last and his hands trembled with eagerness and fear.

But he wasn't yet ready. Before leaving the tent he'd taken the black Dragon helm and the Dragon-fire shield from their crate and given them in keeping his banner-second. She trailed him now and he took these from her, donning both: lacing the helm under his chin, and thrusting his left arm through the fittings of the shield.

Now he was ready for war.

*

As the company came up to him Bera passed along its front rank, shoving warriors into position and adjusting the height of their shields in a show of competence he didn't feel. Now and again an eye would meet his through the slit of a helm and he saw questions there: they wondered whether this Orkh would be true to them, and whether he would lead them well. Bera much to prove and it was here that he would do it, in life or death.

"Ceorl Bera!" This was Dudda and he stood nearby, holding out to Bera a broad strip of white cloth. "Use this!" he shouted, barely heard over the noise of fighting below.

Bera accepted the cloth and the unspoken warning it carried. Then he set the shield against his knees and removed the great helm again to knot the cloth swiftly about its high crest. The white shone brightly in the noon sun.

"Thank you," he said. "The company will move now, on my call." Bera donned helm and shield again and he moved to push himself into the front rank.

"Sir!" Dudda shouted after him. "The rear is customary!"

"You may go there," Bera replied. "Dress the ranks. Encourage the runners. Lead if I fall."

The little man stared at his captain with something that might have been respect in his rheumy eyes, then he turned to hurry away. Bera smiled at this, pleased to see the man becoming attentive to his duty, then he lifted the black shield to set it against the shields of the warriors beside him.

The sword was in his hand and he struck its pommel against the shield, shouting: *"Borkas!"*

The cry was taken up and it spread swiftly across the

company, thrilling Bera's blood. He shouted it again and the company howled it to the sky. Their voices rode over the din of battle until even the black-armored Orkhs breaking the line turned their heads to it in wonder.

Bera grinned. Bera's *Borkas* would turn their wonder into fear. He lifted the sword for all to see and brought down its point.

"Forward!"

They pushed down the slope, through the remnants of the Human line. It was broken now, for the Orkhs had forced the two companies apart, making an ever-widening stretch of open ground between them. A dozen smaller duels raged still in that space, but the fallen were so great now the living stumbled among them as they fought. It was an appalling place: a whirling, confused hell of blood, dust, and fear.

But the approach of Bera's company was seen even so. Orkhish officers in tall black shakos shouted and pushed their scattered warriors back into a shield wall. Horns brayed. Steel clashed. Chaos roared. Yet all Bera could see through the slit of his helm was a narrow arc across his front. He saw Orkhs there, staring back from within their own helms, surely astonished and confused by him. He grinned at this, too.

"Company!" he cried, at the very top of his voice. "Double-time!"

They moved faster now, covering the open ground, rattling against one another and calling out. Ahead Bera saw the first rank of a new wall of Orkhs close its shields and lean forward. The rank behind them leaned on their backs. The distance closed swiftly and then the two foes came together.

*

To Bera it was like striking the earth after a long fall. The breath left him and in the same moment the black shield snapped back to strike his helm a hard blow: metal rang in his ears. He stood bewildered and unthinking for the span of a breath he couldn't take. His jaw thundered with pain, and the shield arm lay numb in its fittings.

But the rage sustained him. His head cleared and he drew breath, and ground his boots into the dust, making a redoubt for himself. Then he set his shoulder to the black shield again.

"Push!" he bellowed. "Push for your lives!"

Bera leaned into the shield, driving the Orkh across from him. But the beast resisted him, shoving back, and the faces of their shields grated together cruelly. The warrior behind Bera pressed his own shield against the back of Bera's cuirass, adding strength to the push.

Then the bright blade of a spear came over the top of Bera's shield. It skittered across metal, searching for flesh. Bera brought up the sword to knock it away.

"Push!" he shouted again.

They did push: calling out war cries and encouragement to one another above the whining grind of shields. Angered by the spear thrust, Bera pushed his sword over the top of the black shield, thrusting down at the Orkh: but the point skated harmlessly over hard leather. As he drew back he saw the Orkh's red eyes through the slit of its helm: they leered at him, bulging wildly. The Orkh shouted to Bera, words, but they had no meaning to him except to convey the Orkh's own dark rage.

Bera reset his feet and leaned harder, feeling the warrior at his back again add his own strength. The battle of shield walls was a test of collective strength and will, won only in small increments. A single step forward was a small success, to be built upon by still another step and then another, until a larger victory was won.

Bera's company had made many such steps, shoving the Orkhs backward and healing the break in the line. The steep pitch of the slope and the Orkhs' own battle-weariness were their allies in this; and soon the beasts were pushed fully from the break and down the slope toward the valley below.

Bera worked the sword as they went, parrying the leering Orkh's spear thrusts and seeking some telling blow of his own. He had opened himself to the rage, letting it drive his arm to swiftness and cunning he'd never known; but the leering Orkh's own rage matched his own and so far the two had fought to a draw.

Suddenly the warrior to Bera's right cried out and she sagged behind her shield. Swift hands reached to pull her back, and the warrior waiting in the second rank stepped forward in a moment to put his own shield into the gap that was made. Happiness came now to mix with Bera's rage, for it was done exactly how he'd trained them.

When finally the Orkhs were pushed against their reserves, they halted, refusing to be moved further. The fight between the walls settled then into a frantic joust of point and shield, fought over a distance of inches. The leering Orkh refused to go down still, but Bera was exultant even so: his *borkas* had closed a near-fatal break in the line, and his first leadership in battle was a plain victory. He threw back his head to cry out in triumph.

But as he did a lash of fire burned his right thigh. He jerked the leg back, but too hard and overset himself: he fell heavily against the shield of the warrior behind him. Hands grasped the neck of his cuirass, seeking to pull him back, but he shook them off and gathered his feet. He stood again, with a push from the warrior behind him, and brought up the black shield. He felt now wet heat gathering at the top of his greave: the leering Orkh's spear blade had found his flesh at last.

Now the rage became a towering pyre, shouting for the Orkh to die.

Now!

Bera pulled his shield back and right, across his body, then slammed it backhanded into the leering Orkh with all the strength he could muster. Their two shields skated left under the impact, creating a narrow gap that was open only for the merest moment. But Bera was ready and he twisted his body to thrust the sword into the gap. But the blade struck hard leather and turned.

He swore and the rage mounted higher. The heat at his thigh was greater, but he ignored it. He lifted the sword high now, clear of the shields, then he brought its hard steel pommel down on the crown of the Orkh's helm. That rust-pitted iron rang under the blow, but the press of the Orkh's shield against Bera's did not lessen.

He lifted the sword again, determined to strike a blow that would stagger this Orkh. But as he did nausea washed over him, making new sweat break on his brow. Heat flashed through his body, and his arm grew weak. His thoughts seemed thin now, and remote.

I'm bleeding out!

This thought was clearer and it galvanized him, but there was nowhere to go. He stood locked in the tiniest of spaces: ahead was his own shield, wedged tightly against the leering Orkh's, and behind was the warrior pressed hard against his back, and next to him were the warriors who fought with him. The shield wall they made together protected Bera, but it was also a vise he couldn't escape.

He would die on his feet.

The fighting receded from his hearing until it became only a murmur of trouble. His legs grew weaker and the black shield dragged his arm ever lower. Now his right foot was warm with blood. A voice roared at him from somewhere.

Get up, damn you! Get up and fight!

Who was it? The warrior behind him? Or Dudda? Or was it the rage itself, berating him for this weakness? Bera didn't know but it brought some clarity to him, and also shame: his duty was to lead, but now he was useless. He cried out and struggled to rise, searching with his elbows for something hard to brace himself against. But strong hands took him up and he was dragged backward, uphill.

No! he shouted to them, or he wanted to. *I can't leave! I have to go back!*

But he was helpless to resist and the black armor ground on and on over stony, war-torn earth. Finally he was dropped and strong hands hauled him around until his head was uphill of his feet. Then a dirty face peered through the slit at him. It was Dudda.

"I'll get you out of this," he said and Bera felt the fingers working at the helm's laces. He used the time to rally his clouded mind: he should return to the fight, and soon.

"My leg," he said, belatedly, willing his voice to strength. "The right one."

Dudda's eyes returned to the slit and he nodded. "Aye, we seen it. You lay there quiet. Ulma's here now and she'll work on that leg. It's your lucky roll that Orkh's blade missed the blood road there, or you'd be a dead'un by now."

The helm was tugged away and Bera's head fell to the grass. Confident hands worked at his leg, and soon something—a bandage—closed around it. A quiet voice muttered something that Bera couldn't understand.

But Dudda did and he laughed. "You been guarding beans and butter too long," he said to Bera, "and forgetting your own blood. Them Orkhs wouldn't've troubled to notice a bed-bug bite like that."

This surprised Bera and he wondered if it was true. He'd never been injured in battle before. Had he succumbed more to the shock of the blow than the wound itself? He didn't know, but he did wonder why the rage hadn't kept him on his feet. Perhaps he hadn't given himself fully to it, not yet, and there remained heights—or depths—to it still to plumb.

The healer drew the bandage tight around Bera's leg then sat back so he could see her face: it was a shocking mess of dirt and dried blood. She looked exhausted.

"You lay out a while," she said to him, wiping her hands on a filthy cloth, "and let your head clear. You can stand then, I reckon, with help. It ain't so deep, but you did bleed like you set your mind to dying."

She left him then, stumbling with fatigue as she went.

Again Bera was shamed: he'd succumbed to a wound like an unblooded child. The anger rose and he put out his hands to push himself up.

"Hold you there!" said Dudda, laying a hand on Bera's chest. "You heard the lady. She said lay out a spell."

"I don't have a spell!" Bera rasped back and he struggled again to rise. But the leg throbbed still and the bandage made it awkward. "Help me up, damn you! And get me my sword and shield! Where are they?"

Dudda made a face at this, but with the help of another he brought up his captain to stand. Bera swayed dangerously, but he knew now it was his head and not the wound itself that threatened him. Turning inward he looked for the rage: he would draw it up to clear his mind of fear and doubt. He knew it would carry him where he needed to go, if he let it.

The Orkhs began to make a great noise then. But this was something new: not their battle calls such as Bera had heard before. Instead it was a harsh croaking clatter, like an army of hungry ravens circling the field.

What now?

Bera leaned on Dudda and together they went back to the crest of the ridge, where he saw immediately the reason for that terrible noise. On the plain below, standing in a wide circle of open ground, was a tall Orkh towering head and shoulders over the others. Like Bera he was clad in black armor, yet he wore no helm on that dark head. It lay bare to the sky, as if the Orkh wished to declare he feared no Human on the field.

Bera cried aloud to see it, for that mighty Orkh was his father: Tsov-ar-kan.

As he watched, the Orkh lifted a double-bitted war axe over his head and shook it: urging his dark legions to greater fury. Bera's own blood was stirred by it, but this was his enemy and even now he looked for a way across to challenge his father. But the Human wall on the slope below was four ranks deep and knit well together; and beyond them the Orkhish horde was massed deeper still. There was no path to where his father stood.

The great Orkh saw Bera then, for he stood nearly alone with Dudda high on the ridge. The Orkh spread his arms wide, the axe held still in one hand, plainly offering challenge. Bera's *orkushna* responded to it instantly and rage flooded his mind, incandescent and demanding. The wound was forgotten and weakness fell from him like a cloak wind-blown from his shoulders. He shook off Dudda and limped down the slope toward his company, holding his father's eye as he went: to say he also held no fear. Although he did.

Suddenly Bera realized his hands were empty. He turned back and found Dudda waiting there with the black sword and the Dragonfire shield in his hands. He carried the helm on his back now.

"I kept them safe," he said. "Not that any would touch them."

"Good man!" Bera shouted and he took first the shield.

But as he did, another shout rose from the Orkhs. Bera looked to it and saw immediately its cause. Goaded to frenzy by their chieftain, the Orkhs had again broken the Human shield wall. This time thirty yards east of where Bera stood. The Orkhs had found or made some weakness there and they pushed into it: coming as a blunt wedge of gray steel. They chanted as they came, driving the Humans uphill before them. Some in the rear ranks drew away already to flee in panic.

He put his arm into the shield and took the sword from Dudda, but there was no time now to don and lace the great helm. So he sent the Second back to the company with the helm, together with orders to hold the shield wall there in all events. Bera hobbled east then, toward the Orkhs and his father, with all the speed he could muster.

By the time he reached the wedge it had broken the wall. Two tall, darkly armored Orkhs stood together at its apex, and they swung about themselves heavy axes that cleaved bone and steel. Bera charged the nearest of them behind his shield and their meeting was like a thunderclap, jarring his leg cruelly. He staggered on the slope, stunned, but kept his feet.

The Orkh did not. It stumbled away to strike the other Orkh, knocking it down the slope; then it fell heavily to the earth, overborne in the end by its own armor. Bera closed swiftly and pushed the point of his sword into the narrow gap between the Orkh's helm and breastplate. The long blade found flesh there and bit deep. Bera's rage roared approval and he leaned into the sword until the giant Orkh lay still: its arms splayed over the earth and the great axe fallen away.

Bera straightened and pulled the sword free. He was wild with rage and now it seemed he could slay Orkhs such as this all the day and into the night without tiring. He looked about for another foe and took long two steps to put a lightning-quick thrust into the shoulder gap of an Orkhish swordsman. The creature fell screaming, its heart torn, and Bera relished its agony.

The second great Orkh had recovered and now it returned to challenge Bera, swinging the great axe with both its hands. Bera ducked beneath the blade and he lunged to butt the Orkh with the flaring shoulder of his cuirass, knocking it off balance again. The wounded leg spoke to Bera then, but it seemed a small cry on a distant wind. The Orkh staggered backward under the body blow and Bera followed, aiming a thrust under the beast's gore-spattered breastplate.

The blade went home and Bera shouted in victory as a vast gout of black blood poured out to rush over the sword and the black gauntlets. The blood ran down his legs and into the Dragon greaves, but now it was not his own but the blood of his enemy.

He'd never felt so strong, nor so dire or so limitless. He knew what it meant to be a warrior. Not a Human warrior, but an Orkhish warrior. And it felt as if he had been born anew.

But a sharp cry pierced his ecstasy. It was a shout of pain and need: a Human shout. Bera turned, looking around himself and holding the sword at guard. The voice spoke his name then and he looked down to see a warrior who lay on the ground nearby. His armor was covered in blood and filth, but Bera knew him.

It was Atul.

The man lay on his back between two dead Orkhs, perhaps

trapped by their fall. A helm that must have been his lay nearby: the edge of it battered by some tremendous blow. There was a ragged wound at his brow, and his hair and face were bloody with it. He breathed in great gasps.

"Help me up, damn you!" he shouted, reaching a gauntleted hand toward Bera.

But Bera didn't move. The rage was in him still, rushing and churning like a great fuming river threatening to flood its banks. He yearned with hollow-bellied hunger to see the man's blood spilled over the earth.

Slay him! None will know it was you!

Bera raised the sword then and Atul's eyes widened. Then they narrowed into knowing, as if Bera had affirmed everything the Human world said of him.

Kill him!

How strong the need was! It came to Bera like a long and bitter thirst only the balm of hot blood could ease.

Yet he held the blade unmoving. He clenched his jaw against the demands of his rage and he turned inward to tame its fury. It bucked him away, roaring defiance: struggling to free itself like a great clawed beast. But he brought it under the lash of a lifetime's mastery.

I will not! he replied to its demand. He would not murder. He would not kill for the sport of it, nor for revenge or merely in cold malice.

So he subdued the rage, and he let the sword fall, knowing as he did something more about himself. He was not Orkh, nor was he Human either. He stood instead between those two things: a third thing, yet complete in himself. He was not Bera the Half-Orkh. He was only Bera.

*

He shifted the sword to the other hand and reached down to Atul, who had drawn his own hand back. "Take it," he said to the man. "Fight still, if you can. Go to the rear if you cannot."

Atul eyed Bera, then he said, "I can fight still. Help me up." He reached then to clasp the Bera's hand strongly. "But I did believe you meant to kill me," he said, "for a moment."

Bera hauled the man to his feet. "I did," he replied, "for a moment. You are the very son of a dog."

Atul grinned at this, showing bloody teeth. "Aye, surely I am. Now this son of a dog must find his own company and set together what remains of it. Yes, Wulfric returned me to mine. Perhaps he caught wind of . . . this." Atul gestured to Bera. "You have changed, Ceorl Bera. Or something has changed you."

Bera didn't reply and Atul said no more, but he bent to pick up his sword and helm and move away east. Bera turned back to the fighting below.

A knot of Human warriors were bravely counterattacking the Orkhs, who had gathered themselves against it: forming a bristling black hedgehog of shield and spear. But it remained high on the slope, and resisted repulse. Below, Tsov-ar-kan and his captains exhorted their reserves to move up in support of the hedgehog.

It seemed to Bera his first task here was to organize what resistance remained. He reached out to grab the arm of a warrior who seemed to wander the battlefield without purpose.

"You!" he shouted to the man. "Stand there!" Bera pointed

to a patch of trampled earth behind the warriors engaged with the hedgehog.

He did the same with another warrior, then another; and so he worked across the ridge crest, rerouting stragglers to make the beginnings of a new shield wall.

Just then Dudda clattered up, the black helm still on his back. A large group of warriors came behind him, perhaps four or five score. Plainly, it was all that remained of Bera's *Borkas*.

"I got most of'em out, sir," Dudda said. "Most as was left, any rate." The man's head was a bloody mess and his armor was slashed and scored. He unslung Bera's helm and offered it across silently.

Bera took the helm and regarded the remnants of the company. They were ragged and worn, and frightened. He smiled at them, not caring it bared his long canines.

"You are well-met, Second Dudda!" he said. "Form the company with those over there." He pointed to the little force he'd assembled.

Dudda nodded and called for the others to follow him. As they filed past him, Bera found the looks they gave him had changed. Where before he'd seen hard-eyed stares, or even refusals to acknowledge him, now he saw a careful nod here and a straightened back there. Twice, he saw a tired smile and he treasured these.

He raised his sword in salute as they passed. "Hurry now, my warriors!" he called to them. "The honor of holding the line here falls to Bera's *Borkas*! We will drive the Orkhs back to their own lands!"

A cheer rose from them, and it was taken up by all who

stood near. The sound of it was washed away swiftly by the din of battle, but it was enough: the warriors of Bera's *Borkas* moved into position on the slope with more spirit and purpose than he'd seen them do anything.

They were few now, but they were becoming his own.

Bera leaned the sword and shield against his hip and took the helm in both hands. The white cloth at its crest was grimed and blood-spattered, but still it held fast. It would ward him again in the fight to come. He ducked his head and lifted the helm.

But as he did so, a vast booming groan shuddered the air over the field. It drew out, on and on: long, warbling, and hideous. Never had Bera heard its like.

He looked west then, whence that sound seemed to come, but he saw nothing there, even to the far distance. Then another noise came from there, rising to mingle with the first. It was like the first, yet higher and seeming more urgent. And together the two calls wound about each other to form a noise he could not guess.

The fighting on the slope slowed now as every head, Orkh and Human, turned in search of the thing uttering that terrible noise. Then yet a third sound came. But now it was the shout of Orkhish voices, rising from the west. It grew louder as it came near, sweeping across that dark army until the whole of it hooted like a flock of feral birds greeting the last sunrise of the earth.

Then Bera saw it, far in the west, and he gaped, unbelieving. Moving there, across the open fields west of the ridge, was a beast that could only be a Dragon, emerging from the twilight of distant legend. Then a second came behind it. It was smaller than the first, yet each was greater than any building in the town above.

But the wonder of the Dragons was banished from Bera even as it came. For the Orkhs of the hedgehog below locked their shields again with a great noise of steel on steel, and they uttered a terrible war cry: high and bestial. And they stepped forward to push up the slope again with renewed vigor.

The king's warriors, confused and disheartened by this new terror, gave way before them. The retreat was a trickle at first, as one warrior fled alone or a few together. But soon that few became many, and many became a flood, and the Human line on the ridge disintegrated before Bera's eyes.

12

OF EARIC AND ZARA

Earic raised his hands to clutch his head, staring.

Two Dragons!

Not in his darkest imaginings had it occurred to him there might be more than one. This was too much, far too much: no mere cleverness would avail them now. Brute strength and terror would surely prevail in the end.

The first Dragon moved over the fields now on legs like ancient trees. The second trailed it by two hundred yards or more, its bulk concealed still by the trees. The first wore no constraints, but walked freely. On its feet were three great toes and a long thumb behind, and each toe bore a long curved talon that made dark furrows in the earth and scattered the stones of the gray field walls. The hide of its back was green and brown mottled, and its scales glittered like armor in the hard sunlight. Beneath, the skin of its wide belly was pale, nearly white, but it was horned and seemed no less yielding.

Then a breath of southerly breeze brought the stench of it to Earic's nose: it was the same fetor of decay he'd smelled before, as if the creature wore rags of rotted flesh in its teeth.

Sheep meat, he thought.

One Dragon was altogether greater and more terrible

than Earic had conceived, but two coming together was a nightmare with no waking. Already panic swept over the warriors in the fields: he could see the weakest of them fleeing already, sprinting back toward the town and the pass. Those who remained stood bravely, but in the face of imminent death. Surely even they would flee as the Dragon drew nearer.

This was ruin.

But they had to do something. "We must stop them!" Earic cried out, hearing the foolishness of his words even as he said them.

"Stop them?" a voice sneered. It was Salf. He'd returned with the *kansa* and stood again on the gray wall. "You would easier stop the seasons in their turning!" he said. "It would be madness to ride against them."

"Yet we shall," Zara said.

Earic turned to her, surprised. She sat on Te'a still, by the wall, but looked north, not south to the Dragons. She'd not forgotten the approaching riders and Earic saw they were now half-again closer, but fighting reluctant horses.

Zara turned her gaze to Salf. "You will move the *kansa* into the fields, *Ritzar*. Now."

The Second stood unmoving. "I will not," he said clearly.

Zara stared at him, surprise on her sharp face. But there was something else there, too: anticipation or eagerness.

"You dare refuse me?" she said. Her voice was cold and stony.

Salf leaned forward on the wide stone where he stood, as if to find a better balance from which to hurl his next words at her. His mouth and the scar were twisted cruelly, as if it galled him to speak.

"There will be no more slaughter of Aelf-kin here!" he said. "Too many warriors cat-sí have been commanded to their deaths by you, here. Their deaths were needless and foolish. And now you wish for more to die, all of us, assailing these beasts. It is madness and I will not!"

Zara's eyes went to the messengers again, calculating, then she cried aloud in her own tongue and sprang from Te'a's back to stand on the wall again. She drew the white-handled knife from her belt and lunged to thrust it at Salf, offering at the same time a cunning flourish of misdirection with the other hand. But the tall Aelf wasn't fooled: he twisted away and snatched out his own white knife to meet Zara. Their two blades seemed matched in length and design.

Earic cried out protest and scrambled down from the wall, but neither Aelf heeded him. Zara closed on Salf again and thrust her knife in a strange, spiraling motion that seemed designed to confuse him. But he dodged left, avoiding the point, then moved to stand on another stone, higher.

"Never in my darkest dreams did it come to this," Salf said to Zara. "Desist, wife."

Aere cried out and Earic drew in a breath of surprise.
Wife?

"I command," Zara responded. "You follow. There is no other way, even husband you may be. Yield to me!"

But Salf only stood on the stone, staring at her with anguished eyes. "Would you truly kill us for your pride?" he said.

"I will not be denied my chances, Salf!" Zara raged now.

"Not by you, not by anyone. I deserve a way back from shame, and I have had to look for it myself. You never wanted enough for me, Salf!"

"This is madness!" he cried. "We have enough for *us*, Zara-ena. Come back to me!"

She sprang nearer to him, the white knife held ready. "Yield to me!" she demanded.

"I cannot!" he said and he uttered a wail of misery. "It has come now to what I feared most! You make me choose, you or the *kansa*, and I will not have more fruitless blood on my hands. Ward!"

He lunged at her then with his own knife. But Zara leaned far back, farther than Earic thought possible, and the blade passed across her front, slicing only air. Then she retreated across the wall, her feet deft on the uneven stones.

Salf followed, pressing his attack, and their blades turned and flashed in the sun like fish darting in clear water. It seemed to Earic each meant land a blow that would kill, yet their sabers lay untouched at their backs.

Aere heeled the bay over to the commander of Zara's guard. "What foolery is this?" she demanded of him. "Stop them!"

But the Aelf didn't take his eyes from the duel. "It is our way," he said, although his accent was so great the words seemed a foreign tongue. "He challenged her right. The *k'nar* will decide."

"Aren't you sworn to her?" Earic said. "She's your captain!"

The commander's face remained impassive. "There is doubt now," he said then he repeated, "The *k'nar* will decide."

Frowning at this, Earic turned back to the fight on the wall.

He called out to them: "Gods damn it! We don't need this now!"

But the Aelfs ignored him. They were inhumanly nimble, moving over the jumbled stones in a flutter of swinging arms and shifting feet, each keeping the finest of balance. And so Earic's despair grew deeper, for not only could they not sally against these terrible foes, but they fought still amongst themselves.

He looked to the Dragons again. The first was taking arrow fire now from the remnants of Cenred's first line of defense. As Earic watched, many score arrows flew at the Dragon in a deadly cloud and all sprang away from its hide like hailstones from a sturdy house. A moment later the noise of the volley came to Earic's ears as an angry hum of bees followed by a thin and futile rattling. Another volley came after, but the arrows were fewer now as more defenders broke away to flee north over the fields.

The great beast stopped then and it swung its long, narrow head around to look back at the second Dragon. Earic followed its gaze. The second had moved out from the trees and Earic could see now it was bound with great chains that hobbled its rear legs. The same chains, surely, as Zara saw. And also unlike the first, the second Dragon had a wide ring of many Orkhs about it: to ward it or contain it, or both.

More curious still were four gangs of tall Trolles that walked beside the second beast, one gang close by each of its great legs. The Trolles carried in their hands overlong steel-tipped lances, far heavier than any an Aelf or Human could wield. And the Trolles prodded the beast with their lances, finding places on its hide to make it flinch and draw away. Earic wondered at this: perhaps scales had been torn from the creature's hide, just as the skin of its wings was cruelly cut away to bereft it of flight.

Then the second Dragon opened its jaws to utter a forlorn cry that passed over the fields and echoed from the foothills beyond. The note of it was bleak and miserable, and the first Dragon took up that call, matching its note, so it seemed to Earic the great beasts keened together in grief.

It was then, in that trembling moment of sound, that all became clear to him.

He understood now how the Orkhs had brought these unwarring beasts to battle, and how they would be made to fight. But also he understood how they might be sent away again.

Aflame with this new knowledge, Earic turned back to the Aelfs fighting on the wall. "Stop this!" he cried to them. "You must stop this, damn you!"

Still they gave no sign of hearing, and no one moved by the gray wall, as if these Dragons had not come and the king's Fyrd did not flee across the fields before them. Even Aere seemed mesmerized by the spectacle made by the Aelfs.

Salf's greater height and reach was telling now, and Zara drew back before him, hopping backward over piled stones. But then, before Earic could speak again, Salf grew still and he lowered the white knife to his side. The scar on his face was flushed and his mouth was a wound of reluctance and grief.

"I do not wish to slay you, Zara-ena" he said. "Your death would not please me."

"Then you may yield," she replied. "Know that I will never yield to you."

Salf lifted his hands as if appealing to the heavens. "I know that well!" he cried. "How well I do, and what a fool I was! I went to your father and I begged him to be your Second. I *begged* him. He knew my heart well so he granted my boon, and I was happy. Oh, what a happy fool I was!"

He lowered his arms, looking at no one. "I do not wish to go on with this," he said. "I have no desire to slay you, nor to make you yield under my *k'nar*. Both are far from my heart, for you are wife to me. But you ask too much. The *kansa* cannot bear more. I cannot bear more. I will not have more death and more sorrow for naught. We must leave this place, or you will destroy us all."

Zara glanced again to the riders, who were near. "Perhaps we may leave, but first you must yield! Now!"

"No!" Earic cried. "You can't leave! There's a way—listen, there's a way to defeat the Dragons. I see how it can be done, but you must listen!"

Salf turned his eyes to Earic, but as he did Zara lunged at him. A broad hump of stone lay between them and she crossed this with two quick steps to swing the white knife across his front then back again, crying out in fury. The artful jabs of before were gone now and she pressed a brutal attack.

Salf stepped away, but the heel of his boot caught a lip of stone and he fell, landing on his back across a wide, round-topped stone. The breath left his body with a sharp wheeze and he lay stunned. Zara closed on him. He brought up the white knife to meet hers but she batted the arm aside with ease. Now she stood with the sole of her boot pressed to his wrist, holding the knife firmly against the hard stone.

She bent to put the edge of her own blade to his throat.

Earic and Aere cried out as one, then Earic said: "Enough of this, Zara! We need him!"

Still Zara didn't seem to hear him. "Yield!" she said to Salf. "Yield to my right, or the *k'nar* will drink your craven blood!"

He glared back at her. His chest heaved on the stone. "Slay me now!" he cried. "For surely you shall slay me later with your heedless ways! It matters not which."

"Yield to her!" Earic said. "There is a way! Yield to her and I will tell it. We have no time for this foolishness."

The Second twisted his mouth into a snarl and the scar followed. "Very well," he said. "All of us will die by these Dragons in any count, since we do not leave. I yield to you, Lady Zara Thu'sem! You command by your father's word and now also by right of the *k'nar*. I am bound."

She held the knife to his throat a moment more, as if thinking to rid herself of her Second even so, but at last she drew away.

"My right is absolute," she said, returning the white knife to its sheath. "You may not deny it again in this life."

Salf pushed himself up to stand. He put away his own knife and nodded to her, then rubbed his neck where the blade had been. Earic had known Salf but an hour or less, but already his heart went out to the tall Aelf.

The messengers came up then, along the stone wall. Their mounts were winded and pranced beneath them, and rolled their dark eyes at the Dragons.

One called out: "I seek *Ritzar* Salf Kve'ma the Aelf, in the name of Aetheling Cenred!"

Salf eyed her then glanced at Zara. "I am he," he said.

The messenger guided her horse closer to the wall, removed a folded paper from the cuff of her glove, and offered to the Aelf. Salf took the paper and unfolded it; and for a moment there was silence by the wall as he read it. Then his scar flushed and the fingers holding the message trembled.

"Did you know of this?" he said to Zara.

"He has no right," she replied. "I was granted leadership of this *kansa* by my father, the king. No other may take it from me. Not you, not him. No one."

Salf crumpled the paper then opened his hand so it fell between the stones of the wall. He seemed bereft now, and he turned to gaze over the remnants of the Aelfin company as if doing so for the last time.

"I am bound by our law, my lady," he murmured. "Command me. I may not refuse you again."

Zara didn't reply to this, but looked to Earic now. "Speak," she said, "and swiftly. How do you see hope in this despair?"

Earic moved to climb the wall again, to see the field, but the leg balked and in the end he was brought up only by a heavy push from Aere. From the wall he saw the messengers, their errand complete, riding away north, fleeing the Dragon. To the south the first Dragon had scattered the forward lines of the Fyrd and many tiny figures fled over the fields and along the cart paths between them.

"That is the King's Own that flies, there," Aere said, coming up to stand next to him. "My people. I should be with them, perhaps holding them firm."

"You may do a needful duty here as well," Earic murmured, but his mind was on the Dragons now, for he trembled with the need for haste. Warriors were dying out there, and here at the wall far too much time had been lost already.

"Look at the second Dragon," he said to them, pointing. "See how it's restrained and how the Trolles harry it with their lances?"

The second Dragon was closer now and he could see the glittering tips of the Trolles' long lances hover by wide gaps rent in the creature's scaly armor: ready to inflict injury there, or even a mortal wound, at need. The fiendish cruelty of it was ingenuous, and Earic wished greatly now to free the beast.

"The creature is enslaved," Zara said. She'd brought out the glass and was examining the second Dragon and its minders through it. "It is a terrible wrong, as was the shedding of the beast's wings." She added something harsh in her own tongue.

"Yes," Earic said, "and the first Dragon fears for the life of the second. Thus is it goaded to assail us."

"They're mates!" Aere cried. "We must free them!"

"Perhaps we may," Earic said. "Here is a plan. I say we ride to the aid of the second Dragon and free it from the Trolles. Then the first will no longer be coerced. The Dragons can free themselves then, if they have the wit to do it. It can be done, with luck, and by us."

"That is no tactic!" Salf cried. He wore a look of deepest scorn. "Nor will any tactic suffice us. It is a deadly errand, however done. We are too few, and there is a ring of Orkhs there, and I see more Trolles under that Dragon than I have in all my other days set together."

"Then tell me your better plan!" Earic said. "We can't remain here fighting among ourselves! They need help—all of them, those fleeing in the fields and the Dragons." He flung an arm at them. "And Cenred has more than his hands full in the center. We must do something!"

Salf said nothing more, but only glared at Earic. Zara brought down the glass and nodded as if to herself.

"We will do what we may," she said, "as Lord Earic says. Perhaps this is the moment for which all others stepped aside." She turned to Salf then. "Bring up a mount for Lord Earic's use. When he is accepted we will ride forth to doom or eternal glory."

The Second's mouth was set in a grim line but he said nothing in reply before stepping down from the wall and moving away toward his waiting riders. Earic watched him go, thinking the tall Aelf was likely not wrong: any attack would come to grief. But it must be attempted, for only they here by this wall stood between the Dragons and the ruin of the King's Dominion.

Zara turned to Earic. "Salf will bring you a mount," she said.

"A cat-sí?" he asked, suddenly wary.

She nodded. "We have no other, and you must certainly ride for we all do. Although the beast must accept you first."

"How will I do that?"

Her eyes shifted away. "Each cat-sí is different, as each of us is different," she said. "But ware any falsehood, Lord Earic, for they are knowing creatures."

He flushed at this and looked to Aere. He felt false to her and wondered whether she felt the same.

"Will you remain here?" he said to her. "It would do my heart good."

Aere's look was scornful. "Do you truly ask this of me? I am a warrior, my lord, and my brothers and sisters die even now!" She flung a despairing hand at the rout in the fields.

Then she leaned close to him so only he could hear. "You do not pledge yourself to me, Earic," he whispered, "yet you seek to put your thumb on me! Others have tried this and failed. I will not have it!"

There was nothing he could say to this: she was right, and in truth he'd known she would not remain. Aere would go where she willed and the day would end as it would. His heart would simply have to bear it.

But he laid a hand on her arm. "I'm sorry I took you from your company," he said. "Perhaps it was wrong of me. Can you accept my heart was in the right place?"

She pulled away. "Perhaps, but that is not enough."

Earic opened his mouth to reply, but the thought strayed when Salf approached them leading a saddled but riderless cat-sí. The creature was tall for its kind and broad-chested. Its fur was tawny like summer hay, a pattern of black spots dappled its long back and sturdy legs, and its eyes were pale green like the leaves of early spring. These regarded Earic now, the black of them narrowed to tall slits against the afternoon light.

When the cat-sí stood before Earic, Salf let its reins fall. Earic made no move to retrieve them. Instead he stood motionless before the cat-sí, quieting his anxiety. He couldn't fail in this, for he could neither run nor walk far, and it was very far indeed to the second Dragon.

He spread his hands to show they were empty of threat then bowed low to the cat-sí. "What is his name?" he asked Salf.

"None know his true name," the Aelf said, "save the luckless rider who fell this morning last." The Aelf's tone was even, but Earic saw his eyes shift to Zara.

Then, of its own accord, the cat-sí stepped forward until Earic could feel the wind of the creature's breath on his face; and its great head stretched to either side of him nearly as far as he could reach with his arms outstretched, and whiskers stretched farther still. A dry smell of clean fur came to Earic's nose.

But he held himself still, and soon he felt a push. Not against his body, for the cat-sí hadn't moved again, but a push within him. This came from the cat-sí, but the creature didn't thrust itself upon Earic, or seek to rummage in the inner things of him. It pressed only lightly, feeling along Earic's outermost walls. Looking, perhaps judging, Earic didn't know. But it was plain the cat-sí's presence was benign: it meant him no harm.

So Earic opened a door in those outermost walls of himself, and that presence put itself inside. But only partly so: as a housecat might peer into an unknown room from a doorway. So Earic came to meet it; and acting on an impulse that seemed right to him, he brought forth to the cat-sí his feelings for Aere. These surprised even him now, for they were stronger than he'd believed. Growing in him without his noticing.

The cat-sí sniffed at these, inwardly, and outwardly it regarded Earic with its spring-green eyes. But it didn't speak to him silently as he expected. Rather it offered him both an image and a feeling that together formed a single thought that Earic understood to mean: 'the tall one who lies overlong in the shade.' He smiled at this and bowed again, thanking the cat-sí without words.

Then he turned to Salf. "I believe I've been accepted," he said. "He has given me his name."

"Do not speak of it!" the Aelf said. "It is only for you to know. But now you must give him an outer name. One known to us."

Earic considered this a moment. Urgency rose in him again as the Dragons renewed their cries. "He shall be Dreng, for surely he is a mighty warrior."

Salf nodded satisfaction, and Earic felt the beast's approval press upon him.

He turned to the others, "We must go now, swiftly!"

It was Aere who replied. "We cannot fight all those Orkhs protecting that second beast," she said. "They are too many and we too few. But perhaps some can break their ring like a needle, and others ride through to the Dragon like the thread behind."

Zara looked doubtful, but it seemed to Earic this plan was sound. They certainly didn't have the numbers to engage a broad section of the ring of Orkhs guarding the Dragon.

"Yes," he said, "Aere is right. That is the way. We can punch through the Orkhs, then ride hard to scatter the Trolles. Or at least harry them enough to break the threat to the second Dragon. I believe it can be done, with luck."

"And with the aid of the beasts themselves," Aere added. "As Earic said before."

Salf stood at the edge of hearing, listening to their talk with a frown, but he said nothing.

Zara had turned to study the Orkhs again through the glass. "Perhaps it can be done," she said, "but only perhaps. The *kansa* should be divided into two parts, I think. The first to make the break and the other to ride through without engagement. Otherwise all will be drawn into the effort to make the way, and few or none will pass to the Dragon."

"That is wise, lady," Earic said. "Each part will have its task."

Zara put away the glass and turned back to the others. Her eyes were eager now, as if she'd discovered something that pleased her.

"I will lead the second part," she said, "which shall be the larger. I will ride through to the Trolles and free the Dragon. Lord Earic and Aere will join me. Salf, you will take the first part and make the way for us. Do not fail in this."

The Second nodded, uttering no protest, then turned away to the *kansa*. It seemed to Earic their fight on the wall and its aftermath had damaged something in the tall Aelf, and now he moved as if attending to some ill only his own ears could hear.

When Zara had gone also, Earic turned to Aere. "All my plans have gone awry," he said to her. "I'm happy this one is yours."

"Would you call our child a plan gone awry?" she said.

Earic put up his hands: he'd meant the words as jest. "No! No, I didn't mean—"

She stopped him. "That's the trouble, Lord Earic. What do you mean? You tell me of your troubles as if we will share a pillow into old age, but we will not. And you take this, but not that. You give this, but not that. I will not be a half of anything to you or to any man, my lord. I will fight here, with you, but do not speak to me of aught else but that."

The rebuke stung him. Earic opened his mouth, but then closed it again. She was not wrong. He thought to tell her of his secret, but now seemed even less opportune than before. He would wait. But now even that waiting seemed wrong, as if still he hoarded things from her, keeping them for himself, as she said.

Dreng butted his massive head against Earic's chest then, seeking attention; and he scratched the cat-sí's broad cheeks with both hands, knowing somehow the beast wished it.

"Very well," he said to Aere, hating this new distance between them. "As you wish. But please help me mount Dreng. Too much time has been lost already."

With her help Earic scrambled up to the cat-sí's back, where he sat awkwardly in the saddle on sore hips. Aere mounted the bay. Some yards away, the *kansa* had arranged itself into two squadrons under Salf's direction. The first was spread across the grass east of the wall in a narrow point, like a chevron. This would pierce the ring of Orkhs protecting the second Dragon and hold a way open.

The second squadron, larger than the first by half, stood behind, taking no particular shape. It would burst through the gap made in the ring and ride swiftly to engage the Trolles. It was a sound plan for what little they had, but Earic felt only small confidence it would succeed. Much depended on speed and quick success.

Salf, who commanded the first squadron, drew his saber and rode to the front. There he raised his blade so it flashed in the sun, and he uttered the high, yodeling war cry of Aelf-kind. The *kansa* responded to him, raising their own sabers to the light. Aere lifted her bow with them and called out. Earic lifted his sword and made the cry of his House. Dreng pranced under him and the cat-sí's eagerness to run on the grass rose into Earic's mind, thrilling him. His confidence grew.

Then the horn-aelf winded his horn twice, and the scarlet and green swallowtail moved forward. And Zara's Company came after it, moving over the fields toward the second Dragon, gaining speed as it went. Earic and Aere rode among the Aelfs of the second squadron, side-by-side, near Zara; and together they went to free the Dragons.

13

OF BERA

Resistance on the ridge below Bera collapsed. The warriors there, pushed hard by the Orkhs and wearied by long fighting under a hot sun, were undone by the Dragons. And now they fled around Bera, toward the town and the pass road. An happy few proclaimed doom as they ran, urging all to flee. Far more flung away their weapons and shields, or even stripped off armor, running in their small clothes to escape quicker still. A great many of these were unharmed, or injured only slightly.

Bera called out to them as they passed, urging them to join him. But few heard, and fewer still heeded his call. In all, two score warriors whose will to fight was not utterly sapped joined the ranks of Bera's *Borkas*. It was far too few, but there was no time to rally more, for the hedgehogged Orkhs were driving up the slope again, seeking to hold open the break they'd made.

All that remained to oppose it was Bera's company of Provisions Guards.

Dudda had pushed them into ranks, together with the extras, and now Bera took the Dragon helm from the Second and gestured for him to take a place on the right of the line.

He wouldn't order the man to the rear: not for a charge that might be the company's last. Dudda nodded without protest, and Bera reviewed the company with a glance. They could just manage three ranks. It wasn't enough, but it would have to do. He put himself into the first rank again, shoving out a space for himself between two shields.

The wounded leg was stiff now, and he limped around it, but Ulma's bandaging held still and Bera felt equal to this task ahead. The rage simmered in him, brooding and impatient, looking always for an outlet, but he held it in check. It would rise swiftly to his need when the time came.

Bera donned the great Dragon helm and returned the Dragon-fire shield to his arm. Then he raised the black sword for all to see, calling "Ready!"

The company shouted as one in response, and Bera drew the sword down to point toward the Orkhs below.

"Forward!"

So again Bera led his *borkas* against the Orkhs, and again they followed him. Seeing their approach, the hedgehog halted and the Orkhs gathered their shields closer to meet this new threat. Their meeting came swiftly and the company slammed into the Orkhs with an impact that jarred Bera's leg cruelly. He set his jaw against the pain and put his shoulder into the shield, pushing with the other leg.

Then the rage came and he slew the Orkh before him with a deft thrust beneath the rim of its shield, held a fraction too high. Another came forward to take its place, trodding on the body of the first, and it sought to slay Bera in return.

The fighting on the slope was fierce and sharp: steel struck on steel with a thousand clattering, clinkering blows. Human and Orkh both uttered fierce war calls, and they cried out at wounds given and received. Again and again Bera shouted encouragement to his warriors over the din, and for a time they fought as well as he could desire.

But it was not enough: the Orkhs were not pushed back. Bera lifted his head to look down the ranks, left and right, and WHAT he saw there shocked him. The company's wall was no longer straight: instead it curved forward so each of its ends hung now, vulnerable, in space. In a moment, he understood why. The center of the line had struck the curved front edge of the hedgehog and stopped, but the ends had carried farther down the slope, seeking to come to blows with the Orkhs across from them.

Now, instead of forming a straight-ruled line that could disengage and retreat swiftly, the company was a great arc with its ends pointing down the slope and engaged with the Orkhs there. Bera cursed himself: he should have foreseen this. It was a terrible mistake, and he must fix it quickly or the Orkhs coming up from below would take the ends from three sides and roll up the wall.

And even as the thought came to him, the event came to pass. With a dark shout a brigade of Orkhs came up the slope to assail the right. Bera shouted in anguish: collapse could come in moments, and when it did the Orkhs would move swiftly to cut off the company's retreat up the slope.

He was afraid now, and angry. Not at the Orkhs, but at himself. His victory earlier had made him overconfident: he hadn't paid then the inevitable price of inexperience. He would now.

*

Bera roared at the warriors next to him to close their shields, and then pulled his own shield from the wall. Then he shoved himself back through the ranks, the leg weak and sharp with pain, until he came out the rear of the formation, nearly falling. He limped along the rear rank, toward the right of the line. A fire drove him, but it was more panic than rage.

What was I thinking? Damn me! Damn me to hell!

He found chaos on the right: the end of the line had come apart under attack by Orkhs on three sides, and the fighting was now only a score of small, desperate duels between individuals and groups. Some were evenly matched, but others were merely massacres of one side by the other. Many had fallen on both sides, but it seemed more of the dead were Human than Orkh.

Bera keened with grief. This was his fault: he should have foreseen the breakdown of the shield wall when it met the rounded hedgehog. He'd betrayed his *borkas* with reckless inexperience, and now men and women were dying around him as he watched.

Fool!

He'd been so proud of himself.

Arrogant fool!

He saw Dudda then and his anger turned outward. The little man was beleaguered by two Orkh axemen. They were tall and towered far over Dudda but he fought them with courage and skill: heaving his sword and shield around to meet their heavy blows.

But then even as Bera watched Dudda missed his footing on the broken earth and stumbled. His shield fell from high guard and the blade of a heavy war axe split the shoulder of his cuirass, above his sword arm. The hard leather parted and red blood rained from the rent.

The axe was wrenched away and the man staggered, but he found his balance again and brought his shield back up to guard. But now his sword hand hung limp at his side, empty. Blood ran from it in long red lines that stained the dust.

Bera lifted his own sword. This, at least, he could make right.

He ran at the nearest of the Orkhs, leading with the black shield. The wound slowed him but the way was downhill, lending him speed. He struck the Orkh squarely in the back and the beast lifted from its feet and fell far down the slope. It landed hard and rolled farther still, carried by the weight of its own armor.

Bera staggered, wheeling on the injured leg, until he too fell. He landed on the shield and some part of it struck him a hard blow. He lay on the ground for a time, stunned, as fighting passed over him.

It was the rage that saved him. It rose like an angry giant to shrug off its chains: it cleared the mist from his mind and gave him the will to rise again. He pushed himself up to stand and as he did he threw out the shield to knock away a sword stroke that might have slain him where he lay. He riposted with a thrust quickened by his *orkushna* and the blade bulled past the Orkh's guard to drive into deep the slit of its helm. Black blood welled out as Bera tore the sword free.

He turned to Dudda and saw the man leaning drunkenly, but he held his shield high still against the blows of the second

Orkh. Bera went to him and slew the Orkh with a shield slam and a thrust of the sword that found a gap between helm and cuirass.

When the Orkh fell away Dudda turned to peer at Bera through the slit of his helm. A fierce light was in the man's eye.

"I ken it now!" he shouted, though weakly. Bright red blood sheeted over the cuirass from his shoulder.

"Ken what?" Bera said.

"*Boor-kas*. It ain't no different from us. It's all the same."

Bera nodded. "Aye, it is. We're all warriors, Orkh and Human." He sheathed the sword and held out a hand to the Second. "Come! We'll find you a healer, Dudda. You'll do no good here now."

The man hesitated and Bera thought he knew why. It wasn't because he wanted to remain, for surely he didn't. No, Dudda hesitated because this was new ground between them. A good Ceorl and a good Second leaned on each other: they made each other better. But Bera hadn't been a good Ceorl, nor had Dudda been a good Second. Each had wandered in a world of his own, stubbornly lost. Bera pursuing his futile quest to be accepted as something he wasn't, and Dudda seeking to preserve the little fief that gave him purpose even as drink corroded his body and spirit. Bera wished now he'd done more for the man.

But the moment passed and Dudda nodded agreement. He dropped his shield and shuffled closer to Bera, leaning over the wound. It was surely deep and he'd lost far too much blood.

Bera put his arm around the man, bearing him up. "We

must hasten," he said, for the fighting here raged still and he wished to return to it swiftly.

As he turned Dudda to face upslope, Bera saw that three warriors—two men and a woman—had come to stand around them, fending away any Orkh who drew near. He was silently grateful to them, and together he and Dudda hobbled away from the fighting.

But the little man faded, shifting ever more of his weight to Bera's arm. Their pace slowed.

"We're nearly there," Bera said, but it wasn't true. The crest of the ridge, and the healers there, lay far away still. "Only a few steps more, my friend. You can do it."

Dudda pulled from Bera and put out his good hand to lower himself to the earth. His voice was a feeble gasp now.

"Let me be, gods damn you!" he said. "I'm killed and I know it. It don't matter where I die. Let me be."

"No!" Bera cried. "We'll find a healer! Don't let go!"

Bera fumbled for a grip on the man's armor, to drag him up the slope. But Dudda shook him off again and sank back to lie on bloody dust, uttering a breath of relief.

Bera drew off his helm and knelt beside the man. "Perhaps some water then," he murmured and he looked around for a skin-carrier, but saw none.

Dudda shook his head. "No—no water. Get this damned thing off me." He tugged weakly at his own helm.

Bera untied the laces and pulled away the helm, setting it aside. Then he lowered the man's head to rest beside it. He looked to the wound then: perhaps there was something he could do.

"No," Dudda said, more firmly than before. "Forget that. Listen to me." He took Bera's arm in a strong grip. "Listen to me!"

Bera leaned close. "I hear you, my friend," he said.

"I'm sorry," said Dudda. "I'm damned sorry for it all."

Bera shook his head. "No! There's nothing—"

"Yes!" The word was harsh and compelling. "I'm sorry for being such a gods-damned sot. I'm damned sorry. Drink is my mistress. I can't leave her. She's cruel."

"I could have helped you."

Dudda coughed and shook his head. "I was never fit to hear any man tell me how to be. But you showed me something to-day, surely." The man's eyes met Bera's now and he smiled with bloody lips. "You took your gods-damned time about it though, damn you."

Bera nodded. "Aye. I was lost, too."

Dudda's gaze looked beyond Bera now. "I reckon all of us is lost sometime," he said. "Blind 'til the light's forced on us. Some as never see. Make Esma your Second after me. They trust her and she's got a way with'em. Better than me. No, don't you stir. I can feel the bleeding in me. No healer can fix what that damned Orkh gave me."

Grief rose in Bera, hard and demanding. He nodded. "I will raise Esma," he said. "A wise choice." Then he slipped off the black gauntlets and took Dudda's hand between his own. "Do you have kin I can tell of you?"

The man shook his head as if the effort cost him greatly. "Only the company. Yours now. They wasn't before, but they are now. What's left of'em, any rate. Ain't seen such hard fighting."

"I'll do right by them," Bera said. "Better. I promise."

Dudda coughed on blood, spraying it over his chin. "Something else I ain't proud of, but I'll tell it now. It was me as put that paper in your tent."

Bera pulled back. "You?"

The Second's lips twisted with shame or regret. "Took five crowns to do it," he said. His voice was a whisper now. "Didn't know what it was. Can't read. But the Mistress called that day. Told Atul of it. Later. Figuring he'd pinch you for a spy and I'd be shed of you. Wished I ain't done it now. You showed me something. Surely."

Bera smiled at him. "I'm glad you did it," he said. "That paper was from my father. I met him and he taught me things about myself I didn't know. You gave me a great gift that day, Dudda, though you didn't know it. Nor did he. And I came back. I came back to fight with you. And to thank you, it seems."

Dudda's smile was wan and he seemed to settle into himself. "It's good you came back," he said. He squeezed Bera's hand without strength. "Thank you for pulling me out, down there. It was . . . *borkas*."

"Yes," Bera whispered. "It was *borkas*."

But the man didn't hear him, for the life had left his body. There was no struggle: his ravaged spirit slipped swiftly and quietly from its earthly frame, to carry away to those Endless Halls where it might find the peace it was denied in life. Bera wished that for him.

But he felt no peace for himself. Grief held him, but more urgent still was the rage thrashing within him, seeking an outlet to the world. He knew now he would let it free, utterly and completely, without reserve for himself. He wouldn't lose another warrior to the Orkhs, if his life or death could prevent it. That was *borkas.*

He rose from Dudda and donned the great Dragon helm again and drew the sword. First, he looked west and saw there the two Dragons on the fields. The foremost thrashed about itself, surely slaying warriors. Its dire calls could be heard even here. But Bera could do nothing for those caught beneath that monster.

He lifted the black shield from the ground where it lay and limped back down the littered slope toward his beleaguered company. The banner flew above them still, but it was plain his warriors fought for their lives. He had tarried with Dudda overlong.

He struck the Orkhs like a cyclone of black steel. Sword and shield both were his weapons, and he swung them left and right, smashing armor and battering helms. Submitting himself completely to the darkest biddings of his rage, the wound forgotten. His *orkushna* seemed to move him with a will of its own; and a part of him watched in awed silence as he moved and swung, thrust and pushed, striking down all who came within reach with dark fury.

And the Orkhs fell back before him. They didn't rout, for their shields were high. But they seemed to lose their will to defy him. The silent part that watched from afar wondered if these Orkhs saw him now as they did his own father: a mighty Orkh chieftain to be respected and feared, an object of awe and instinctive deference. Bera grinned at this and laughed aloud for the irony of it: for the regard of the Orkhs cut full against all he'd striven for in his life. Yet it felt right even so.

But he knew it wouldn't last. Bera could see now the steel twinkle of more spears moving up from the south, to stiffen the battle-weary Orkhs here on the slope. He looked around for his own warriors and he saw nearly all had used his disruption to retreat up the ridge. This was good. But a few fought near him still and he called to them, swinging an arm to send them back with the others. They'd done well, all of them, even in extremity, but Bera knew the company was near the end of its effectiveness without rest and reinforcement, although the latter was unlikely.

He feared to know his losses. Esma could tell him the number or nearly so, but he suspected the company was now worn down to less than half its strength of the morning. The thought sent him low. The fallen were his warriors, entrusted to him, and he'd failed them. He flushed again at the memory of his mistake against the hedgehog, and at his own arrogance in the crow of victory hours ago, as if that first charge had told all. He knew now there was no glory to be won here. There was only survival to see the dawn tomorrow.

So he retreated up the slope behind the last stragglers of his company, and resolved again to preserve all who lived still. How this might be done, he didn't know, but he would do it.

At the crest of the ridge, he was dismayed by the sight of them. Many lay on the ground, mute and staring, or carried swiftly into sleep. Others stood leaning on their shields or each other, looking as if no force on earth might move them to fight again.

But he said nothing to them, not yet. He went to find Esma, a stern-faced woman of many years service. He told her quietly of Dudda, and of her own elevation to his place as Second.

She took the news thoughtfully. "It's not the way I would have wanted it."

"Nor I," Bera said. "But I have confidence in you. It seems he did."

Her laugh was tired. "That smelly old he-goat wanted between my legs from the beginning. But he did right by his people, or he did when he was sober enough to remember his duty."

"True," Bera replied, "but neither he nor I did our duty to its fullest." He looked down the slope to where Orkhish officers were already re-forming their wall. "I need the company ready to fight again," he said. "There's still a hole here and they're coming again."

Esma looked also. "Are we going down there again, sir?" Her eyes were wary and doubtful.

"No, we haven't the strength," he said. "Not anymore. All we can do now is close up tight and hold our piece of ground here as long as we can. And hope the rest of the line holds theirs."

Esma frowned at this and looked west. "What of the Dragons? I don't believe it even now."

Bera followed her gaze. The first beast rampaged still. The gods knew how many had died over there.

"What of them?" he said, with a roughness that surprised him. "They're not our concern, however strange and unlooked for they are. Our work now is to hold this place." He pointed to the earth at their feet. "Nothing else."

She gave him a careful look. "And if we do not hold? Shall I give thought to how to move the company back over the pass?"

Now that she had spoken of it, Bera gave himself permission to think on retreat. It had hovered, unacknowledged, at the edge of his mind since Dudda fell. Retreat seemed inconceivable once: in Bera's first flush of victory, and in the strength of arms around him and the flower of his rage. But this army below was mighty, and it grew mightier still as more Orkhs came up the roads and emerged from the trees. They seemed numberless now.

"Very well," he said. "Think on a way we might take in retreat. But do no more than that. And do not speak of it!"

Esma nodded and he gave her permission to depart.

But as Bera turned his thoughts from retreat to defense, the Orkhs below began to shout, dark and feral, and they struck weapons and shields together in thunder. He supposed they were again steeling themselves to come against him, but when he looked he saw his father had returned.

That great Orkh had disappeared during the last fighting on the slope, perhaps rallying his forces elsewhere. But now he stood again behind the Orkhs massed below, clad in the same black armor and carrying the same black war axe. He held it aloft now, exhorting his legions as he had before.

Bera watched this and an idea flickered into life.

It was interrupted by a voice speaking behind him, that said: "Is that him?"

Bera turned to find Atul standing near him. The Ceorl's

face and armor were dusty and blood-ridden, and he carried the same dented helm under his arm.

"Yes, that is my father," Bera said. "He is a general, or what passes for such among them. His name is Tsov-ar-kan."

Atul studied the Orkh. "You went to him? Before."

"Yes."

"And you came back?"

"Yes."

They stood in silence, watching Bera's father, then Atul said: "I have misjudged you, Ceorl Bera. I am a man enough to admit when I'm shown wrong—whatever other faults I may have. And no, you may not tell me of them. Where did you get this armor?"

"He sent it to me. Long ago."

Atul ran an eye over Bera and laughed. "I can see why you hid it until now. It seems that Orkh had designs for you long ago, yet you refused them even then. I have indeed misjudged you."

Bera nodded. "You have."

Atul grinned. The blood on his face cracked. "Then I say we should have designs for him, Ceorl Bera!" he said. "Listen to me. I have half again as many as yours remaining in my company. Tell me, if yours and mine together can get you down there, to him, can you slay him? Would you? There's no other here who could."

Bera jerked around to look the man fully in the face. It was his idea exactly! Although he'd thought it foolish in the first. The germ of it was his memory of the Orkhs falling back before him in the bloom of his rage: so betraying an instinctive submission to a more powerful Orkh. Perhaps this road ran both ways. Perhaps the death of their commander, Tsov-ar-kan, would undo them.

It was a foolish hope maybe: a last, desperate throw of the dice. But if not this, then what? He had no other plan but to stand here and fight to the end; and he'd promised himself to preserve these lives who remained. Yet he feared the result: he was not the warrior his father was.

"This was my thought as well," he said to Atul, "but my company hadn't the strength left to attempt it."

Atul's grin was gone now and his face had hardened into resolve. "You have the strength now, my friend. I will join mine to yours, and you may lead us."

Bera frowned at this. "Are you certain? I've led my own near to ruin."

"Every captain might say the same today," Atul replied. "The fight is hard and costly. No, you will lead us against your father, Ceorl Bera. You have shown yourself loyal, Orkh or no. I doubt you no longer."

Bera rumbled a small laugh that cleared away some of his misgivings. "It's good I didn't slay you before."

"Well," Atul said, "as to that, it mightn't have been so easy! But yes, I thank you for your forbearance." He bowed to Bera. "Now, shall we strike a telling blow together?"

Bera caught Esma's eye and signaled her closer. "We shall," he said. "But bring your warriors quickly. The Orkhs will make another try soon."

Atul clapped Bera on the shoulder and moved away, then Esma came up and Bera told her of this new plan. As she listened she gazed down the war-strewn slope.

"So he is your father," she said. "Tell me, Ceorl, do you

believe you can slay him, in the end when your sword lies at his throat?"

Bera was silent. Atul had asked the same question of him and he hadn't answered. In truth he had no answer to give, because it seemed to him he wouldn't know the answer until the price of what he meant to do was set before him.

"I will do what I must," he said, and he lifted the Dragon helm to set it upon his head and hide his face from her.

But she didn't press him but moved away to ready the company. Already Bera could hear Atul bringing across his own warriors with many trampings and jinglings of armor and kit. Soon they would merge their companies into one, and Bera would stride down this slope again, sword bared, to challenge his father.

14

OF EARIC AND ZARA, AND AERE

Zara rode south toward the Dragons and their Orkh guardians. Savage glee bloomed in her heart for she knew her time had come at last. After so many failures, and so much shame, all would be put right again by this single wondrous deed to change the world. She laughed beneath her helm, for she would be Queen of Aelfs in time.

Be damned to all who opposed her!

Salf rode ahead, with his first squadron. They would slash a hole in the ring of Orkhs guarding the second Dragon, then hold open a narrow way there long enough for Zara and her second squadron to pass through toward the Trolles controlling the second Dragon. The *kansa* would have to work fast before the Orkhs collapsed on it; but in the end success or failure turned on the Dragons themselves. Would they understand the Aelfs meant to help them? Would they take this opening they were given to free themselves?

None knew.

Zara set these questions aside, for the van of Salf's squadron had reached the ring of Orkhs, bearing down on a single point as she'd ordered. But the coming of the Aelfs was plain to all, and the Orkhs had moved to their own defense: lifting their black shields and bringing sword and spear to hand, and setting themselves to receive a mounted charge.

But this was no assault of cavalry on ready infantry, as would end in ruin for any riders. The cat-sí slowed as they came to the Orkhs and when each reached the ring it swerved sharply left or right, and its rider leaped from the saddle onto the very shields of the Orkhs. All of Salf's first squadron came in this way, throwing themselves on the Dragon's defenders and pitching them over across an ever-widening front. The cat-sí, now unburdened, turned to defend the flanks with tooth and claw.

The battle grew swiftly and the noise of it was like thunder over the field. For Orkh and Aelf were ancient enemies and they fought now in the closest of quarters: one atop the other, each struggling to rise and live. Anything might be a weapon in that terrible melee: knife and sword, boot and helm, fingers and teeth. It was a contest of steel and strength, and the tall figure of Salf rose to stand within it. He shouted to his charges and worked his saber about him, slaying Orkhs who fought to rise against the weight of their armor.

And slowly a way opened in the midst of that first squadron. But it remained only wide enough for two cat-sí to pass through, side by side and their riders pressed knee to knee. Beyond that narrow way lay a long fallow field of tall grass and yellow flowers that led to the second Dragon. Zara urged Te'a there, signaling to her guard and the banner and horn Aelfs to follow her closely.

There was no time to lose.

*

She urged Te'a forward through the riders of her second squadron, for Zara wished now, belatedly, to be first through the gap. But as she passed toward the van, she was dismayed to see many cat-sí halted before the narrow way, unable to pass through.

It was then she saw her error, and she cried aloud in frustration and anguish.

Her riders hadn't struck that gap like the point of a needle, as the woman had said, piercing it and passing through swiftly. They had instead arrived without common purpose: like a flock of sheep seeking to pass a gate. Those arriving later were put at a stand, milling and jostling one another while they waited for those ahead to pass through.

The entrance to the gap grew still more crowded as Zara watched and it was far too late now to form the squadron into column, as plainly she should have before. She swore in her own tongue. The way must be widened: there was no other answer. Worse, it would need to be held open far longer than she'd reckoned.

With the point of her saber and a shout, Zara directed Gar'an to take her guard and others to lend their weight against the Orkhs on the right of the gap. Then she called for those about her to follow the banner. She would take it left, where Salf was battling a phalanx of Orkhs that had come up from another part of the ring. Zara understood now she'd sent too few with the Second to break the ring, but it mattered not: she would make good on the mistake and then ride to the Dragon.

Arriving directly behind Salf, Zara leaped from Te'a's back

into a small oasis of empty ground. The others dismounted around her, and together they joined the fight against the phalanx. She wouldn't stay long, only what it took to get the balance of her riders through the gap. She had bigger things to do than play this small part in the day.

But the Orkhs refused to play their own part to her liking. The phalanx remained stubborn, and many of the Orkhs who'd survived the first assault were gathering to counterattack.

Damn it! I don't have time for this!

Zara looked back to see many riders waiting still at entrance to the gap. Far too many, and these only sat their cat-sí, watching the fighting rage around them. Zara swore. The balance had to be tipped here, and swiftly, or this venture to free the Dragons would end in the destruction of her *kansa*.

She turned to the horn-aelf and ordered him to sound rally on banner. That was a start: the Aelfs here were too thinly spread to fight effectively. Then she moved toward Salf, pushing her way through the melee. She stumbled on bodies, both Orkh and Aelf.

Move, Zara! You can't stay long!

Then she was surprised by a huge cat-sí, tawny and riderless. It crossed close in front of Zara, moving toward the Aelfs facing the phalanx. It leaped them, twisted nimbly in the air, and swung its heavy haunches around to crash sidelong into the Orkhs. The creature's great weight, and the force of its coming, flung the first rank of the phalanx back on the second, and the second on the third, shattering the cohesion of the formation. Zara saw now the cat-sí was Dreng: Earic's mount.

It was well done, but the Orkhs' disarray wouldn't last. Zara shouted at Salf to order a charge but he was too far and didn't hear. Still, the tall Aelf was an ancient warrior of many battles and knew what to do: he swung his saber high and shouted, ordering a quick charge into the Orkhs' broken ranks.

Perhaps the tide was turning.

Zara looked around for Earic and saw him lying on the ground behind her, in the direction of the gap. He writhed on the grass, his mouth stretched wide, but the screams were lost in the clamor. The impetuous Human had surely desired Dreng to attack the Orkhs before himself leaping from the cat-sí's back, as he'd seen her warriors do. Zara would have laughed at this, had the leap not hurt him so cruelly. But that leap had been wisdom, for Dreng's impact with the phalanx would have surely crushed the man's leg before pitching him head-first into the Orkhs to be slain.

She crossed to him and reached down a hand. "Well done, Lord Earic! That was a needful stroke!"

He took her hand and brought himself up to stand on one leg. Pain sweat stood bright on his brow. "How do I call him back?" he asked her.

"Wish it," she said. "He will hear you." Then she looked back toward the gap. It seemed to have widened now and a much larger part of her squadron was through to the field beyond. But it wasn't nearly enough, not yet. This place was a trap for her dreams: she needed to get out.

Suddenly Earic pointed over her shoulder: "Ware!"

Zara spun to see four Orkhs moving close to her. She

brought up the saber even as she summoned Te'a silently. The cat-sí sent back a smeared, anxious image of hard fighting with Dreng.

Zara cut at the nearest Orkh but it lifted its scimitar to knock the saber aside. She set her feet properly then brought the blade back to parry the beast's return swing.

The other Orkhs moved closer, spreading out to either side. Zara thought to step back, giving herself more room, but Earic came up then to stand beside her. He held a sword but awkwardly, as if the handle ill-fit his hand. When he was slow to parry a blow, Zara lashed out with the saber to deflect the Orkh's blade.

Earic stepped back. "I'm sorry!" he shouted. "I'm no good with this thing! I'm a tent officer, not a warrior!"

Zara didn't reply: her mind and eyes were on the Orkhs. But soon three Aelfs came near to drive them away and she turned to Earic.

"I must go!" she said, raising the saber to point toward the second Dragon. "Our time grows short!"

Earic's face closed against her. She ignored him and turned to look for Salf. He wasn't near. She grabbed the arm of a passing Aelf carrying a bloody blade and a look of fear.

"Where is *Ritzar* Kve-ma?" she asked him. "He was here! Just now!"

"He lies there, lady!" the Aelf said, pointing. "He is wounded and cannot rise."

Zara shoved the Aelf away in frustration and looked toward the gap again. Somewhat more than half her squadron was through now, but some who waited still had drawn their sabers to join the fighting.

No, damn you! Go through! Go! Her time was bleeding out, one irretrievable drop at a time.

Earic was before her again, seeking her gaze with his. "You can't leave us!" he shouted, waving his hands at her.

She avoided his eye. *Of course I can leave you, foolish Human.* But aloud she said: "I must! Salf will command here."

Earic shook his head. He looked frightened and dismayed. "Salf can't lead! He's fallen! Who else can command here but you?"

Zara grew savage. This was her moment to seize with both hands, and it was the greatest that might ever come to her. She refused to be denied: not by Earic, not by anyone.

"You will lead!" she said. "I will give the order!"

His face was aghast now. "Me? I can't walk! I'm worthless without Dreng, and even with him I'm no damned good with this sword!" He held out the weapon to her as if he didn't know what it was.

She knew these things were true, but she refused to yield to them. Life had been unjust to her. That thing she'd done was so long ago, yet it hung over her still like a black storm no wind could carry away, pouring an endless rain of shame on her head.

She jerked the saber angrily. *Be damned to the gap!* She would go to the Dragon. She would free it, and get the glory she deserved.

Earic seemed to see this resolve in Her eyes for he limped closer. His mouth twisted with pain and determination.

"You have to hold the way open!" he shouted. "If you don't,

they'll die!" He stabbed a finger at the gap and the riders waiting there still. "All of us will die! *She'll* die!"

Zara didn't answer. Her mind was ablaze with denial. *No! No! I cannot stay!*

"Zara!" he cried. "Look at me! Look at me!"

She did.

His eyes were anguished. He thrust his hands at her in supplication, the sword held still in one. "Zara, have you ever done anything just for someone else?"

She stared back at him, outraged. Had *he*? Yes, he had. He'd given much, perhaps everything he had, to protect that woman. He'd sacrificed his station in life and his health. And when his army found him, they would take his freedom also and maybe his life. He'd given everything he was for that woman and now he stood here looking at Zara as if the gods themselves had turned their faces from him.

Have you ever done anything just for someone else? Had she? Did it matter?

It did. She knew that in her heart. It mattered because all of this mattered. The Orkhs must be stopped. The Dragons must be freed. Some here must live to go on with the world.

Why shouldn't that be me? I had such plans! I have waited so long!

All these thoughts came to Zara in a moment, and when that moment had passed she knew she couldn't go. There was no one else who could command here. No one else to stand against this growing disaster that threatened them all.

There was only her.

And hope died within her. She would not be queen someday. She would not rise above her station as the least of her father's brood, and the one who had shamed his house. She would remain who she was: only Zara.

But even as she mourned the death of her long-held hopes, a fire kindled elsewhere within her. She could make still a reckoning upon the Orkhs their children's children would remember.

That at least was left to her.

"Take the banner," she said to Earic, "and my horn-aelf. My part of the *kansa* will follow you with them, and with Dreng. Go now! Bring them through and free the Dragon!"

Zara held his gaze as she said this. Too many Aelfs had been lost already, yesterday and today, and it was her doing. She would pay her penance here. Earic nodded in understanding, and it seemed to her also gratitude. She signed for the banner and the horn to follow him, ceding to him the outward tokens of her authority. Dreng arrived a moment later, his fur black with Orkh-blood.

She helped Earic up to the saddle. "Lead them to victory," she said. "We will hold the way open, if steel and valor may do so."

Earic made no reply, but touched his heart to her before wheeling Dreng to bound away toward the gap. She watched the banner and horn Aelfs urge their own cat-sí after him. Neither Aelf looked back, content it seemed to follow another, even if Human. Zara supposed the rest of the *kansa* might fall away just as swiftly. The thought gave her grief.

She felt a tug at her thoughts and turned to find Te'a waiting nearby. She crossed to the cat-sí, determined to give what remained of herself to the task of keeping the way open. Sensing this mood, Te'a pranced and threw off a tart eagerness for battle. But as Zara lifted a foot to the stirrup, something else came from the cat-sí also: something unlooked for.

It was an image, clear and bright, of an unweaned kit with Te'a's coloring or near to it. The kit growled and pulled at the tail of a far larger cat-sí, perhaps its mother. Puzzled by this, Zara paused with her foot lodged in the stirrup. But then it came to her that Te'a was offering Zara her true name.

Zara hadn't sought to know that name when the cat-sí was first given to her, although the beast allowed itself to be ridden even so. She had believed then it was her right to ride cat-sí, and to make them her servants in work and war. Other, lesser Aelfs might devote themselves to their mounts: she would not.

But now it was different, or she was different. Or the lifting of some burden now permitted her to see as she hadn't before. She accepted the image and when she did, she found a feeling came with it: a sense of fierce determination of purpose, playful in kittenhood, but which had carried forward into the greater matters of life and war. This also was the cat-sí's name.

Zara pulled her foot from the stirrup and stepped back. "I'm sorry," she said to Te'a, meaning much more but finding she lacked the words.

Te'a turned then and she placed the crown of her great head against Zara's chest and she pushed lightly. Zara rubbed the cat-sí's cheeks, wordlessly, then returned to the saddle, where she swung herself up and tied herself in. They would fight together until the end.

*   *   *

It was true Earic would have been useless without Dreng. The tawny cat-sí warrior was a courageous mount and immensely strong: he carried Earic when he couldn't walk, defended him when he couldn't use a sword, and covered him with authority when he dared command Aelfs in place of Lady Zara. Earic felt already a powerful bond with the beast.

He and Dreng were beyond the gap now, standing on a fallow field within the great ring of Orkhs. The Aelfin riders Earic had found here were leaderless and disorganized, and he had used Dreng and the presence of the banner and horn Aelfs to assert command. He organized the Aelfs into small troops each with a leader, and he sent these farther into the field to wait, making room for those coming through the gap behind. This arrangement had worked well, and now Aelfs and cat-sí moved through the gap without pause.

Best of all, Dreng had known somehow to find Aere in the crowd of cat-sí that milled beyond the gap; and now she waited by the banner-aelf, sitting atop the bay still. Earic wheeled Dreng to her.

"Aere!" he said. "Take all who are through and attack those nearest Trolles." He pointed to them. They moved in a tight group by the Dragon's foreleg, pressing their over-long lances against its hide. "You have enough here at least to harry them," he said. "I'll send more after you, and come myself when I can!"

It grieved Earic to send Aere into harm, after he'd worked

so hard and given so much to keep her from danger. But there seemed no other way now: their assault on the Trolles must begin now, before the fighting here drew in and destroyed Zara's remaining strength for no greater purpose. But also this was fit work for Aere, for Earic knew well the fire and determination that lived within her. If any could do this, she would.

Yet her eyes on him now were wide with apprehension. Earic smiled encouragement to her and lifted a hand to make a fist of strength. She saw this and nodded, then wheeled the bay toward the Dragon and called out to the Aelfs around her to follow.

Earic turned to the banner-aelf. "Go!" he said, pointing to Aere. "Follow her wherever she goes!"

The Aelf obeyed, urging her cat-sí after the bay and taking the scarlet and green with her. Then, unbidden by Earic, the horn-aelf sounded a high three-note call that rose over the din of fighting; and Earic's heart lifted to see the Aelfin riders he'd sent into the field now send their cat-sí racing after the banner and Aere. He nodded to himself, satisfied: the main work of the day had begun at last.

Before turning Dreng back to the fighting, Earic watched Aere's receding back. Even riding on the bay she seemed far too small and far too frail beneath the awful loom of the Dragon, and Earic yearned to go after her and call her back to safety. But he was needed here, to bring through the rest of Zara's squadron; and she was needed there, to find a way to victory under the Dragon.

When he turned back to the gap, he saw it had narrowed once again. Riders pushed through it still, but only two could come at once and even these jostled one another to win free. A large part of Zara's second squadron waited on the far side still to come through. They were needed at the Dragon and swiftly: the weight of their sabers and cat-sí mounts might carry the day for Aere.

He saw immediately why the way had narrowed: a broad wedge of Orkhs had come up from another part of the ring to push against the Aelfs holding the south side. Still more hurried over the fields behind, drawn by the battle for the gap. They were many and Earic wondered for the first time whether he would survive this fight. Perhaps Aere could escape, in the end, through a weakness in the ring. He yearned still to follow her, but knew his work now was this wedge from the south.

At its point was an enormous Orkh: a giant of its kind. Its armor was the blackest of steel, giving back no part of the afternoon sun; and it wore on its long arm a black shield fully the height of a tall Aelf; and a broad, curved scimitar lay in its hand. The Aelfs had retreated before that great Orkh, leaving a ruin of bodies behind and pressing their backs against the fragile gap.

Earic hesitated. This Orkh was not for him. His sword arm was weak and unhandy, and the pain in his leg, now risen to his hips, made even his seat on Dreng infirm. But he'd done much wrong of late, and he wouldn't add to the miserable tally by abandoning the Aelfs here. He would do what he could, whatever that might be.

Earic understood now somewhat of his emerging link with Dreng and he gave the cat-sí an image of standing defiantly before the giant Orkh. The response from the cat-sí was immediate: Dreng sprang forward to weave a cunning way through the melee, aiming for the Orkh. The noise of battle was tremendous here: the very air seemed fearsome and deadly, and death might come from any quarter, swift and unseen. Earic drew his sword, but it seemed puny and effectless in his hand, and he was afraid.

But Dreng preserved him. The cat-sí was a wily creature: stepping lightly here, bulling through there, always sparing his rider the worst of the melee. Until at last they emerged into a clearing of bloody grass before the great Orkh. Earic could see now its dark armor was scarred and dented by a thousand blows, and the scimitar it swung was crude and unadorned: a common tool brought to the work of war. The eyes of the beast were hidden from Earic by a squat, brutish helm, but he knew that bitter gaze now fixed upon him.

The field grew quiet then, or so it seemed to Earic, as if all here paused in their terrible labor. Then the great Orkh spoke in its own tongue and it lifted high the scimitar so the blade became like a dark comet in the sky, portending doom. And behind the giant the lesser Orkhs began their war chants: harsh, roaring, and pitiless, and the air quivered under the sound.

All seemed to watch Earic now, but he knew he couldn't duel this Orkh, even on Dreng: he was no warrior to slay Orkhs. But he was also no longer Earic the Master of Cenred's Scouts, who made plans in a tent and pushed counters over a map. That time was gone. Now he was Lord Earic Eadwulfing, Ceorl of Aelfin Cavalry.

He was a war-leader, and he would lead.

*

So he lifted the sword in his hand, as he'd seen Zara do. The blade was useless to him as a weapon of war, but that was not his purpose for it now. He pulled at Dreng's reins to whirl the cat-sí in a tight circle, and drew breath to cry out for the Aelfs' allegiance over the chanting of the Orkhs.

But he stopped, the breath held, and turned in the saddle to look north. For he could hear now the sound of strange horns. It wasn't the flat bray of Orkhish war horns, nor the high trills of Aelf-kind. Instead it was a sonorous drone unlike any sound he'd heard before, even the Dragons. It carried on and on, growing louder, until every head, Orkh and Aelf, turned in wonder. Then, from atop Dreng, Earic saw what lay on the fields and he shouted for joy.

The Dweorg had come.

It was not all of them, surely, for they held still the left of the line. But even so their numbers darkened the grass to the north and the east; and they came swiftly against the ring of Orkhs under banners of black and gold. Earic laughed: for the Dweorg had indeed chaffed under Cenred's yoke, and the coming of these Dragons was a temptation far too great for their proud souls to bear. Cenred likely knew nothing of this mutiny: or if he did, the Aetheling raged in his tent even now.

Let him. We will win this war here.

A new fire came to Earic and he felt Dreng take it up eagerly. The Dweorgs' attack would slow greatly the flow of Orkhs coming from elsewhere in the ring, and those here already would cast a wary eye elsewhere. Earic turned back to the great Orkh and he lifted the sword again, now with greater confidence.

"The tide has turned!" he called to the Aelfs about him, hoping it was so. "The Dweorg have come and the Trolles are assailed! Keep the way open and the day is ours!"

Even as he shouted these words Earic feared they would fall on deaf ears. But then Dreng settled back on his haunches to rise and rear beneath him. High the cat-sí rose, and higher still, huge and tall: stretching even above the tall helm of the giant Orkh. And Dreng brought out his claws to rake at the air and scream a challenge. Courage and determination flooded into Earic from the cat-sí, filling his soul, and he lifted the sword high to make the call of his House.

The Aelfs were moved from their dread. They lifted their sabers and shook off weariness and fear. Determination returned to their faces. Leaders and their Seconds, recalling their duty, reached out to pull warriors into sturdy ranks. Earic whirled Dreng and shouted encouragement to all who stood near, calling for swiftness and courage. He was pleased with himself now: perhaps the tide had truly turned here.

There was one thing more he could do to ensure this. Earic turned Dreng toward the great Orkh, summoning as he did an instruction to his mind. But the cat-sí needed no command. Knowing his rider's mind, or only the need of the moment, Dreng pushed off with his back legs and lunged to slam his broad shoulder into the great Orkh's massive shield.

The Orkh was truly a giant of its kind, but the greater weight of the cat-sí told and the Orkh staggered backward under the blow. It threw the scimitar and the black shield about itself, struggling to keep its feet; but in the end the constriction of its own steel armor overbore it, and the beast toppled with a roar of protest into the Orkhs behind.

That was enough. With a shout, the once-beleaguered Aelfs surged forward, giving the giant Orkh and those behind it, and beneath it, no time to recover. And as the Aelfs came forward, they drew away from the gap and it opened wider behind them.

Earic ordered Dreng there and together they stood by the exit, urging the remaining Aelfs of Zara's squadron to move through swiftly, and to gallop on to Aere at the Dragon. Each Aelf who passed him carried a little higher Earic's hope the suffering and death around him was not in vain.

Soon the last of the Zara's squadron was through and it was time for Earic to go to Aere. He paused to look over the roaring melee on the north side of the gap and saw Zara there. She rode Te'a still. The cat-sí bucked and spun in a dense crowd of Orkhs, but Zara kept her seat, calling out to those around her with words Earic couldn't hear.

The Aelf fought like a creature possessed: turning this way and that, her eyes seeing everywhere at once and the long saber flashing in the sunlight: cutting, blocking, striking, shoving away. Earic found he was happy for Zara, even in her extremity. Not because she fought so well, but because she'd laid aside something she didn't need. Something that held her back even as it goaded her forward.

And as he looked at her, she raised her eyes to meet his. It was only a moment, for a moment was all she could spare. Earic raised his hand to her and spoke words he knew she couldn't hear.

"Go well, Lady Zara," he said. "Your sacrifice will not be forgotten."

But she did not raise her own hand to him, or make any sign of acknowledgment, before the fighting swirled her away again.

Earic turned his gaze to the Dweorg now and saw they were engaged with much of the ring to the north and east, stopping the flow of new Orkhs coming to Zara's company from there. Then he looked north, to the first Dragon. It had moved deeper into the fields, toward the town and the pass, and Cenred's legions fled before it. If this second Dragon couldn't be freed, defeat would come swiftly.

Earic turned Dreng toward the Aere and the Dragon, and he urged the cat-sí to find the uttermost limit of his speed.

The Dragon lay two hundred yards south, and although Earic stood as well as he could in the stirrups, he saw nothing of Aere there. Too many cat-sí late through the gap ran between here and there. So new imaginings came to torment him as he rode: Aere lying broken on the grass, struck down by a hammering fist or impaled on a long lance. He drove Dreng harder and the cat-sí responded with swiftness that made the wind sing in Earic's ears.

Halfway to the Dragon the view opened suddenly, and what Earic saw there took his breath. His heart thundered in his chest.

What is this?

He saw that Aere hadn't taken the first cohort of Aelfs and cat-sí straight in, to attack the Trolles directly. She had instead done something far more ingenuous. She and her Aelfs now rode their mounts around the Trolles in a ever-revolving wheel, riding even under the belly of the beast and around its great leg before emerging into the open again.

And they harried the Trolles as they rode. Earic watched as two cat-sí darted inward so their riders could strike with swift sabers before dashing clear again, unhurt. Earic grasped Aere's tactic immediately and it was brilliant: she was goading the goaders.

And so she forced the Trolles to choose. They couldn't control the Dragon with their long lances while at the same time defending themselves against the quick, slashing strikes of the Aelfs. One of those things must be abandoned in favor of the other, and Aere had wagered she could provoke the Trolles into abandoning the Dragon.

Earic believed this also: for Trolle-kind were dull brutes, driven more by instinct and emotion than by the small intellect they possessed. Soon the beasts would suffer no further injury without responding in kind.

That time seemed to come already, for a few of the long dark lines that were the Trolles' lances drew back from the dragon's flank, and they came down toward the earth, slowly, their blades flashing like sparks of silver sunlight. Down and down they came, until they were leveled against that turning wheel of riders. But these weapons, though great, were unhandy: they were too long and too unwieldy even for the strength of Trolles, and the cat-sí avoided them.

Now Earic could see Aere riding the bay within the great wheel, just now coming out from under the shadow of the Dragon. The scarlet and green swallowtail floated after her, and she vexed the Trolles with her longbow, driving white-fletched shafts deep into their gray hide.

Earic was aflame with happiness for her, and pride. He shoved aside the pain of his leg and stood on Dreng's stirrups to thrust a fist at the heavens as he rode, shouting Aere's name as if she could hear him and respond. For she was so much more the warrior than he—far more. And she showed it now, bringing a bitter taste of war to the Trolles. Should victory come here, Aere could claim as great a share in it as any.

And he would take her for his wife, if she would have him.

But victory had not come yet. Earic drove Dreng to the front of the riders approaching the Dragon and signed for them to follow. He led them past the first group of Trolles and Aere's wheel, onward to the Trolles that walked by the Dragon's tall hip. Their long lances goaded the beast still.

But like the others, these too had lain hard on the horns of a dilemma. Would they go to the aid of their kin now harried by Aere, and sacrifice their own control of the Dragon? Or would they hold their stations here and watch the fight ahead unfold as it would? So far, they'd chosen to watch.

Earic was determined to make their dilemma more dire still, leading his Aelfs into a second wheel of death. Round and round the Trolles they rode and the Aelfs turned inward, in ones and twos, to slash at the beasts and yodel their keen calls of war. When Earic rode into the cool under the Dragon, its wide belly loomed over him like a living roof and he marveled such a wonder would come to him.

When the end came, it was swift. Under merciless pressure from Aere's Aelfs, the first group of Trolles wholly abandoned the Dragon to turn their lances on the Aelfs, plying those awkward weapons as well as they could. And the Trolles within Earic's wheel began to bring their own lances down.

"Now!" Earic shouted to the Dragon and waving his arms at it. "Now is the time! Free yourself!"

The beast certainly did not hear him, but it did see well enough the consternation of its tormentors. Unhindered now by the prick of lance blades against its left side, the Dragon brought down its serpentine head and snapped at the Trolles with its great jaws. Long yellow teeth severed heads and cut massive bodies in half, and the Dragon whipped its head to fling the pieces far over the fields.

That was enough: it was time to leave and let the Dragon do its work.

Earic turned Dreng toward Aere's wheel, looking for her. He came to the horn-aelf first and jabbed a finger back toward the gap.

"Sound withdrawal!" he shouted. "We must leave!"

The Aelf bought the horn to his lips and blew a high, twittering call that he repeated twice more. Immediately cat-sí broke from the wheels to run back over the fields toward Zara and the others fighting still at the gap. As they streamed past him, Earic spared a moment to look and he saw no Aelf or cat-sí fallen beneath the Dragon. Their victory here had been complete.

As the Aelfs left, the Dragon, now free of any Trolle, threw back its massive head to utter a long honking call that made the air in Earic's ears shudder. The note was exultant, but also terribly and fearfully angry. The first Dragon, ranging far ahead, turned its head at that sound and it was then Earic knew the two were mates.

For the first sprang about with a leap beyond what Earic would have credited in so vast a creature, and it bounded back with a vigor born surely of joy and rage alike. The earth shuddered and the heavens rang with the violence of its calls. Earic didn't envy the Orkhs the swift justice that would surely come to them.

Earic drew Dreng around and urged him back toward the gap. He fully expected more hard fighting before the Aelfs won clear of the Orkhs, but as he and Dreng drew nearer where the gap had been, he saw the Orkhs already ran south. Fleeing from the wrath of the Dragons, and leaving behind them a wide trail of dropped weapons and kit of war.

Earic smiled then: for the victory, and for his vindication. But most of all he smiled for Aere, who rode toward him now on the bay, her face afire with joy.

15

OF BERA

Bera watched as Esma used a sure hand to shepherd the remains of his company into ranks again. She had been a wise choice. A few yards away, Atul and his own Second placed their warriors, encouraging each with a few quiet words. The two companies were set together now, side by side, so no difference could be seen between them; and the whole was no larger than what Bera had begun the day with.

When Atul and Esma nodded readiness, Bera stepped forward to speak to the companies as if they were one, and his own. Now he didn't raise the sword, and he raised his voice but a little, letting his height and his conviction carry the words to them.

"Warriors!" he said. "Many of us have fallen today! Too many. Some we knew long and well. We honor them. But we who remain must fight on. I know you're battle-worn. I know you're tired and blood-sick. And these Dragons yonder are a mystery none looked for. But even so we must go down to meet the enemy again."

There was a stir at this, but no one spoke aloud.

Now Bera raised this voice. "But lest you think this a

doomed charge, I will tell you this! That great Orkh down there, the one in black armor like mine." He pointed. "He is my father!"

There was a greater stir now but Bera couldn't divine its mood. Would they turn on him finally, now that Dudda didn't stand by his side? Had they had enough of their bungling half-Orkh commander? Perhaps so, but all he could do now was press on and hope.

"He is my father!" Bera said again, louder now. "But he's also my enemy! *Our* enemy! And I mean challenge him! Orkh to Orkh, sword to sword! And I mean to—" He paused then. What did he mean to do? Could he truly slay his own father?

"I mean to defeat him in single combat!" he said finally, avoiding the question. "So I ask you now for a last labor! Will you come with me? Will you get me there, to him?"

Bera stopped then and waited, hoping. His question to them hanging still in the air, unanswered. Then his heart fell as some in the ranks turned their backs on him, as if to watch some commotion behind them. Did they see the first sparks of rebellion against him? Had he pushed them too far? Did he ask too much?

Then, suddenly and unlooked for, the banner pole rose in the midst of his part of this new company, borne aloft by many reaching hands. Up and up it came and Bera saw the pole carried a new standard.

It was made from pale cloth that might have been some-one's shirt once, and when the pole stood straight, a puff of wind caught the cloth to unfurl it. Bera saw there the letters "BB" drawn in blunt lines, perhaps with the charred point of a stick; and surmounting these letters was a sketch made in the same blunt lines, yet cleverly made. It was the image of a great black helm trailing a twisting scrap of cloth.

At the sight of their new standard a cheer rose from both companies; and Bera's heart leaped in his chest and he cried out for the joy of it. He had a place now: he'd been accepted. Not as Human—for that had been a fool's errand from the start—but for what he was and what he had done.

A bright new energy rose to fill him, and it was cleaner and more wholesome than the rage. And this pleased him, for he saw now there were other well-springs of purpose and power within him apart from the rage. Springs that surely rose from his mother's people. He had much to do to bring together the two halves of himself, Orkh and Human, and he looked forward to doing it.

But there was work here first. Bera drew the sword his father had given him and lifted it in his hand. With the other he held aloft the black helm, trailing still the strip of dirty white cloth.

"We are *borkas*!" he cried. "Warriors for each other, perilous and strong! These Orkhs below fear us now!"

This might have even been true, for the Orkhs had lingered strangely long at the foot of the slope. Even the urgings of his father had moved them little. It occurred to Bera that perhaps the day had gone somewhat better than he'd believed, and the Orkhs too were sorely battered. But he knew this reprieve wouldn't last. They would come in time and in greater force, and when they did they would sweep from the ridge all who remained here.

Bera searched for more to say to these warriors, thinking it was expected, but he found there was nothing that suited. He intended this to be his fight now, and they would have to find inspiration in what he did, not what he said. So he donned the helm again and put his arm into the black shield. Then he turned from them to stride down the slope, sword in hand, to where the Orkhs waited.

He didn't call the charge, for he knew now they would follow him. Nor did he put himself into the first rank of shields, as he had before. Rather he wished his father to see him, and to come out to meet him here on this torn ground between armies, so the lives coming behind him might be spared. He had little doubt that great Orkh would be drawn out so, for Bera's own *orkushna* demanded this meeting, and he was his father's son.

The Orkhs were drawn into ranks again, with their shields set together; and Tsov-ar-kan paced behind them, exhorting his warriors in a voice of command that carried up the slope. But when he saw Bera coming toward him, he stopped to watch from within the tall black helm he wore now. Bera called out in challenge and raised the black sword to shake it, bidding his father come.

The Orkh did come. He pushed forward, battering his warriors aside with the shield on his arm, until he stood alone at the front: tall, dark, and forbidding. Bera halted twenty paces from him. Now he could see a design was laid into the Orkh's black armor in the same manner as his own. But whereas Bera's was red and formed a Dragon, the Orkh's was green and seemed to form a demon-like creature, perhaps a fiend living near Orkhish lands or in their legends. The facets of it were brilliant in the sun, so the fiend seemed to leer at Bera with malevolence.

In his right hand Tsov-ar-kan held the great axe still, but now he cast this aside and drew a sword from his waist. Its blade was the same make as Bera's, but it was longer and broader matching the Orkh's greater height and breadth. And on his left arm he wore the shield, and it too was much as Bera's, but for the green of its inlaid design.

And so they stood facing one another: alike yet different, each with an army at his back. Each looking out from the depths of his helm, wondering at the other.

It was Bera who spoke first. "You may not enter these lands!" he said in a voice that carried to all standing near. "Go back to your own lands and do not return. These are my people and I will defend them to the last!"

"Your people?" the Orkh replied. His voice was scornful now and harsh, sounding to Bera more like a crow's. "You have chosen your people poorly, *sashna*. I will prevail here. Surely even you can see this. Look you there: even now my brother's Dragons ravage the west. No, you are wrong, *sashna*. I will enter these lands you call yours and I will take them for mine. I will rule these weak creatures you call your people and be their master."

He stepped closer to Bera. "But I can be a generous master when I choose, so I will permit you to choose again because you have become a true warrior today. Perhaps one worthy of ruling by my side. We will see in time. Come to me, *sashna*. Come to me now, or you will die like the rest of your broken army."

Bera gave no answer. Instead, moving with calmness he

didn't feel, he shook the shield to settle better on his arm, then he turned to look back at the warriors waiting above him. The banner-woman had brought the new standard forward to thrust the spike of its pole into the earth close behind him. Behind her the two companies stood in their silent ranks, shields held high. Atul stood some way to Bera's right, watching him in the hush that had fallen over the ridge.

All waited for his answer.

Bera knew the Scales of Fate hung finely balanced here between victory and defeat. Each word, each gesture, and each action and intent tipped that Scale one way or the other, until all here had laid their weights upon the pans. Then the doom of this place and time would be known.

Bera knew where he would set his own weights.

He turned back to his father and said to him in a clear voice that again carried to all, "I refuse you still! There is nothing here for you. Leave this place and do not return."

As he said this, Bera pointed with the sword toward the Southlands whence the Orkhs had come.

"Your loyalties are misplaced, *sashna*," Tsov-ar-kan replied, "but you have indeed become a warrior. This pleases me. Now it will be a worthy deed to slay you with my own hands."

Saying this, the great Orkh raised his black shield and set it against his shoulder. Then he advanced on Bera, covering the ground between them with long strides.

Bera lifted his own shield and stepped down the slope to meet the Orkh. But as they closed he felt a chill of doubt. Could he truly best this battle-hardened warrior? Or would he be struck down and slain out of hand? Perhaps challenging this Orkh was yet another foolish mistake: born not of naive thoughtlessness, as at the hedgehog, but of arrogance unearned.

But whether this was mistake or no, it was now far too late to back away: Bera had made his choice and now the Scale was swinging.

He stepped down toward his father crouched behind the Dragon shield, moving lightly and remembering his footwork. But when they came together there was no dance of sword and shield. Instead the great Orkh crossed the last yards between them swiftly and raised the black sword to batter it on the face of Bera's shield. It was a long rain of hard blows that made sword and shield alike ring like bells.

Bera drew back, looking for an opening to riposte. But his father gave him none, following him across the slope to press his savage and potent attack. It was plain the Orkh meant to overwhelm Bera and unnerve him, forcing a fatal mistake early.

But Bera wouldn't be cowed so. That time was over. He leaned into the shield and pushed with his legs to bull-rush his father, crashing past the Orkh's sword and shoving him off-balance. It was a crude tactic, and did no real harm, but it put an end to the furious assault. Already Bera's shield arm was sore, and the quick rush and shield-blow had reawakened the wound in his leg.

He drew back again, wary, keeping his shield held high; but this time his father didn't follow. Instead the Orkh shook off his own shield and let it fall to the battle-scarred earth.

"I am not a common warrior," he said to Bera, "nor are you after me, *sashna*. Let us contest this as our grand-sires did, in the days of glory." The Orkh unlaced his great helm and drew it from his head. This also he cast aside and it rolled some way down the slope to rest on the dust.

The Orkh's face was as Bera remembered it: proud and stern, even noble in its savage way, and looking very much like his own. But a dire light shone in his father's red eyes, and Bera knew was the Orkh's own *orkushna*, loosed by their fighting. Bera's rage rose eagerly to meet it and he too cast away his helm and shield. Then they stepped together again to trade blows with swords alone.

Bera now let the anger rule his arm, and it carried him far beyond what he thought possible. He matched the great Orkh blow for blow and their swords rang as they fought across the slope: thrust and parry, swing and block, move and counter. The few blows Bera could not dodge or parry were blunted or turned aside by the hard scales of the Dragon armor.

After a flurry of blows from which neither took advantage, Tsov-ar-kan backed away to lower his sword. The green demon on his armor glittered at Bera with ill-intent.

"Tell me, *sashna*," his father said. "Did your mother speak of how you came to be? No, I thought not. That would be a hard burden for a Human child bear." He sneered this. "I will tell you of it."

Bera's breath hurt his throat and he was tired, and his leg ached, but even so he thought of attacking the Orkh again. For he feared to hear what his father might say: there were things he didn't wish to know. But there remained yet a quiet part in him, beneath or beside the rage; and this stilled him with the thought there might be things he needed to know, whether he wished it or not.

Tsov-ar-kan spoke into the quiet between armies. "I took your mother for a slave in The Great War," he said. "Of which this one is yet but a pale shadow. We roamed far into Human lands then, slaking our thirst with blood. Our *orkushna* was great and it drove us like fire. She was a warrior and I took her in battle, making her serve me in my tent. Yes, the same as you saw. Your mother knew that tent well, *sashna*. But she was wily and sly, and strong, and she escaped me." His father laughed harshly. "She could have been a she-Orkh."

Bera listened keenly now, his urge to attack forgotten. He hadn't known his mother was a warrior once: she hadn't told him. He felt a fierce pride for her.

"I did not pursue your mother," his father said, "for I knew she was with child. In time I would have an Orkh of my own kin among my enemy. An Orkh who understood my enemy's ways like no other might. A spy among them I could get in no other way. So I let her go, so that one day I would have you." He gestured to Bera with the sword. "I sent you in secret these Orkhish tools of war you wear now. Armor as mine, sword as mine, shield as mine. That you might know me when we met."

"You let me go," Bera said, divining this only now. "Before."

"Yes. I believed you would return to me when you came to know your *orkushna*. I believed you had only a thin veil of Human taint to throw off and you would join in secret with me. I was wrong, and now three times you have refused me. I will not be shamed further by a fourth. You know the truth now, *sashna*. Now you will take it into the earth with you."

The Orkh lifted the black sword again.

But Bera didn't move, nor did he reply. He knew now his youthful fancies about his father were lies. That despite the Orkh's pretensions to a crude kind of gentility, he was like any other Orkh: brutish, warlike, and driven by a feral barbarism that knew no greater impulse than its own dark rage. This had been a shock to Bera, in the beginning, but since then he'd come to understand its inevitable truth.

But now he knew it was worse than that. This Orkh had never seen Bera, his own son, as more than a tool to be used: a spy to be wooed with gifts and promises, and then moved across the board like a pawn to serve the Orkh's own dire ends. Pawns were sacrificed at need. And then there was what this Orkh had done to his mother . . .

Rage as Bera had never known came to him then. It was a mighty deluge no force of mortal will could cage or turn aside. It picked him up entire and carried him to a place he'd never been: a place where nothing could touch him and defeat was impossible. It frightened him even as it exalted him, and the quiet place in him seemed to shrink and flee before it, leaving behind a frothing torrent of power searching for outlet.

Yet as Bera lifted the sword, he saw the rage was different now. It was not merely a wanton force seeking to rampage without scruple, as it had been before. Instead, it seemed a righteous anger. For all its fire, it did not urge him to seek destruction for destruction's sake, but rather to right an ancient wrong. It was purer now: cleaner and more purposeful. And Bera knew then that quiet place in him had not fled. It had instead gone into that flood and altered it.

For he was Human, also.

He smiled. The sword felt light in his hand and the black armor seemed comforting and supple about him, as if grown from his very skin to ward him against harm. He drifted toward his father on cunning feet, offering a feint then a hard thrust to a shoulder gap. But the Orkh wasn't fooled and he struck the blade away.

Bera pressed harder. Their blades clashed and grated. He worked on the Orkh's guard, seeking a way past it, letting the new righteous force of his rage drive his arm. Once, as his father stepped back from a flurry of blows, Bera saw for the first time doubt in the Orkh's eyes.

Good! Let him fear me!

He struck again and again: a hard rain of swift blows that kept his father ever on the defensive, much as the great Orkh had sought to do to him. Atul shouted once, but whether it was in warning or encouragement Bera didn't know. He had no thought to spare from the swing of the blades and the motions of his foe. His *orkushna* drove him still and it was powerful beyond anything he'd known, but it was not reckless now or hateful. It had become an alloy of Orkh and Human, as Bera was himself: drawing something essential from each while allowing neither to rule completely.

The Orkh retreated before Bera, taking many unparried blows to his black armor. Chips of green garnet spun away in the sunlight and the demon became less fearful. Finally the Orkh's heel caught on a hummock of grass and he fell, landing hard on his back.

Bera closed swiftly and struck the sword from his father's

hand with a powerful backhanded blow. The dark blade spun far before falling at last to the earth.

Yet the Orkh only laughed. "Well done, *sashna*!" he said. "Well done! Your *orkushna* is strong, very strong. But do you have the stomach to strike the last blow?"

That was the question. Did he? Bera raised his head to gaze up the slope to where the companies stood in ranks, watching, silent and graven. The banner-woman stood nearer but Bera could see no judgment on her face for good or ill. Finally, his gaze went to Atul. The man stood helm-less with a sword in his hand and a gray shield on his arm. A tatter of his bloody leggings fluttered on the air. Nothing else on the slope seemed to move.

Then Atul drew himself up straighter, as if in salute, and he nodded to Bera. The man's eyes held neither contempt nor scorn for Bera, as they once did, but only the quiet respect one warrior might give another.

Bera had long wished for this, but now it didn't feel as he thought it might. There was no pride in him, nor satisfaction or contentment, but only a great weariness of body and soul. And a fervent wish that all this death and terror had never happened.

Fingers grasped his knee. They were strong and gripped him tightly, seeking to pull him down. Bera brought the sword around, thinking to drive its point toward the Orkh's neck, but the Orkh was swifter. He released Bera's knee to bring up both hands and seize the blade, stopping its descent. The Orkh's fingers were preserved by the black steel of his gauntlets but the point of the black sword—the very blade he'd given his son long ago—hovered at his throat. Bera shifted his feet and leaned over his father to push the stroke home, knowing now he must but fearing still to do it.

Their faces were close now but Bera kept his eyes on the dark blade, away from his father's, fearing his will would fail. As they struggled the keen edge of the sword ground deeper into the steel of the gauntlets, making a terrible sound Bera shuddered to hear. Black blood ran over the blade, but still the Orkh held death at bay.

"I did not judge you rightly, my son," he gasped. "You are more than I believed. Yet also you are less."

Bera answered him through clenched teeth. "You have no idea who I've become."

His father's voice was a cold whisper now as he struggled against the blade. "You have defeated me," he said, "and shamed me before my *borkas*. They will not hear me now, nor follow me. There is nothing left now for me but death."

The great Orkh opened his hands, releasing the blade. Bera's weight, bearing hard on the sword, drove the point down swiftly. It passed through Tsov-ar-kan's neck and went deep into the ground until it was stopped by a stone. Black blood welled freely around the blade and Bera wept to see the light of *orkushna* fade from his father's eyes.

He leaned over the Orkh for a time, his head bowed, speaking silently a prayer to send his father's spirit flying true to the halls of their ancestors. Then he raised his head and stood, and he pulled the sword free to face the Orkhs below, straddling still the corpse of his father.

They returned his stare, their ranks hushed and still. And Bera knew then he could have them. He could go down among them and win his father's place as their leader, if he chose. He could command that great, dark legion and it would do his will.

He did wish to command them, but only once. He raised the dripping sword to point south and shouted: "Go back to your lands! There is nothing here for you but death! Go now!"

He saw them waver, for there were none left to gainsay him and each Orkh now stood upon his own doubt. And the moment lay trembling, and the Scales of Fate moved toward balance.

Then a great note of sound rolled down the ridge and all looked west in wonder. They saw there the Dragons still, but the beasts no longer strode on far fields. Instead they came east, among the Orkhs: shattering their ranks and scattering them like ants from a flooded hill. And behind the Dragons came companies of Humans that drove the panicked Orkhs south across the fields and into the trees, and back down the roads whence they'd come. And with the Humans came Dweorg.

Seeing this new doom come upon them, the Orkhs below Bera dropped their shields and flung away their weapons; and they too ran south, fleeing the wrath of the Dragons and the might of Bigan Heolfbera.

THE END

EPILOGUE

What remained of Zara's *kansa* was scattered over the fields. Some were mounted still, but others had lost their cat-sí and many cat-sí had lost their riders. Te'a was among the latter, for Zara had fallen in the last defense of the gap.

She lay now where they'd placed her: in the shade of a tall pasture oak that spread crooked limbs over a wide sward of soft grass. The scarlet and green banner was thrust into the earth beside her, marking it as a place of honor.

Earic spent some time there, resting with Aere in the cool and grieving for the Aelf-lady who'd rescued him from his dire need. Te'a came to lay by her former rider and she placed her head on Zara's shattered cuirass. Earic didn't know how to comfort the great beast, but other cat-sí came to lay with her and groom her fur.

The Dweorg came, too. A delegation of five that included the older Dweorg with the leaping stag pendant. Earic greeted these and bid them welcome, expecting nothing more. But the older Dweorg addressed him, speaking through the same young Dweorg as before.

"This Aelf wrought a great harm on my people," he said. "Long ago. I saw it with my own eyes and I will not forget it." The Dweorg looked around the fields and frowned. "But in this place she fought well, and died well. A warrior's death. I saw this also with my own eyes. This also will be remembered."

Earic thought to respond, but the old Dweorg turned from him to give Zara a slight bow. The others did the same, and they left the tree, returning over the fields to their own war-weary remnants. Earic watched them go, wondering what Zara would have said to the grudging respect they'd paid her.

Salf lived still, and when he came to the tree he sent Earic and Aere with others into the fields to bring in Aelfs and cat-sí who wandered in the aftermath. There were many of these. Once, when Earic returned to the tree on Dreng leading two riderless cat-sí, he found Cenred there speaking with Salf.

The Aetheling took in Dreng, then said: "You remain absent from your post, Earic, and a fugitive from the king's justice."

Earic nodded. "Yes, sir. Both are true. I will surrender to—"

Cenred held up a hand to stop him. "However, this Aelf, Salf, has told me of your deeds today. I owe this victory to many, it seems, but you not least." The man paused then, seeming to gather his thoughts, and said, "My Lord Earic Eadwulfing, by my power and authority, I hereby grant you clemency for your offenses against the king and the Fyrd. You are free of any charge or constraint, or any taint of dishonor. Earic, let's put the past behind us, shall we? Victory cleanses all ills, as they say."

Earic bowed from his seat on Dreng. "Thank you, sir."

"But I cannot restore you to my council."

Earic nodded: he wouldn't have expected so much. He'd lied to this man, twice, and he would accept the consequences.

Cenred continued. "But I can forgive you, Earic. You acted wrongly in the beginning, very wrongly. But you did rightly in the end. In honesty, I'm amazed you risked so much to tell me of this new foe. That took courage, as did assailing the Dragons with so few. For myself, and for the Fyrd and our king, I thank you."

Now it was Cenred who bowed to Earic.

"There is another who deserves greater thanks," Earic said. He gestured to Aere, who had ridden near on the bay, bringing with her two Aelfs that sagged low over their cat-sí.

Cenred turned to Aere and looked at her keenly. "To whose company do you belong, warrior? Or are you yet another absent from her post?"

Aere flushed at this but her answer to him was lost in the sudden sound of many hooves. Earic turned to see a retinue approaching the tree. Floating over it was a tall white banner bearing a device of gold stars set in a circle. In the center of the retinue was a straight figure on a tall white horse. He sat on a saddle of white leather, and from beneath that saddle fell a broad blanket of gold that trailed near the ground and shone brightly in the sunlight.

The king had come.

He was the first to dismount, and he rushed forward into the shade of the tree. He was a boy of fifteen but looked younger still, as if life had yet to touch him with its pain. He wore a suit of silver parade armor and carried by his hip a longsword far too ornate for true use. Yet his face was open and generous, and it was alight with excitement.

"What a victory, Cenred!" the boy cried. "What a victory! Well done!"

The Aetheling bowed to the king, and Earic slipped carefully from Dreng's back to lower himself to kneel on the grass. Aere dismounted also and she knelt beside him.

"Tell us!" the king said. "Tell us how it was done, Cenred! This instant! What a victory this is!"

As all there listened Cenred recounted the final act of the battle, giving Earic's role no stint. He told the king of Earic's suspicions, and of Cenred's own doubts, and of Earic's riding with the Aelf company of Lady Zara Thu'sem to challenge the Orkhs and Trolles, and to free the Dragons to turn on their captors.

"He is Earl Eadwulfing's youngest son, sire," Cenred added when he was done.

The king turned to Earic. "Is you?" he said. "Then we congratulate you, my lord! And we shall make you a knight of our Dominion, as befits your deeds and our generosity."

The king moved then to draw the ornate sword, but Earic raised a hand to stop him.

"I thank Your Majesty for this honor," he said. "Most humbly. But I crave leave to refuse it. It's not fitting to raise me. Beg your pardon but I will be leaving your service, as soon as I may, and renouncing my birth."

The boy's hand left the sword and he scowled. "Renouncing your birth? Great gods! Whatever for?"

"I wish to wed a common, Majesty."

The king blinked as if he'd been told the sun wouldn't rise tomorrow. "Wed a common? Cenred, has your hero lost his wits to the Dragons?"

"I knew not of this, sire."

"Who is this woman?" the king said.

Earic gestured to Aere, who knelt beside him still. But her face was stern and she whispered under her breath.

"Whatever are you about, Earic?" she said. "We cannot wed! You have told me so. And you have not asked me any rate. I will not be taken like a village maid waiting for a husband to come for her!"

Earic said nothing to this. Instead he told the king of Aere's own deeds that day. How she'd led the Aelfs and defeated the Trolles by cunning stratagem, and freed the second Dragon to turn the battle from a slaughter into victory. The pride he felt for her shone in his words, and when he was done he told the king he wished to make Aere his wife. Howsoever he could, even if it meant renouncing his birth.

The boy considered this for a time, seeming perplexed. Then he addressed Aere: "Is what this man says the truth of it? Did you do these things?"

Aere replied without raising her eyes. "Yes, Majesty. I done those things, but maybe not so glorious as he made it seem, Majesty."

"We shall be judge of that, good woman," the king said. Then he blew out a breath and looked around, shedding some of his air of formality. "Well then, we cannot have nobles wedding commons, can we, Cenred? That will not do. Not at all."

"Sire!" Earic cried, fearing his sole desire would be denied out of hand. "As I say, I shall renounce my title and birth. We will live as common folk."

"No," the king said. "That will not do either. Tell me, good woman, would you have this man for a husband, were he not as he is? Of noble house."

Hearing this, Earic reached out to take Aere's hand, hoping silently that what he'd done and what he'd said was enough. There had been no clear moment after the battle to tell her of his intent to wed her, if she willed.

When Aere didn't speak for a time Earic's heart quailed. But then she said, "I would wed him, Majesty. If it please you."

"No, it does not please us," the king said, "or not as things are." He reached again for the sword and this time he drew it fully. Then he looked to Cenred, the sword in his hand, and said: "Lord Raedmund has this place, does he not?"

Cenred nodded. "He does, sire."

"Where is he? We don't see him."

"I know not, sire," Cenred replied. Then he added more carefully: "Retired from the field, perhaps."

The king frowned at this and a dangerous look came to his eye, but it passed swiftly.

"Yes, well then," he said. "I suppose it's all the better we should bestow our honors here, where they're deserved. Don't you think, Cenred? That ratty old bag shan't miss this place overmuch anyway. He has all this Southland to carry on his damned hunts."

Cenred nodded politely but he looked as perplexed as Earic felt.

The king drew himself up to stand straight in his silver

armor, and he lifted the sword high so he could bring down the flat to lay on the crown of Aere's head. Then he spoke.

"We are most pleased," he said, "to make you now, by right and rule, The Lady Aere, Baronetess of Suthgaet. We command you to enter into this place, and to rule by and under our sovereign right. We swear to you such right and title we grant shall be yours utterly and forever, so long as faith be met with faith, and demand be met with service. Do you so swear?"

Earic looked to Aere as the king spoke. Surprise lay on her face, and fear also. He squeezed her hand, and when the king had finished she turned her gaze to Earic, studying his face long as if seeing it for the first time.

Then she looked up to the king and said to him in a voice that trembled, "I do so swear it, Majesty, though I know not what else to say for it."

"No more is needed, lady," the king said. "You may rise now and be greeted, Dame Aere."

She did rise and Earic with her, and the King came forward to embrace them both. Many had gathered under the tree now, and all breathed in the joy of their victory and Aere's raising. Even Cenred smiled as he embraced her, and he shook Earic's hand with a sincere and gratifying warmth.

Salf came also but he did not embrace Aere, and he seemed not to share in the happiness about him. He moved carefully and wore a broad bandage about his chest.

"My lady," he said to Aere with a small bow around his wound, "you may take Te'a for your own, if you wish it. And if she will have you as rider, although I do not doubt she will."

Aere clapped her hands with happiness. "I do wish it! Her heart is broken and I will do my best to heal it."

The Aelf nodded to this then turned to Earic. "And you, Lord Earic, may take Dreng for yours. Know well the honor of these givings! For the care and keeping of cat-si has never before been given to any Humankind. Guard and care for them well."

"I'm sorry for your loss of Zara," Earic said. "I didn't know, or guess."

"None knew," Salf replied, "outside our own realms. There was no need. I came here in part to save Zara-rena, as I could, but she would not be saved. In her pain I had become an enemy to her, though I loved her."

Aere moved to hug the tall Aelf then, putting her arms around him gingerly. He looked awkward but bore the gesture silently.

"What will you now?" she asked him.

Salf looked away then. "Return with her, and the *kansa*, or such as remain. Grieve. Continue." He smiled a small, sad smile. "I will fare well, I believe, and may you fare well also."

Saying this, the tall Second bowed to them again and moved away. It seemed to Earic it was an unfairness that he should gain a new wife here, while Salf should lose one so long held. Silently, he wished peace upon the heartbroken Aelf.

The king had remounted his horse, and with a last wave to those under the tree he rode east over the fields with his retinue, drawing Cenred after him. As Earic watched them go, a new westerly breeze caught the white banner with its gold stars, and it flapped confidently as if knowing a lasting peace had been won here.

*

When finally they were alone beneath the branches of the great tree, Aere turned to Earic. "You have not asked me," she said.

"What?"

"For my hand. You have not asked me. I might refuse you and take another. I'm a proper lady now, with lands."

"Oh, you are?" he said. "I don't believe a proper lady trysts in haylofts."

She drew up. "Earic Eadwulfing! I shall surely refuse you now! And banish you from my lands. Ware well, for your feet stand upon them even now."

He laughed. "You will need a guard to see me off. I shan't leave."

She crossed her arms. "Ask me."

Earic stooped again to a knee, carefully, and took her hand in both of his. "Will you wed me, Dame Aere?" he said. "I am but the youngest son of a minor Earl, with no lands or inheritance of my own. Indeed I no longer have any place in the world, while now you have lands and people of your own. But I do love you, Aere, and I love our child you bear. You heard me tell the king I meant to give all that remained to me to have you for wife. Will you have me for husband?"

She looked down at him, studying his face, then she smiled. "Yes," she said.

And so it was they were wed that next spring, upon a cloth of gold and beneath a bower of purple-flowering vines. The king himself joined their hands together. Then they went into the Town of Suthgaet and made it their home and work, although much time passed before all was set right again.

In time Aere caused a wall to be built, tall and strong, from the west end of the ridge to the foothills, so no enemy might pass there easily. And the building and walls of the farmstead between the hills were cast down and their stones went into the making of that great wall.

In later years, Earic was sent by the king in embassy to the Dragons of the south. To make himself known to them, and to seek their friendship however he might. But he did not find them, though he searched long. He found instead only a rumor of their passing into the uttermost reaches of the Earth, out of history and into legend forever.

*   *   *

Of Bera, there is less to say. The king did not come to him, nor make him a knight, nor a lord. When the Orkhs had gone, he sat on the ruin of the ridge, near the corpse of his father, and rested.

He thought of Dudda and others who'd fallen here. They lay about him even now, for the storm of battle had only just swept away its gray skirts. Soon the corpse-bearers would come and the funeral pyres would light the evening sky; and by tomorrow all that remained of the fallen here would be white ash and blackened bone, and the memories of the living.

At length Atul came to sit near him, resting his battered helm on the ground between them. And together they watched the Orkh fires that burned still on the fields, until the man said: "That was the damnedest thing I ever saw, you know. I wouldn't have wished it on anyone."

Bera thought about this. "Nor would I. My father was not as I wished him. But I've learned that wishing is a trap. It conceals what's truly there, leading the wisher astray. I wished to be something I am not, instead of being who I am. My father was led astray by his own wishes, for he also wished I was something I am not. We each wanted the other to be in our own image, and we both suffered for it. I am sorry for my attempts to be Human."

Atul grunted. "As I said, I misjudged you. Not as a wish, but in pride. I may be the son of a dog, as you say, but I do know worth when I see it. You're a warrior, Ceorl Bera. You showed that today. And I know you're not a traitor. You gave much for this victory, more than most who lived."

Bera nodded. Yes, he had given much. And he'd done his part well enough. He stood and with a parting nod to Atul, he walked back toward the town and the pass road. He meant to find his tent again and sit at his little desk, and there he would finish the letter to his mother, for he had much to say to her.

ABOUT THE AUTHOR

The Author lives in The Berkshires of Western Massachusetts with his family, two dogs, a cat, and a flock of chickens. John B. Cheek was his great-great-grandfather, an Arkansas farmer, carpenter, and cobbler.

Sign up at www.johnbcheek.com to be notified of new releases.

Also, please consider leaving a star rating or a written review on Amazon or Goodreads. Independent authors like me rely a great deal on reviews and ratings from readers like you to gain a wider audience and to continue writing stories you enjoy.

www.ingramcontent.com/pod-product-compliance
Lightning Source LLC
Chambersburg PA
CBHW051011180726
48291CB00006B/2058